Game ON

DANICA FLYNN

GAME ON

A PHILADELPHIA BULLDOGS BOOK

DANICA FLYNN

GAME ON

ISBN: 978-1-957494-26-5
Cover Art: Qamber Designs
Editor: Charlie Knight

AUTHOR'S NOTE

Content Warning: This book has mentions of growing up in an abusive home. There are no scenes of domestic abuse, just references to the past.

To Bethesda Softworks for creating The Elder Scrolls video game series but specifically Elder Scrolls Online which inspired Dragonspire in this book. LOL!

PLAYLIST

"Super Mario Bros. Theme" By Retro Crowd
"Electricity" By Flora Cash
"Toss a Coin to Your Witcher" By Sonya Belousova, Giona Ostinello, Joey Batey
"The Dress Looks Nice On You" By Sufjan Stevens
"Dragonborn" By Jeremy Soule
"I Was a Fool" By Tegan and Sara
"Get Lucky" By Daft Punk, Pharrell Williams, Nile Rodgers
"Wildcat" By Ratatat
"An End, Once and for All" By Clint Mansell & Sam Hulk
"Fire" By Waxahatchee
"Drink Up, There's More!" By Percival Schuttenbach
"When Am I Gonna Lose You" By Local Natives
"(Do You Wanna Date My) Avatar" By The Guild, Felicia Day
"Ocean Eyes" By Billie Eilish
"Harder, Better, Faster, Stronger" By Daft Punk
"Dragon Age Origins" By EA Games Soundtrack
"When I'm With You" By Best Coast

CHAPTER ONE

LOGAN

"Bro, you never come out with us!" my teammate TJ whined.

I thought now that TJ had settled down with his fiancée and had twins on the way, he'd be less annoying. Not the case. Especially after we had a win.

"No can do, man. I gotta get home," I said with a shake of my head.

My teammates couldn't relate to me being a single dad on a short-term contract that expired after this season. They didn't understand the uncertainty. Especially since the team called up another rookie while G, our captain, was laid up with knee surgery.

"Dude, you're wound so tight. You need to get it in!" TJ laughed that hyena laugh of his.

I rolled my eyes as I stripped off my jersey and took off my pads. He wasn't wrong, but I didn't have time for that shit. Occasionally, I'd take a bunny to bed, but only when I was on the road. When we were at home, my sole focus was on my nephew Liam.

"T, leave him alone," my buddy and defensive partner, Blaise, came to my rescue.

Blaise was a recent addition to the team last season. Fans loved him because he was a hometown boy, and his dad was a Bulldogs legend. You became close when paired together, but when I confided in him about my struggles, he and his girl became my support system.

"I gotta jet and relieve the nanny," I explained as I rushed off to the showers. Thank the hockey gods I didn't have to do a post-game interview.

"Maybe she can relieve something for you!" TJ shouted after me, but I shook my head at him.

Never change, T, never change.

I took the quickest shower I could and changed back into my suit. I wouldn't mind having to wear suits to the arena for game day if I had a better one. Being on a two-way contract, I wasn't getting paid the big bucks. I had three suits to my name, and the boys always gave me shit for how ugly the brown one was.

"You good, man?" my teammate Mac asked. He ran a dark hand across his jaw as he peered at me.

I nodded and took a check out of my jacket pocket. "Here, this month's rent."

He waved me off. "Dude, I know what it's like being a rookie."

Mac was a veteran on the team, and when I got called up, he took me under his wing. He lived on the Main Line with his family, closer to our practice facility, but he sublet his condo in Old City to me.

I shoved the envelope in his hand. "I'm still gonna pay you for letting me stay at the condo."

Mac nodded. "All right, kid. How's Liam doing?"

"I don't know. It's hard. He cries for my sister every night."

When my sister Rose and her abusive husband got into a car crash that killed them both two years ago, I got custody of her son. Did it rock my world that I became a father when I wasn't prepared? Absolutely. I had just gotten the call-up to the big leagues and was working toward a bigger contract. I was finally living my dream, playing with the Bulldogs, but my priorities shifted when Liam came to live with me. Did it suck that I couldn't stay out late partying with my teammates? Sure. But after Rose's death, I made a promise to myself I'd take care of her son over anything else. Even my own career or happiness.

"Hey, you should talk to T's girl," Mac suggested.

I furrowed my brow. "Why?"

"T said she was the sole survivor in a car crash, and she's in therapy. It might help your little guy."

"Hmm. Maybe. I gotta jet."

"How many nannies have you gone through?"

I groaned. "Four. I hope this one works out."

Mac clapped me on the shoulder. "Good luck, kid."

At twenty-four, I was still a 'kid' to most of the guys on the team. It was the usual shit you dealt with being on a hockey team and having to be the rookie. Although, since Cally got called up, he was Rookie now, and I was back to being Cully. God forbid hockey players call each other by their given names.

I walked out of the arena and toward my car in the player's parking lot. I drove on autopilot back to my condo. This was the fourth nanny I had hired this year alone. Why? These women saw dollar signs in their eyes when they found out what I did for a living.

I made more than the average person while I was up in the big time, but I was still on an entry-level contract. I wasn't making millions like my teammates Noah or TJ. Or hell, even Blaise. And I had a kid to worry about. Something TJ would understand in the months to come.

The last nanny I hired had been young, and that worried me, but Mac and his wife had used her before, so I thought I was in good hands. Until I came home and she was naked in my bed.

She had been hot, and any other time I'd have taken her up on the offer, but fucking the nanny was a bad idea. I went through an agency for this new one. I asked for someone older, hoping to get a sweet old lady, but no, they sent another young thing with a smoking hot bod. I hoped she knew how to be professional.

When I keyed into the apartment and found it dark with no immediate sign of Crystal, my stomach dropped. First, I freaked out and checked Liam's room. That was my biggest fear with leaving a stranger with him. What if he got kidnapped?

Since becoming Liam's guardian, I was in a constant state of worry that something bad would happen to him. I couldn't protect my sister, but I'd make damn sure I protected her son. Guilt wrapped itself around me every night, knowing I hadn't got my sister out in time. At least now I could show Liam that real men didn't hit their partners. I wished getting him away from his shitty father hadn't cost my sister her life.

I slowly opened the door to his room, in case he was asleep, and breathed a sigh of relief when I walked in the room and found the four-year-old asleep in his own bed. For once.

My biggest challenge was keeping him out of my bed.

Before Mac let me sublet his condo, I was rooming with one of the other rookies, and Liam slept in my room. Despite having his own bed, he always managed to find his way into mine. That hadn't stopped when we moved. Despite all my trying to get him to sleep in his own bedroom in his 'big boy bed.'

I peered down at my nephew, grateful that Crystal got him to sleep in here instead of in my bedroom, but then his blue eyes popped open.

Dammit. I was hoping he would stay asleep.

"Buddy, go back to sleep," I whispered.

"No," he argued, even as he yawned. No, had been his favorite word since the moment he moved in with me.

"Buddy, you need to sleep. Sleep for Uncle Logan, okay?"

He shook his little head and clenched his fist. "Want Mama."

I sighed and smoothed down his hair. "Buddy, we talked about this. Mama's with the angels now."

"Mama!" he wailed.

Fuck, I didn't know how to help my nephew. I wished his mama was here, too. I sang his favorite song that my sister always sang to him until he settled back down.

This single dad thing was tough work, and some days, I didn't know if I was doing any of it right. I had to be on top of my game all the time. For him. I worked myself to the bone in the weight room and studied game tape as much as I could because I wanted to keep my spot on the team. For this little guy who needed me more than anything.

I quietly left his bedroom after he closed his eyes and fell back asleep. I had to find out where the hell his nanny got to.

The door to my bedroom was closed, which sent alarm

bells off. I closed it when I left, but with Crystal nowhere in sight, I had my hackles raised. I had a bad feeling about what was behind it.

I opened the door, and on my bed was Crystal in sexy lingerie. "Welcome home," she said with a smile.

I clenched my jaw. This was what I was afraid of.

My dick kicked against my pants. She was hot as hell, but this was inappropriate. Everyone knew you didn't sleep with the nanny.

"Crystal," I said flatly. "What are you doing?"

She crooked a finger at me. "C'mere big guy. Let me help you relax."

"No. Put your clothes on and get out of my bed."

Her face fell. "Don't you want to fuck me?"

Of course, I wanted to fuck her. She was hot as hell and waiting in my bed. But I wasn't gonna fuck the woman I hired to take care of my nephew. You don't shit where you eat.

"Crystal, you're a gorgeous girl, but this is wildly inappropriate. Get your things and leave. I'll make the payments through the agency, but I'm not looking to hire you again."

She jumped off the bed in a huff and rushed around to get dressed. She bumped me with her shoulder and gave me a glare on her way out. I don't know why she was so pissed off at me; I had set the ground rules with the agency that I had several problems with women thinking I wanted a sexual relationship with them. Crystal had excellent reviews, and she never had a complaint before. Well, she would now.

Since I was a hockey player, people assumed I wanted every single woman I laid eyes on. But who wanted to be the stereotypical athlete who banged the nanny? A lot of these women weren't my type, anyway. They were gorgeous, sure, but I liked my women a little nerdy.

I changed for bed and composed another email to the agency, telling them again that I was interested in a seasoned nanny. I needed to find someone reliable. And no more puck bunnies.

I lay in my bed and pulled out my phone to charge for the night. I saw a text from Blaise.

BLAISE: How'd the new one work out?

I sent him three angry face emojis in response.

My phone beeped with another reply.

BLAISE: BRO!! Want me to ask V to watch him next time?

ME: Maybe. I gotta figure something out.

BLAISE: We got you.

I was grateful for Blaise and his girlfriend, Veronica. Blaise had even offered to let me move in with them, but I didn't want to put him out. He and V had just moved in together, and he let it slip they were expecting their first child already. I didn't want to cramp their style, and I felt guilty when V rearranged her work schedule to watch Liam for me.

I grabbed my game controller and turned on my game console. There was one way for me to ease the stress right now — playing Dragonspire. I put on my headset so the noise of the game wouldn't wake Liam.

My teammates loved playing the latest sports video game, but that was boring. I loved a good role-playing game, or RPG, as we called it in the gaming world. I had been playing Dragonspire, a fantasy-style multiplayer online game since I was sixteen. If a game had dragons and elves in it, I was in. I didn't have a guild, and most hardcore gamers called me a 'casual,' but I had people I played with regularly.

Like FlowerChild183.

If I was being honest with myself, she was probably my best friend. Even if I didn't know her real name. Or what she looked like. We had been playing together since I was in high school. When I was nervous about getting drafted into the league, she talked me down. Although I lied and said it was a college admissions interview, but her advice had been helpful all the same.

She disappeared last year, and it was rare to see her online lately. I didn't have room to talk since I only had a few spare minutes between all my hockey and parental duties. When I found the time to do a quest, I always searched to see if she was online.

To my surprise, her gamertag popped up on my friends list when I signed on, indicating she was online.

I shot her a message.

GINGERPOWER33: Yo, Flower! Dragonspire?

FLOWERCHILD183: Ginge! I could do a dungeon crawl. You need a wood elf archer?

GINGERPOWER33: Hell yeah, girl! I'm logging in. Switch to voice chat?

FLOWERCHILD183: On it!

I logged into the game and saw a notification pop up

that said, 'FlowerChild183 wants to group.' I logged into the voice chat. "Hey, girl, long time no game!"

"Ha! Could say the same about you."

"I travel a lot for work. It's been busy. How have you been?"

She sighed. "Ugh. Long story, had a baby, got married, and then divorced."

That story sounded eerily familiar, but I couldn't place why. Did she tell me that before? I felt like I would have remembered that, and I couldn't remember the last time we gamed together.

"Whoa, I get that. I have custody of my nephew. Single parent life's rough! You got time to play tonight? I need to relieve stress and kill some dragons."

"I have time for one dungeon," she said.

"Works for me!"

She did only have time for one dungeon crawl, and when she logged off, I couldn't help but think that her voice sounded familiar to me. Which was weird. Of course it sounded familiar – I'd had her voice in my headset for years.

Playing with her had relaxed me, but I still had to worry about getting a new nanny. That was a problem for future Logan.

CHAPTER TWO

LILY

I walked out of the courtroom with my head held high. DONE. I was finally done. Had a baby, got married, and divorced, all within two years.

I turned to my lawyer. "That's it, right?"

The older man with thinning hair and a dark complexion nodded. "Unless he files for custody. You had a mutual consent case."

"Seth won't file for custody. We agreed to share Rosie," I said.

My lawyer gave me a tight smile, but then he reached into his briefcase and handed me his business card, even though I already had it. "Call me if anything comes up. Good luck Lily."

I pocketed the business card and waved goodbye to him, then I went to find my car. My friend Veronica had agreed to watch my daughter while I dealt with the hearing today. Thank god for her.

My daughter was the best thing that ever happened to

me. She may have been an 'oops baby,' and I was dense to believe all of Seth's lies, but Rosie was my everything. Now that I was divorced, I could get back to focusing on my career and my daughter. Nothing else mattered.

I got into my car and made my way to the other side of the city. Veronica's fiancé Blaise played for our city's hockey team, making millions of dollars shooting a puck around the ice. Last year he bought a swanky townhouse in Rittenhouse Square. Now that she moved in with him, she always offered to help me with Rosie. I didn't ask her all that often, but being a single mom was hard, and I'd take all the help I could get.

After circling the block for a parking spot, I walked up to the townhouse, only to find Logan Cullen already on the doorstep about to knock.

Logan was one of Blaise's teammates. We had met at Blaise's housewarming party last summer after Veronica moved in. He was a tall attractive man with a lean, athletic build. I wouldn't have remembered him if not for the fact he sported a shock of bright red hair, making him stand out from the rest of Blaise's teammates.

Clinging against his leg was his little boy with that matching red hair. "Mama!" the little boy cried as he looked at me.

Logan grimaced at me. "No, buddy, that's... I'm sorry, what's your name again?"

I hid my laughter. "Lily."

He shifted the four-year-old off his leg. "That's Aunt V's friend Lily."

"MAMA!" the little boy yelled.

I must have looked like Logan's baby mama. I was aware that with my petite frame and blonde hair, I looked like the hockey WAG stereotype.

I didn't know much about Logan. When we met, we made small talk, finding out we were both single parents and agreeing about how hard it was. It had been the strangest thing because while having that casual conversation, I felt like I'd known him forever. His voice sounded so familiar to me, but I couldn't place it. I chalked up the immediate connection to finding someone who dealt with my same daily struggles. We had a kinship in that regard.

Logan gave me a 'HELP ME' look, but then Veronica answered the door with my sixteen-month-old on her hip. Veronica had changed her hair again for the hockey season. She wore it long with black on top that faded to a different color on her tips. Today she had fire-engine red tips. It always looked great with her whole aesthetic. She was a tattoo artist and was covered in a sleeve of colorful flowers. She looked like a rockabilly pin-up girl.

"Hey, you two. Come in," she said as she handed off my baby.

Surprisingly, Rosie was asleep, and she didn't wake when I took her in my arms. "Thanks, V. I owe you one."

"Take a seat. You want coffee?" she asked.

"Please," I said and took a seat on the couch.

Logan and his son walked into the living room behind me. Logan knelt in front of the boy. "You be good for Aunt V, okay, buddy?"

The little boy nodded, but he reached out to hug his father, clinging onto him for dear life.

Aw, poor little guy. With the way Veronica bemoaned Blaise being gone all the time, I was sure it was tough on the player's kids.

It startled me when I heard the clomping of feet down the steps. Blaise walked into the room wearing a nicely tailored suit, and I realized for the first time that Logan was dressed similarly. That must have been a hockey thing.

"Hey," Blaise said to his teammate. He reached down and ruffled the little boy's hair. "Liam, buddy!"

Veronica mentioned Blaise was good with kids because he helped raise his younger siblings. I got distracted when Rosie stirred and let out a tremendous wail. "Mommy!"

I rocked her in my arms. "You're okay."

"Mommy!" she cried again and pulled on my hair. That was Rosie's MO.

"Oh, sorry, Lily," Veronica said when she came back into the room and set a cup of coffee on the table in front of me.

I squinted at my baby and tickled her tiny belly. "Ouch. Hurts Mommy."

Rosie laid her little head on my chest. "Miss Mommy."

I kissed the top of her head. All the problems with my ex melted away when our little girl was in my arms.

Veronica gave Blaise a look of longing as she watched him with Logan's kid. "Baby, I can't with you right now."

"What?" Blaise asked with a raised eyebrow as Liam talked his ear off.

"I already have baby fever!" she squealed.

I smiled to myself and shifted Rosie in my arms. Veronica mentioned they were trying for a baby already. They had just gotten engaged, but they wanted a family as soon as they could, and it didn't matter when they got married. Their baby fever was why they were always eager to help me out with childcare. I loved them for that.

"Did she eat?" I asked Veronica as I bounced my daughter in my arms. She was getting a little cranky and had been having difficulty eating since I weaned her off breastmilk a couple of weeks ago.

"She was so good," Veronica said.

"Were you good for Auntie Veronica?" I asked Rosie.

"She's so cute and getting so big!" Veronica said to me and smiled at my daughter.

Oh God, her baby fever was bad. Maybe I should leave Rosie with her overnight more so she'd really learn what she was getting herself into. Loved my little girl, but the lack of sleep, not so much.

"Come on, dude, we gotta get to the arena," Logan urged Blaise. He crouched down to say something to his son, and then the little guy nodded and hugged him tight again. Aw, that was cute. Liam was the spitting image of his dad.

Blaise came over to Veronica and planted a kiss on her lips. "Are you gonna come to the game, sweets?"

She glanced my way for a second. "Nah, I think we'll hang here."

I pretended not to notice them having a quiet conversation with their eyes. He kissed her one last time, and then the two men left.

Rosie went back to sleep for once while Liam crawled into Veronica's lap. She stroked his hair, but he stared at me.

"Hey, buddy. Remember me?" I asked.

He nodded, but he hid his face in Veronica's boobs. That made us both laugh.

"How did it go?" she asked.

"Fine. It's done."

"Good."

I grimaced. "I'm sorry."

She furrowed her brow. "For what?"

"You know."

She gave me a hard look. "Lil, I don't blame you. You didn't know Seth was engaged to me before you started dating him. It's not your fault he left me or that he cheated on you. Is he gonna fight you for custody?"

I shook my head. "Nah. We agreed to share custody."

It looked like she wanted to say something about that, but she bit her tongue instead. I didn't blame her. I had doubts Seth would follow through with the terms we talked about, but I'd deal with that later. Right now, all that mattered was our daughter.

"What's the deal with Logan?" I asked.

"Oh, he had to fire another nanny."

I gestured to the little boy in her arms. "No. I meant, what's the mother's like? Liam called me 'Mama' when I got to the door."

"Logan doesn't talk much about his sister. Maybe she had blonde hair like you. He took custody of his nephew after she died a few years ago."

Wait. Nephew?

"I thought he was his son."

Veronica ruffled Liam's hair. "It's the red hair."

"How many nannies has he gone through?"

Veronica laughed. "Too many."

"Why? Does he keep sleeping with them and have to fire them?"

That sounded like something a douchey hockey player would do. Not that Logan gave off those vibes. He was a little quiet like he had a lot on his mind weighing him down. I recognized that in him the moment we met.

Veronica shook her head. "No, the opposite. He keeps on hiring women who see hockey players with WAG expectations. But Logan's on a two-way contract, and he's not making a lot of money. He lives in one of the veteran's old condos, and I'm not even sure he pays Mac rent."

I didn't know what she meant. Veronica wasn't a huge

fan of hockey, so I wasn't sure if she even knew and was just repeating what Blaise told her.

"He looking for an accountant?" I asked.

She laughed. "Maybe."

"I could use the work."

She squeezed my arm. "You'll figure it out." She paused and shifted on the couch. "Are you wearing strong perfume today?"

I raised an eyebrow. "No."

She rubbed her temples and looked a little green.

I peered at her suspiciously. Did her boobs look bigger? I tilted my head at her, remembering how she canceled plans on me last week because she got food poisoning.

Oh my God. Blaise worked quick.

"V!"

"What?"

I stared at her stomach. "Did Blaise already knock you up?"

She gave me a sly smile.

"Really?"

She nodded. "I have to admit, I'm surprised. I did the math, and I'm pretty sure we conceived before we even started trying. But I was still on the pill, so I'm not sure how that's possible..."

"Well, the pill isn't one hundred percent, and Blaise's family's fertile."

She laughed. "I know! Wasn't expecting it so soon, though."

"I'm so happy for you. You deserve everything you're getting with Blaise."

"You'll find that too."

A part of me wondered if that was true. When I started dating Seth, I didn't know he not only had another girlfriend but a fiancée. Or that when I got pregnant, he left her a week before they were supposed to get married. I had no idea about any of this until after I married him and he cheated on me. Veronica should hate me, but she'd never blamed me for what happened and instead took me in as a friend. I'd never understand why.

I looked down at my sleeping daughter and smiled. It would be me and Rosie against the world. I was a strong, independent woman, and I'd survive on my own. I didn't need a man.

"Do you want to go to the hockey game tonight?" Veronica asked.

I shook my head. "No. I'm gonna get out of your hair."

"You sure?" she asked.

Veronica was a good friend, one I didn't deserve, and it was nice she was offering her time to hang out, but I'd rather get Rosie home. Once back at my mom's place, I could work on applying for more jobs. When the baby was asleep, I could melt my brain with video games. I much rather do that than watch hockey.

"I got work to do. Thanks, V."

"I'm here if you need me, okay?"

I gave her a hug and tried not to squish Rosie in between us. "Thanks, hun. I appreciate you."

"Seriously, call me if you need company."

"I'm good," I said to her one last time.

Then I left for another fun night of trying to get my career and life back on track.

CHAPTER THREE

LOGAN

"Bro, I don't understand. Why don't you just fuck them?" TJ asked from above me as he spotted me while I lifted the barbell above my head.

"Because I don't shit where I eat," I grunted out.

"Truth!" Benny called from the other side of the weight room, where he was doing squats with a ridiculous amount of weight. Benny was the biggest guy on the team, and he lifted weights like you wouldn't believe. He was a beast.

"Another one?" Riley asked as he did pull-ups next to Benny.

"Yup. Not naked this time, wearing sexy lingerie," I said with another grunt, finishing up my set.

"Was she hot?" TJ asked.

I rolled my eyes. "Fuck yes, she was hot. But I'm not doing the nanny."

"Fuck," Riley swore.

"What's wrong?" I asked.

He groaned as he hopped off the pull-up bar and wiped the sweat from his brow. "Do I have to worry about that soon?"

Riley and his wife had their first baby last month. Not the best timing with how much we were on the road.

"What do you mean?" I asked. "Doesn't your wife work from home?"

He nodded. "Yeah, but she goes to a lot of signings and conferences. I only have eyes for my wife. I don't want puck bunnies coming onto me as the nanny."

I sat up and wiped my face with a towel. "Maybe it's different because you're married."

He didn't look convinced.

Riley had gotten a wedding ring tattoo because we couldn't wear rings while we played. He was hardcore in love with his wife, and I didn't blame him since Fi was a smoking hot redhead. He wasn't the type of guy who cheated. TJ told me even when Riley was doing the bunny circuit, he never cheated if he was in a relationship. That wasn't always the case in our line of work. Some guys were douchebags who cheated on their wives, but I tended to stay away from those guys.

"You'll find someone soon," Benny reassured me.

I wanted to believe him, but so far, I had little luck. Liam was with my neighbor, who was a sweet girl, but she worked nights and so she wasn't a good option. I wished she was because Liam liked her.

After spending time in the weight room, we had some much-needed time in the media room. We were already on the ice earlier, running through drills, but I needed to focus.

Coach paired Blaise and me together, but he was switching up the lines a lot. I thought Blaise and I were better together because he was good at being a stay-at-home defenseman while I was good at the two-way system. Also why Coach kept putting Blaise and Riley together because Riley was a stronger defenseman than I was. I had been doing a lot of drills with him lately. I hoped it meant I had earned my place on the team for good.

Back in the locker room, Coach asked us to stay for a few minutes before we left. Cally and I shared a look of concern. We both thought that meant one of us was getting put on waivers. I needed to stay in Philly. I needed stability for Liam.

Coach cleared his throat. "Boys, no easy way to say this..."

We waited with bated breath for whatever shitstorm Coach LaVoie was about to drop on us.

"G's not coming back."

I released a breath, and then my brain processed his words. G was only out for knee surgery; him not coming back didn't make sense. Yeah, he was in his thirties and that was old for a hockey player, but he still had a few years left in the tank.

"What does that mean?" Riley asked the question on all our minds.

Coach gave him a tight smile. "G decided to retire. He spent a lot of time thinking about it, but he wants to spend time with his kids, and the injury was a wake-up call."

"So who's the captain?" Noah asked.

"Glad you asked, Kennedy," Coach said with a grin. One of the equipment managers walked over to Riley and handed him a white letter 'C.' "Congrats, Riley. You earned it. Now keep these assholes in line!"

With that, Coach breezed back into his office.

Riley stared down at the 'C' in his hand, at a loss for

words. Benny clapped him on the shoulder and congratulated him.

That wasn't a shock to me. Riley was the alternate, and he had leadership qualities on the team. He and Mac had taken me under their wings when I got called up—Mac by helping me with my living arrangements and Riley with improving my game. Only shock was G deciding to retire.

"Whoa. G, retired," Blaise said.

"Whoa is right, dude," I agreed as I shrugged on my jacket.

"He's played here a long time. My sister's gonna lose it."

That shouldn't have made me smile, but it did. Blaise's little sister was probably the most hardcore Philadelphia Bulldogs fan I'd ever met. She wasn't afraid to tell you when you played like absolute shit. The first time I met her, she asked me if I forgot how to block a shot. Blaise said she might not be faster than him on the ice, but she had a shot that would make any player jealous. It made sense considering who their dad was.

"You want to grab lunch?" Blaise asked.

I shook my head. "Nah, my neighbor has Liam. I want to get back as soon as I can."

Blaise nodded. "Right. Let us know if you need help. Seriously, V and I are here for you."

With Veronica being pregnant, I didn't want to stress her out any more than necessary. Blaise was ecstatic, but I could tell V was nervous about their first baby.

"Nah. I don't want to put you out. I gotta jet."

I took off so he couldn't convince me further and headed back to my condo. Once I got to my condo and onto my floor, I knocked on my neighbor Cynthia's door. She answered with a sleepy Liam clinging to her leg.

"Hey," she said, untangling Liam's hands from around her body.

I bent down to his height. "Come on, buddy. Let's go home."

He reached out for my hand and I took it, nodding at Cynthia. "Thanks. I owe you one."

She waved me off. "He's the sweetest. I don't mind."

"I really appreciate it. I need to find a new nanny."

Her eyes went wide. "You fired another one?"

I nodded. "Yup. Another one looking for a meal ticket... sorry, is that sexist?"

She laughed. "I don't think so. You want someone to help you with your nephew, not a wife."

"You know of anyone good?"

She squinted. "I'll have to think about it, but nobody comes to mind."

"Honestly, I think I need a sweet old grandma type."

"Good luck with that."

I groaned. "Anyway, thanks. I'll get out of your hair." I ruffled Liam's hair. "Say bye to Cynthia and thank her for watching you while I was at work."

"Bye, Liam!" Cynthia said to him.

"Bye, Cece," he said. Cynthia was still hard for him to say, so 'Cece' had always been what he called her.

She made a cooing noise. "He's so cute. You'll find someone soon."

I wished she was right, but I was having my doubts. I even asked the GM's assistant if she could help me. She put feelers out, so I could find someone soon, but nothing so far.

I walked into the condo and sat Liam down at the table in 'the big kid chair' and made us lunch. I sliced apples and spread creamy peanut butter on bread while I asked him if he behaved himself at Cynthia's.

I watched him as he munched away at lunch until he asked if he could play. I set him up in the living room and watched him play with his toy truck and dinosaurs while I checked my email. I sighed when I didn't see a response from the nanny agency yet. I needed someone permanent for Liam. I couldn't keep asking my friends for favors.

Liam fought me when I put him down for a nap—another sign he was starting to grow out of them. The fight was more because he wanted to be in my bed and not in his own room, no matter how much I encouraged him to sleep in his 'big boy bed.'

I probably should've taken a nap too, but instead, I logged into Dragonspire.

I smiled when I saw FlowerChild183 online. Outside of my teammates, I didn't really have friends. It was hard when all you did was eat, sleep, and breathe hockey. It was why the team was so close-knit and was always all up in each other's business.

I requested a chat with her and slid on my headset.

"Hey," her soft voice cheered in my ears.

"Hey," I sighed.

"Oh no. What's up?"

"Ugh. I had to fire another nanny."

"Oh no! What happened?"

I sighed again. "Um... so I'm single, and they keep coming onto me."

"Oh."

"Yup. I just need someone who can take care of my kid when I travel for work."

"I get that. I'm technically still on maternity leave. If you count quitting your cushy corporate job because you're gonna be a stay-at-home mom but then you find out your husband's a piece of shit cheater, so you have to get divorced and move back in with your mother."

My mouth was agape at her admission. Sure, we'd played Dragonspire for years together, but we never said anything so personal before.

She sighed. "Shit, sorry. That was too personal."

"He sounds like a dick."

"You know what's the worst part?"

"There's a worst part?"

The hair on the back of my neck raised as the worst came to mind. I watched my mom take hit after hit from my dad until I was big enough to push him back. Then my sister turned around and found a man just like him. The only thing worse than a cheater was a man who laid his hands on their partner.

I touched my bicep where Veronica tattooed the rose for my sister. So I could remember her and teach Liam that real men weren't like his father. Or his grandfather. That they never laid a hand on their partners or berated them in front of their children.

"I was the other woman, and I had no clue. The woman who he cheated on is a friend now," Lily explained.

This story sounded familiar, but I wracked my brain for why and came up empty.

"Umm."

"Ugh anyway! Can we kill some dragons and pretend they're my ex-husband while my baby's sleeping?" she asked, trying to lighten the mood.

"Hell yeah, girl!"

She laughed. "Thanks, Ginge. Sorry to unload. I know we don't talk about personal stuff."

"No worries. I feel you."

"Was that weird? We've been friends for years, but we don't even know each other's names."

"Not weird. It's a gamer thing."

"Agreed. Let's do this dungeon crawl!"

"Atta girl. Let's fuck 'em up!"

We played for a little while until I heard a cry in the background, and she had to hop off. By the time I signed off, Liam was waking up too. With a blood curdling scream for his mama. Fuck. I was not prepared for this at all.

CHAPTER FOUR

LILY

I glanced over at Veronica lying on the couch in the tattoo shop's office. She looked a little green, and I knew that pain of early pregnancy morning sickness. I felt for her, I did, but I was trying to work on the shop's books, and she was distracting me.

I searched for the correct receipt in the piles she had handed to me when I came in. I rocked my foot against the stroller Rosie was sleeping in, hoping she'd stay quiet. I loved that the tattoo shop didn't mind if I brought her in, especially if I'd be working in the office and out of the way.

The first thing I did when I started working for the shop was install accounting software and transfer the data from their manual excel report to my program. My friend was an incredibly talented artist, but she wasn't good at numbers or keeping records straight. It took me about a week because it was a lot of manual work, but it would be better in the long run. Especially when I did the taxes for them later.

I looked up when the door opened, and Olivia, the shop

manager, came into the office. The petite Asian woman gave me a smile. "Oh hey, Lily. I didn't know you were back here. How are things looking?"

I gestured to the piles of receipts.

Olivia gave me a tight smile. "Sorry. V never lets me help. I could definitely make it more organized."

"That would be amazing," Veronica said.

Olivia handed her a cup of tea. "Here, drink this and hurry because you have an appointment in five minutes."

"I feel terrible," Veronica admitted.

"You want me to call them and cancel?" Olivia asked.

Veronica shook her head and sat up. "Nope, I'm not canceling a client last minute. Wish I didn't feel like I was gonna puke again."

"It'll pass," I told her, not looking up from my spreadsheets.

"Are you sure, V?" Olivia asked.

"I haven't told Alex or Eddie I'm pregnant yet. They'll treat me like glass."

I smiled. They were rather protective of her, but they meant well.

My phone vibrated on the desk, but I tried to ignore it as I crunched numbers. It kept vibrating, and Veronica and Olivia were already distracting me too much anyway, so I picked it up.

I scowled when I saw a text from Seth.

> SETH: Gotta reschedule. Can't take her this weekend.

"Asshole," I seethed.

I didn't realize I said that out loud until Veronica and Olivia looked at me in alarm, and Rosie started to cry. Because of course she did. She had been fussy all day.

I took her out of her stroller and rocked her in my arms, but she wasn't having it.

"What's wrong?" Veronica asked.

"She's just fussy. Huh, baby?" I asked my daughter.

"Mommy," Rosie said as she promptly pulled on my hair. I loved my daughter, but the hair-pulling had to stop.

I unclenched her fingers from around my hair. "No, baby. Hurts Mommy. Ow! Okay?"

"Otay," she said and laid her head on my chest.

Safe to say I wasn't getting any more work done today.

"Are you okay?" Olivia asked me.

She and Veronica peered at me in question.

I sighed. "No. Seth was supposed to pick her up and take her for the weekend. I'm sorry, I gotta cancel tonight."

Rosie perked up her head. "Da-da here?"

I stroked her head. "No, baby. Daddy's at his house. You'll see him later."

God, I hated Seth for doing this to her.

"Bring Rosie!" Veronica said. "Logan can't get a sitter again, so I'm bringing Liam. It'll be fun."

Despite the fact that Seth was a diehard hockey fan, I'd never been to a game. My family was more football fans than anything else. Veronica had invited me to the game tonight since I was supposed to have the night to myself. I would have much rather spent the night baby-free playing Dragonspire, but I wanted to spend time with V.

I shook my head. "Let me try my sister. Rosie's too cranky today."

"Gimme that sweet little baby," Olivia said.

I wanted to kiss her when she took my daughter. Olivia knew when people needed something and was more than willing to step in. I'd take all the help I could get right about now.

I walked out of the office with my phone in hand and went outside. I called Seth first.

"What do you mean, you're rescheduling?" I screeched into the phone as soon as he answered.

That might have been an immature thing to do, but Seth had rocked my entire world and cut me into a thousand pieces. I was done caring about decorum when it came to him.

When I got pregnant, I thought that was the end of my world, but he reassured me everything would be fine. For a while, it was, and we were happy. Then I met his ex-Veronica.

Seth got cagey when I asked when they broke up, but Veronica had been so kind to me. When my friends ditched me at my wedding, she helped me with my baby, so I could get my pictures taken. It only took a couple of months to figure out Seth was cheating on me. That's when I found out I had been the other woman. When I got pregnant, Seth was telling Veronica he was going to marry her, but then he left her for me.

I wished Veronica had told me at my wedding. I would have never asked her to watch Rosie while I went to get pictures of me marrying her cheating ex. I never would've married him in the first place. I wished someone had warned me about Seth.

Okay, my mom did, but I was too in love to listen. He reminded her of my dad. The one who walked out on her with another woman when I was a baby and she had been pregnant with my sister. I wished the cycle of cheating men hadn't repeated itself with me.

"Well?" I asked when Seth didn't respond right away.

"Katie and I..."

I stopped listening.

Katie. That was the girl he had been cheating on me with.

I only figured it out after I was doing our bills and noticed one didn't look right. It was for an expensive hotel in Vegas. He said he had a tattoo convention, but that seemed steep. Seth had been working here at the shop, and they were brand new, so I knew they were still finding their footing. I called Olivia to confirm if it was something the artist took out of pocket or if it needed to be expensed, and she had no idea what I was talking about. Because Seth had called out sick those days. I might have caused a scene by coming into the shop and throwing my ring at him. That's when Veronica and I really became friends.

Should I blame this Katie woman for being with Seth? I didn't because who knew what lies he told her? I was the other woman and had no idea. If Katie knew, if she was with a man who cheated on his wife, I didn't want to know.

"Lil?" Seth's voice pulled me out of my wandering thoughts.

"Sorry, I stopped listening to your lies. This is your daughter, Seth. We agreed on a schedule for her, so we can both spend time with her."

"I know, it's just—"

"Fine, then don't have this weekend, but don't expect me to bend over backward for you. And don't expect you can have her next weekend either. That's not how this works. You don't get to pick and choose when you want to be in her life. We agreed to shared custody."

"Lil, come on."

"No. You know what? Fuck you!"

I punched the end button on my phone and ran a shaky hand through my hair.

Was that smart? Absolutely not. I rarely lost my cool

like that, but he made me so mad. If he kept messing with her schedule now, it was only going to get worse as she got older. I didn't want to have to explain to my daughter why her dad didn't want her. God, I can't imagine all the questions I asked my mom when I was a kid. I didn't want that for Rosie.

I should go home and take a raincheck with Veronica. She seemed like she felt too sick to go to the hockey game, anyway.

That didn't stop me from texting my sister.

ME: Guess who canceled on me?

MARI: What an A-hole! I'll take Rosie for the night.

ME: I don't want to put you out.

MARI: Bring that sweet little baby! You deserve a break.

I owed my sister so much. The only reason I didn't move in with her instead of Mom was that Mari lived in a tiny one-bedroom apartment. Sometimes I wondered if that would have been better than dealing with Mom's passive-aggressive 'I told you so' moments. My sister was a professional nanny, and since she was between families right now, she helped me a lot with Rosie. I did her taxes and bills in exchange for the childcare.

I walked back into the tattoo shop and saw Veronica at her chair, tattooing a big burly biker. She was smiling while chatting him up and tattooing a gigantic piece on his back. She still looked a little green, but she was pushing through it. Olivia was at the front desk and was listening to Rosie babble at her.

"Mommy!" my little girl cried. "Want Mommy!"

I mouthed 'thank you' to Olivia, and she waved me off like it was nothing. I lifted Rosie up into my arms. "Okay, my sweet girl, change of plans. You're gonna go hang out with Aunt Mari tonight."

"Da-da?"

I shook my head. "No, baby. Daddy had something come up."

"Want Da-da!" she cried.

I shifted her on my hip. "You'll have so much fun with Aunt Mari, okay?"

Then she started to cry again, on the verge of throwing a tantrum. I sighed and walked into the office, where I tried to calm her down. She inched closer to toddler tantrums lately, and I'd admit it was in these moments that being a mother was really freaking hard.

I put her back in her stroller and closed down for the day. I hated having to leave before I was finished because my daughter was having a meltdown. This single-mom thing was the hardest thing I ever had to do. Some days, like today, I wasn't sure how I was going to manage. Thank God for my sister coming to my rescue.

CHAPTER FIVE

LOGAN

I needed to find a new nanny. I couldn't keep relying on my friends.

"You okay, man?" Blaise asked.

"Huh?" I asked and realized I had wrapped tape on my stick way too many times.

Blaise raised an eyebrow as he laced up his skates next to me. The other guys were getting amped up to go out for warmups before the game started, so no one else was paying attention. They were getting in their game day zone while my thoughts were all over the place.

He nudged me with his stick. "You taped your stick so much, I thought you were Riley."

Riley glared at him from his other side. Everyone gave Riley shit for how much he did that.

"I'm good," I reassured him.

"You sure?"

I nodded. "Yeah. I got this."

He squinted at me but didn't press me on it before getting up and walking out to the hallway with the rest of the team. I couldn't afford to mess up my career because I was worried about my nephew. I had to play well here, so when my contract was up, they'd re-sign me, and I could stay in Philly.

I undid the tape on my stick and redid it the right way before walking into the hallway.

"You okay?" Cally asked.

I nodded.

Cally and I were both fighting to earn a bigger contract next year, but since we were on entry-level contracts, we roomed together on the road. I wasn't as close with him as Blaise, but he was a good guy. Noah had taken him under his wing, so much that Cally was living with him and his fiancée. Noah had offered that to me too, but with Liam, I didn't want to impose.

"Still dealing with trying to find a nanny," I explained.

He nodded. "I don't envy you. But you'll have your head in the game, right?"

"I'm good."

We shuffled down the tunnel, getting amped up to get out on the ice for the first time tonight. Riley was at the back after Metzy, our goaltender. Since Coach put the 'C' on his chest, he'd taken it to heart. At the front, TJ was yelling to pump us up. Actually, right now, he was yelling in Noah's face. The stoic giant stood there, letting him do it. It was their weird pregame ritual that no one else questioned.

Blaise turned around, and we bumped fists before we took off down the hallway and skated out on the ice. We skated around the zone until we came around to the glass where the girls always sat. I watched, amused, as he and

Veronica did that heart-tapping thing they always did with each other. He tapped two fingers against his heart, pointed at her, and then she repeated the action to him.

Alarm bells went off in my head when my nephew wasn't with her.

Blaise grabbed the sleeve of my jersey, sensing my panic, and pointed to the cute blonde next to Veronica holding Liam. Lily was holding Liam in her arms and pointing at me. Instead of waving at me, Liam crushed his face into her boobs.

Me too, little guy.

Okay, maybe TJ was right that I needed to get laid.

Not gonna lie, V's friend was smoking, and my internal caveman beat at his chest when I saw her holding Liam like he was her own. I couldn't go there, though. Veronica might stab me with her tattoo machine if I slept with her friend.

When I met Lily last summer at Blaise's barbecue, there was something familiar about her. At first, I thought it was because she had blonde hair in the same bright-white shade as TJ's girl, but when she spoke, something inside me calmed. Like I had heard it before. I couldn't put my finger on it, but something about her gave me a sense of déjà vu. I'd never met her until that day, though, so I didn't understand it. Maybe it was because she looked like all the other WAGs – blonde and petite. That had to be it.

"He's good," Blaise reassured me.

I nodded and looked at Lily from behind the glass. She shrugged and looked down at the little boy in her arms. I hoped he didn't call her mama again. Any blonde woman he came in contact with, Liam called her mama because he missed his own, and I didn't know how to keep telling him Rose was gone.

Lily got him to turn around, and his eyes lit up when he saw me. He waved to me, and I waved back. I gave him a thumbs up, and he nodded before curling up into Lily's neck again.

I owed her a drink for that.

Blaise and I did a couple more laps and stretched out on the ice. I shook my head when Blaise started chirping the captain of the Montreal Saints, who was his oldest brother. Fans loved a sibling rivalry story, so tonight's game would be fun.

We went back into the locker room for a bit and amped ourselves up for the game before going back out. I stood behind the bench during the national anthem until the first line started it off. I sat on the bench next to Blaise, watching my team trying to set something up at the other end.

"Come on, boys!" I called out in encouragement.

I watched in amazement as Noah finessed the puck on his stick and got it away from the Saints d-man. Him, TJ, and Benny on the ice were a dream line. With Riley and McCarthy backing them up on D, it was a strong opening shift.

Blaise and I hopped over the bench on the shift change, and we skated our hearts out as we chased after the Saints, trying to make sure we didn't lose our steam. It was scoreless so far, but I definitely wanted to change that. I could defend our net, but I also wanted to score the game-winning goal. That's why Blaise and I worked well on the ice together. He was a traditional defenseman protecting the net, while I was aggressive on the puck, wanting to put it in play. We filled the holes in each other's game to be successful on the ice.

The Saints had our number on this shift. They went hard at the net, forcing Blaise and me to work for it to get it out of our zone. Try as I might, I couldn't get the puck past the Saints all shift. When the shift changed and we hurried back to the bench, I hung my head in defeat.

"Good work, boys!" Riley called to us.

It didn't feel like good work if we were still scoreless.

I wiped a towel on my eye shield and stared out at the ice. Instead of studying my teammates and looking for the holes in our game to fix in my next shift, my eyes wandered over to the section where the WAGs sat.

What was my problem? Lily was hot, but not hot enough that I lost my head during a game.

"Dude, head in the game," Blaise muttered next to me.

I nodded in agreement. I needed to be in tip-top shape tonight.

Our teammates set up the play on the other end of the ice. Hallsy passed it to Mac, and then the big guy flung his stick back and took the risky shot. The whole bench erupted into cheers and stood up when the red light behind the Saints' goalie lit up. The Philly crowd was going wild as the in-game announcer told them who scored the first goal of the game.

Mac and Hallsy came back to the bench, where they skated down the line, giving us all high-fives. Determination coursed through me as I watched the next shift change. I had to prove my worth to Philly, and I was about to do that, no matter the cost.

"Fuck yeah, that's how you do it, boys!" TJ danced into the locker room at the end of the game.

It was still early in the season, but a 4-0 shutout win was nothing to sneeze at. Especially for Metzy.

"Wait!" Riley yelled at us. Coach handed him the silver

helmet we always gave to the player who played the best in a game. "Before you assholes try to slink out of here, we have one thing to do first."

Riley handed off the helmet to our goalie. "Metzy, you fucking beauty, you played your ass off tonight!"

Metzy put on the silver helmet while the rest of us whooped and hollered at him. "Well, boys, I had a good D in front of me tonight. Let's do it for the rest of the season."

"Atta boy, Metzy!" TJ cheered.

I stripped my jersey off and gave Metzy a nod of approval. I wasn't sure I played my best in front of him, but once I got that burst after my first shift, I skated my ass off. I didn't score any goals, but I kept a lot more out, and that was my job.

"Yo, Holmsy!" Cally called to Blaise.

"What?" Blaise asked, stripping off his jersey and throwing it in the bin.

"Who was the hot blonde next to V tonight?" Cally asked.

"Oh, that's V's friend Lily."

A smile curled up on Cally's lips. "She single?"

"Not for you!" Blaise quipped.

I arched an eyebrow at Blaise. That was news to me.

Blaise gave me a curious look, but I turned away and shed the rest of my gear in silence. I walked to the shower, taking one as quickly as I could.

Blaise and I stepped out of the shower and back to our cubbies at the same time. We dressed in silence, but he shuffled his feet, waiting for me to finish getting dressed.

"Bro, what?" I asked.

"Do you have a thing for Lil?"

"What?" I balked.

He narrowed his eyes at me. "You do, don't you?"

I shrugged and adjusted my tie. "She's hot, but I don't have time for that shit."

Blaise ran his hand down his face. "Lil's been through a lot, and she doesn't need some horndog hockey player on her heels. You got me?"

I held up a hand. "Loud and clear. Like I said, I'm too busy with my kid."

He nodded. "Okay. I'm just looking out for her. Things haven't been easy for her."

If she was off-limits, that made it easier for me to resist the temptation.

"Come on, let's find the girls," he said, pulling on his jacket.

"Yeah, I better get Liam home."

"He was fine with Lil and V."

I followed Blaise out of the locker room and into the family lounge, where the WAGs sometimes waited to meet their families. The guys with kids usually left as soon as possible, their wives leaving before bedtime. Those without kids usually met at Eileen's. Since Veronica was supposed to have my kid, we planned to meet here when we were done instead of at the bar like usual.

When we walked into the lounge, my eyes were laser-focused on the cute blonde kneeling on the floor and talking to the little redheaded boy. She listened intently while he told her something that was of the utmost importance, and she acted like it was so interesting to her. It surprised me he was still awake.

"Uncle Logan!" he cried when he saw me.

Lily turned around right as my nephew sprinted toward me. I knelt down, wrapping him in a big hug. "Hey, buddy. Were you good for Lily and Auntie V?"

"Yes!"

I looked up at Lily, and she nodded. "He's so cute, and he knows it."

I stood up, letting Liam cling to my leg. "Yeah, he does. He gets so many C-O-O-K-I-E-S from me because I cave too easily."

She smiled at me. "Oh, I'm familiar with that bribe. You just gotta be firm."

Something was firm for sure when I looked at her. She wasn't even wearing anything that revealing, but the way the purple blouse accented her features and how her jeans looked painted on made my dick perk up in interest.

Do not go there, Logan. No way.

"Where's V?" I asked.

"She went home early. She's not feeling good."

"Damn, sorry. I didn't mean to put you out."

"Damn!" Liam repeated loudly.

We both cringed and tried not to laugh. If we laughed, he'd know that was a bad word, but if we pretended not to hear it, maybe it would be okay.

"Bye, Liam. It was fun watching hockey together," Lily said to him. "You be a good boy for your uncle, okay?"

He nodded. "Bye, Lily!"

Lily smiled, and then she took her phone out, and I saw she was calling up a car service.

"Let me drive you home," I offered.

She waved me off. "It's no trouble. I have to go to my sister's first."

"I'll drive you. Consider it payment for watching Liam for me."

She chewed on her lip for a moment, but then she nodded. "Okay."

"I promise I'm not a serial killer."

She laughed. "That's what a serial killer would say!"

"Well...." I trailed off, and we laughed. "Come on. Help me wrangle him into his car seat, and I'll take you to your sister's."

She nodded. "Okay."

CHAPTER SIX

LILY

Getting into a car with a man I barely knew wasn't a smart idea. But from the moment I met Logan, something about him felt familiar. Like we knew each other already, but that was impossible.

The only reason I got in the car with him was that Veronica liked him, and I sensed his desperation as a fellow single parent. The man looked exhausted. I knew that look. I'd worn that look since the moment I found out my husband was cheating on me.

"Thanks for hanging with him tonight," he said after we had been driving for a few minutes in silence.

"No worries."

"Sorry V bailed on you."

Veronica should have stayed home tonight. She struggled all night, going back and forth to the bathroom. I was the one who told her to leave. It pained her to do it, but she looked worse for wear. I'd have to see if I could find my relief band or get her those morning sickness lollipops that helped me when I was pregnant with Rosie.

"Oh, it's okay. She didn't want to, but she wasn't feeling great tonight."

I paused before I mentioned her pregnancy. I wasn't sure if Blaise and her had told anyone yet. She said Blaise and Logan were close, but I didn't want to divulge her secret.

"Is it because of the baby?" he asked.

"Yeah...I didn't want to say anything if you didn't know."

The corners of his lips turned up into a smile. "Yeah, Blaise was too excited not to tell me."

"He's going to be a good dad."

Logan nodded. "Yeah, he will. Parenting isn't easy, but he'll figure it out."

"You have to," I agreed.

He gave me a small smile, recognizing our shared plight of single parenthood. Maybe that's why I felt such a connection to him. We bonded over our struggles.

I studied Logan's profile as he drove us to my sister's place. He had reddish-brown scuff on his face but was groomed neatly, and his hair was styled so it was long up top and brushed back out of his face. He wore a navy blue suit that fit him like it was made for him. They probably were. Veronica said Blaise had to get his suits tailored to fit his hockey butt and tree-trunk thighs.

I felt heat color my face when I thought about what other thick things Logan had. I definitely shouldn't be thinking about him that way.

"This is it?" he asked, pulling me away from my horny thoughts.

I peered up at the old brick apartment building my

sister lived in. It was old but not as expensive as when she lived in Fishtown. Even though her place was small, her last place was even smaller and for way more money. I was glad she was only a few minutes from Mom's place now.

"Yeah, this is it. My car's here, so thanks for the ride," I told him.

"No, thank you."

I cocked my head at him. "For what?"

He pointed his thumb at the backseat where his nephew slept soundly. "Taking care of him while Veronica couldn't. I'm having a hell of a time trying to find a nanny."

My hand froze on the door of his car. Something about that statement felt familiar. It must have been because Veronica told me that, but something nagged me in the back of my mind.

"We're square. See you around, Logan," I said before getting out of the car and walking up to my sister's apartment building. I noticed he didn't drive off right away, and I waved to him as I walked through the lobby door.

Logan seemed nice but had a lot of weight on his shoulders. I had to admit, it was nice to chat with someone who understood the burden of being the single provider for the little being you loved the most.

I walked up the flight of stairs and knocked on my sister's door.

She answered it and gave me a big hug. "Hey! How was the hockey game?"

"Good! How was Rosie?"

"Fussy, but otherwise okay. You got a climber on your hands."

I sighed. "I know."

Mari smiled at me, and I took in her appearance for the first time. Her dirty blonde hair was in a messy bun, and she was wearing sweats and leggings. Mari had been babysitting for as long as I could remember and had been a full-time nanny for a family for the last couple of years. Once school started again, they didn't need her anymore. By the tight-lipped expression on her face, I guessed the strain on her finances drained her.

"Did you find a new family yet?" I asked.

She shook her head. "Not yet, but I can't wait around until the summer. I'll need to find another job in the meantime."

"But you love being a nanny!"

She sighed. "You know anyone who needs one?"

Her words hit me, and suddenly, I had the perfect solution. For both her and Logan. Why hadn't I thought about it when he asked me earlier?

"Actually..."

She perked up. "I was just kidding, but if you do?"

"I should have given him your card."

"Who?"

"Logan."

She raised an eyebrow at me. "Who's Logan?"

"Logan Cullen!"

Her eyes widened. "The hockey player?"

"Yes!" I cried. "He drove me here after the game since Veronica felt so sick she had to go home. I spent the game with his nephew on my lap. He needs a nanny."

"But you need me," Mari insisted.

"Yes, but...I don't pay you, and he could pay you a lot. He doesn't make as much as Blaise—"

"He still makes way more than you and me combined."

I opened my mouth and then closed it because she was right. His salary had to be decent because I saw Blaise's finances. Although, I wasn't sure of the difference between their contracts.

"Okay, I'll talk to Veronica to get his number. He's having a hard time and keeps firing his nannies."

She crossed her arms over her chest. "Why does he keep fucking them or something?"

I shook my head. "Veronica said they have WAG aspirations."

Mari laughed. "Well, I'm gay as fuck, so he won't have that problem with me!"

I laughed. "You'd be perfect."

"That would be amazing. I need the money."

I nodded. "Okay, where's my baby girl?"

She nodded toward her bedroom door.

I crept inside and found my daughter sleeping in the crib we kept at Mari's place. Rosie was getting so big every day, and soon she wouldn't be my little baby anymore. She was already walking and talking more and more each day.

I lifted her up into my arms and said a quiet goodbye to my sister. I got Rosie into her car seat; miraculously, she didn't wake up. My sister was magic with kids. I didn't know how she did it.

I drove a few minutes away to my mom's row house. Of course, she had waited up for me, even though I told her not to.

"It's late," Mom said with a raised eyebrow.

"I told you I'd be home late," I said through gritted teeth.

Nobody did passive aggressiveness better than an Irish-American woman from Northeast Philadelphia. No one else was like Violet Mathews. Maybe moving out and struggling with bills would have been better than the judgment I faced from my mother on a daily basis.

Rosie stirred, and I took that as my opportunity to rush upstairs. She started to cry, and I tried to soothe her while I got her ready for bed. I put her down on the changing table and changed her diaper while singing to her. That usually calmed her down.

My heart was full when I set her down in her crib, and she went back to sleep. I watched her for a few moments, and it reminded me that all my struggles were for her. This little girl was my entire world, and I'd do everything in my power to make sure she was taken care of.

I should go to bed or study my notes for the meeting I had tomorrow with Blaise's dad, Hal. He was going to hire me for bookkeeping at his bar, but I was certain he was only doing it because Blaise asked. I was desperate for more work, so I didn't care why Hal wanted to hire me.

Instead of doing either of those, I powered on my laptop and started making a website. I could do this freelance thing. I didn't have my CPA yet, but I could finish my credits later. I could do this. I *had* to do this. If only to prove to my judgmental mother that I wasn't a total fuckup. That I wasn't exactly like her.

CHAPTER SEVEN

LOGAN

"Did you figure out what you're going to do?" Blaise asked as he raised the barbell above his head while I spotted him in the weight room.

"I don't know, man. My neighbor can watch him during the day, but she works nights," I said and rubbed a hand across my bearded jaw.

After sending that scathing email to the nanny service, they decided to no longer work with me. Not great because I was out of options for tomorrow's game.

"V would do it, but she's at that tattoo convention," Blaise said. He finished his set and sat up on the bench, wiping the sweat from his brow.

I didn't want to keep relying on Veronica. I had to find a long-term solution, but right now, I needed to find someone who could look after Liam while I was on the ice tomorrow. It had to be someone I trusted and someone he was comfortable with. That was the key problem.

Blaise had offered his dad, but we tried that once, and Liam was scared of him. Hal was this big blonde guy with a booming voice. His grandkids loved him, but to Liam, he was scary. My sister swore her husband never hit Liam, that she took the brunt of his anger, but I knew a scared little boy living in fear of a monster. I had been that little boy, and I never wanted my nephew to be afraid again.

Blaise and I switched places, so he could spot me while I did bench presses. After finishing my set, I dropped the barbell down on the rack with a loud clang. I cringed. That was louder than I intended.

Blaise peered down at me, his blue gaze clouded. "You okay, man?"

I sat up and ran a hand down my face. "Yeah. Sorry. Just stressed."

"Work that out here, but I need you focused tomorrow."

"I got it."

"Let's call it a day, okay?"

I nodded in agreement.

"Let's go to my dad's for lunch. All this weight training's making me hungry."

I shook my head. "I don't think the nutritionist approves of pub food. Unless it's game day."

Blaise laughed. "Yeah, but that's why my brother convinced my dad to add calories to the menu."

"Okay, but only because I love the food there and because your dad always has the hockey channel on."

"That's why I go. And to annoy my brother."

If there was one thing I learned about being buds with Blaise, it was that his large family was all up in each other's business. One of his little brothers was the manager at the hockey bar his dad owned near the arena. It was a hangout for the team and, unfortunately, puck bunnies. Last night we went there after a victory, and there were a lot of bunnies eying me up. With my lack of a nanny, I didn't have time for that.

Well...maybe on the road. Even then, it was a feat.

TJ kept trying to egg me on. Riley said he was trying to live vicariously through me since TJ had settled down. Even more so now that he had twins on the way. He and his girl were the most mismatched couple I'd ever met. Whereas TJ was loud and in your face, Max was quiet and reserved. But when TJ saw Max from across the room, it was like none of us even mattered. If I hadn't seen it for myself, I wouldn't have believed it.

Sometimes I wondered what that would be like. If I'd ever find a love like my teammates had. I thought I had been in love when I was younger. I dated the same girlfriend since middle school until I got drafted. When I got sent to our AHL affiliate in Reading, she went to college across the country with barely a goodbye. That had stung, but I made up for it by fucking my way through girls who heard I was a hockey player and wanted to say they banged an athlete.

All that shit changed when Rose died and left me to figure out how to raise her son. The entire course of my life had been turned upside down, shattering my worldview and leaving me to pick up the pieces. Not gonna lie, I hadn't been happy about getting parenthood dropped on me, but I wanted a better life for Liam. I didn't want him to go through what Rose and I did.

"Bro, are you okay?" Blaise asked.

When I turned to him, I realized he had parked his car on the street outside of the bar, and I hadn't even registered getting into the car. I got so lost in my thoughts and doubts about raising my nephew, I barely said a word the whole ride.

I rubbed the back of my neck. "Not really."

Blaise arched an eyebrow at me. "You wanna talk about it?"

I shook my head. "Nah. Let's eat, then I can go get Liam."

Blaise looked like he wanted to prod, but then he shook his head and got out of the car. I followed him inside the bar, where he didn't even wait for the host to seat him. I gave the flustered girl an apologetic look and took the seat across from him.

"Get out of my section!" a familiar voice yelled from across the bar.

I grinned as Blaise's younger brother Ayden walked over to us. Ayden had a shaved head and a permanent scowl. He and Blaise were night and day. If they didn't have the same piercing ice-blue eyes, I wouldn't have known they were related.

"Hey, Ayden," I greeted.

Ayden looked at me. "I like that one of your friends has manners. Hey, Logan, what can I get you?"

Blaise poked Ayden. "Hey, asshole, nice to see you, too."

"Get me the chicken Caesar salad," I told Ayden, not even bothering to ask for a menu.

"What do you want?" Ayden prodded his brother.

Blaise was staring up at the TV above the bar, catching whatever the talking heads on the hockey network were spotting off. "You know what I want. Hey, is Lily still here?"

My ears perked up at her name. I couldn't get Lily out of my head. There was something about her that called to me. Despite Blaise's warning to leave her alone, my sex-deprived brain couldn't stop imagining her in inappropriate scenarios.

Christ, I needed to get laid next time we were on the road.

"Yeah, why? Don't bother her. I need her to help me figure out how Dad does expense reports," Ayden said.

"Tell her I need to ask her something," Blaise explained.

Ayden rolled his eyes and walked off into the back.

"Why's Lily here?" I asked.

"Oh, I told Dad to hire her to do his books."

"Oh."

Blaise stared down at his phone with a scowl across his face. He wouldn't admit it, but he was a ball of nerves while his pregnant fiancée was away.

"Are you worried about V traveling?" I asked.

Blaise nodded. "She's still not eating a lot. I don't like it. Didn't want her to go to the convention, but it's great networking and to build up her client list."

"She'll be fine, bro."

He rubbed a hand down his face. "I know it's just...our first baby. I hate her not being next to me. I didn't expect us to get pregnant so soon, but I don't regret it. Can't wait to have a family with her."

"When are you gonna get married?" I asked.

Ayden dropped off water for us and went back behind the bar. It was the middle of the afternoon, so it wasn't that crowded at the bar yet.

Blaise rolled his eyes. "My family's making a huge deal about it. Starting to understand why my brother Brendan had a courthouse wedding."

"You could do that," I offered.

He shook his head, and I smiled when I saw the dopey look on his face. "Nah. I want to give her the whole big thing. Her ex was a colossal douche and left her a week before their wedding. I want to pull out all the stops for her. But after the baby comes."

I nodded. That made sense.

"Hey," a familiar feminine voice greeted us.

I lifted my head up and saw Lily standing in front of our table. She wore a charcoal grey pantsuit with a purple blouse underneath, her hair and makeup flawless.

Blaise smiled at her. "How was the interview?"

She blanched. "Don't want to talk about it. What's up?"

"What are you doing tomorrow?" he asked.

"Nothing. Seth has Rosie, so I'll going to do nothing and—"

"Perfect!" Blaise cut her off and then turned to me. "Lily can help you."

Lily and I shared a confused look. The way her brow creased made her look so cute.

Stop it, Logan. Don't go there. She's off-limits, and you don't have time to get involved with anyone.

Lily cocked her blonde head at me. "What's going on?"

I sighed. "Need a nanny. You know of anyone, good?"

"Actually..."

"Really?" I asked.

She nodded. "My sister. I meant to ask Veronica for your number so I could get you her info. Shoot, she's out of town this weekend."

I waved her off. "I get it. I'd still like her number, though."

"When do you need help?" she asked.

No way I was asking her to babysit. She just mentioned having time away from her baby. I felt like a dick asking her to give up her free time to help me with my nephew. But... Liam liked her. He was a chatterbox asking when he could see her again after she watched him during my game. That was rare. Liam didn't trust easily.

"I can do it. Believe me, Logan, I understand your predicament. Let me grab Mari's card for you, though," she said, and then spun on her stiletto heel and disappeared into the back where I couldn't see her.

I wasn't sure what had just happened.

"Problem solved!" Blaise cheered. Then as if on cue, his brother brought over our food.

We ate and talked about strategy for tomorrow night's game, but I was only half paying attention to Blaise. Which was bad. I needed to prove to Coach LaVoie that I deserved my spot on the team.

"Dude, you gotta let that stress go," Blaise said, pulling me from my thoughts.

I took another big bite of my salad and tried to ignore him. My teammates didn't understand the pressure I was under. I was twenty-four and had a kid to take care of while trying to figure out my career. I needed to stay put for Liam's sake. Which meant working my ass off on the ice to make sure I stayed in Philly next year.

"Hey." That sweet, feminine voice pulled me away from my dark thoughts. Lily stood in front of our table again, and she slid a business card my way.

I picked it up and examined the colorful logo. It read 'Marigold Mathews – Nanny/Babysitter. References upon request.' At the bottom was her contact info.

"That's my sister. She can provide references too. She's been a nanny for this one family for years, but the kids are older and in school now, so she's not needed as much."

"Lily, this is...thanks."

She smiled at me. "I get it. Single parenting's so hard. Call me later about what you need for tomorrow."

"I don't have your number!" I called after her as she walked away.

"Get it from Blaise! Sorry, I have numbers to crunch."

As swiftly as she came, she was gone.

"See, I solve problems!" Blaise joked.

I shook my head at him while I composed an email to Lily's sister. I hoped this worked out.

CHAPTER EIGHT

LILY

Should I have said no when Logan needed a sitter? Absolutely. I should have said sorry and spent my Friday night playing Dragonspire and forgetting my problems for a few hours. But I recognized the desperation in his eyes. I saw the way he struggled with the single parent juggle, and I couldn't say no.

"I'm not sure when I'll be home," I told my mom.

She crossed her arms over her chest and raised an eyebrow. "Why don't you know?"

"Because he has work."

"He has work that late? Who is this friend?"

I sighed. "It's one of Veronica's friends. He plays for the hockey team with Blaise. He's a single dad, and he's in a bind."

"Hmm."

I sighed.

Nothing I did was good enough for her. She still shamed me for not listening to her warnings about Seth. I was naïve and in love, and I thought the future he painted for me was a real possibility. I wished I knew then it had all been a lie.

Since I'd moved back in with my mom, she threw all my mistakes into my face. As if she hadn't made the same ones. Like it was my fault I never saw Seth for who he was until it was too late.

"We're barely even friends, Mom. I'm just doing him a favor," I explained.

"Okay."

"I wasn't asking for permission. I'm an adult. I was just letting you know."

Her eyebrow rose again like she wanted to argue more, but then she threw up her hands and walked away.

I put my computer in my bag. Maybe it was a good thing I couldn't spend tonight melting my brain with video games. Once Liam got to sleep, I'd work on my website and get my business up and running. Blaise's dad hired me to do bookkeeping a couple of hours a month. He didn't need as much help as the tattoo shop, just someone to do data entry. But that meant I now had two clients. I was hoping to build up that list and get testimonials I could add to my website.

I had a plan in motion, but I wasn't fully banking on freelance, either. I had a job interview as a staff accountant, but as soon as I told them I was a single mom coming back to the workforce, they seemed to not care anymore. Companies said they were a 'family' and had a good work-life balance, but they treated mothers with disdain. I'd keep trying because I couldn't stay in my mom's house. The passive-aggressive snide comments and interrogations were grating on me. I didn't want Rosie to grow up in a house full of hostility.

I threw comfy clothes into my bag because I figured I'd

want to be comfortable later when Liam was asleep. Logan called earlier and gave me a run down and what time he needed me. It surprised me when he told me what time he had to be at the arena, but I didn't know what hockey players did to prepare for a game.

I called out a goodbye to my mom before I let the front door slam on the way out. Seth had driven such a wedge between me and my mom, but I wasn't sure how to repair it. It didn't matter, though. The only thing that mattered was Rosie. As long as she was happy and taken care of, I'd deal with the passive aggressiveness. For now.

I got into my car and plugged in the address Logan had given me into my phone. It was somewhere in Old City, and judging by how nice Blaise's house was, I bet Logan lived in one of those swanky condos. I drove to the other side of the city, cursing at traffic since I was alone and could say the F-Word without Rosie repeating it.

Logan lived in a fancy condo that I passed while I searched for a parking garage. I cried a little inside at how much it would cost to park there for the night. I should have taken SEPTA instead.

It reminded me how different our lives were when I walked over to his condo and saw he had a doorman. I went to the front desk and told them I was there to see Logan Cullen. They nodded after I gave them my name as if they had been expecting me and told me I was good to go up.

He might struggle as a single parent, but I searched for him online the other night and found out the details of his contract. He wasn't hurting for money. It wasn't a shock since I did Blaise's taxes last year. Hockey was on the low end of sports, but it was still way more money than I would ever see in my entire life.

The elevator doors dinged, and I walked down the hall

until I found his door. I knocked, and after a few minutes, Logan came to the door with Liam climbing onto his leg.

I gulped when I noticed Logan wasn't wearing a shirt, and his pajama pants hung low on his trim waist. He had red hair marking his happy trail that disappeared into the waistband of his pants. I had not been expecting that, and I couldn't stop staring.

I could blame it on the fact I hadn't had sex since before Rosie was born, but Logan was an attractive man with a trim, athletic physique. It was hard not to notice him.

He gave me a sheepish look. "Sorry, I'm just getting up from my pre-game nap."

"Lily!" Liam cheered when he saw me, and his eyes lit up. "Come play with me!"

"Hold on, bud. Let Lily get inside first."

I waved Logan off and dropped my bag on the floor. I let Liam take my hand and drag me over to the living room, where he had a pile of toys. I sat on the floor with him, and he animatedly told me what we would play.

"Go get dressed for your game. I got him," I reassured Logan.

"Lily, watch!" Liam said to me as he played with a mini hockey stick on the carpeted floor in front of a tiny hockey goal.

"Wow, bud, look at you! Just like your Uncle Logan!"

"You be goalie," he told me.

A smile curled up on my lips. Oh, this little boy was going to have me running around all night. I got in front of the goal net and faked trying to block his shots. I played with him on the carpet for a few minutes until I heard Logan walk back into the living room.

I gulped when he came out wearing a royal blue suit that looked molded to his body. He no longer had messy bedhead; instead, he had styled his bright hair to perfection and trimmed his beard.

He walked over to us and held up two different ties to Liam. "Okay, bud, help me pick which one."

Liam pointed to the blue one that matched Logan's suit. "This!"

Logan smiled and then ruffled Liam's hair. "You'll be good for Lily tonight, okay?"

"Okay!" Liam cheered, and then he moved on to playing with one of his toy trucks, the hockey stick long forgotten.

Logan laid the rejected tie on the floor and put the other one on instead. But he messed up and had to redo it. I leaned forward and pressed my hands against his chest. He flinched at my touch, but then he relaxed when I fixed the tie for him.

"Thanks," he said, but neither of us moved. It felt like all the air had gotten sucked out of the room while his eyes bore into my own.

"Umm. So, is there anything we need to go over?" I asked, trying to cut the tension.

He pulled away and stood up, then offered me a hand and helped me off the floor. Liam was preoccupied with his toys on the floor, and Logan pointed to a binder on the coffee table. A thick binder.

"Everything's in here, but you're so good with him, he shouldn't have an issue."

I raised an eyebrow. "Logan, that's a bit much."

He rubbed his beard. "I might be a helicopter parent."

"I'll read it, I promise," I laughed.

"It's mostly emergency numbers and detailed lists about his likes and dislikes. He doesn't have any allergies, but you'll probably only get him to eat chicken nuggets tonight.

I left my card on the counter if you want something else for dinner for you."

"Should I bring him to the game?"

He shook his head. "Nah. It will end pretty late, and I don't want you stuck there all night. I also want to talk about payment."

I waved him off. "I'm doing you a favor."

"That's why I want to pay you. It's a lot for me to ask. You don't know me."

That was true, but I felt a kindred spirit in him. Maybe it was because we were both struggling single parents. When I peered into his eyes, I felt calm. Like I had known this man my whole life. I couldn't explain why.

"Liam likes you. When I told him you were coming over, he got excited, and he doesn't trust very well. Thanks for doing this. I owe you."

"You can buy me a drink later," I told him and gave him a friendly smile.

He cracked a smile. "Okay. A drink. Maybe dinner. Deal?"

I stuck out my hand, and he shook it in confirmation. "Deal. You better get to the arena, right?"

He nodded. "Yeah. I'll be back late."

"Fine. I brought work to do once I get him to sleep. We'll be fine. I promise you."

He let out a long breath like he had been holding it all in. I saw the stress bearing down on his big shoulders. The mama in me wanted to take that all away from him. I had that same expression on my face more than I would have liked.

Logan walked over to Liam and knelt down in front of him. He opened his arms out to the little boy. "Okay, little man, I gotta go to work."

"No!" Liam cried.

"Lily will be here with you tonight, okay?"

Liam balled his little fists.

"Liam," Logan said sternly.

The temper tantrum boiled up to the surface, so I stepped in. "Liam, we're gonna have so much fun tonight. Right?"

Liam's mood shifted when he looked at me.

"Give me a hug," Logan said.

My heart melted when Liam sweetly hugged his uncle goodbye. If you didn't know their relationship, you'd think they were father and son. It was that red hair and even some of their mannerisms. It was clear Logan loved the little boy with all his heart.

"I'll see you later," Logan said to me.

I nodded. He left shortly after, engulfing Liam and me in silence. But not for long because the little boy was determined to wear me out.

"Come on, Liam, bedtime," I tried to persuade the four-year-old.

The little boy in question crossed his arms over his little chest. "No!"

I read through the very thorough binder Logan had put together while I cooked dinner and Liam sat with his tablet. In the binder, Logan mentioned bedtime could be a fight. Before now, Liam had been a little angel. He kept me on my toes, having me playing mini-sticks with him for most of the afternoon. He even behaved when I gave him a bath and got him in his jammies. When I told him it was time to get into bed, that's when he pushed me.

"Liam, it's time for bed. I'll read you a story."

"No bedtime."

"Yes, bedtime, mister."

He scrunched up his little face and shook his head. "No!"

The binder said Logan was trying to get Liam to sleep in his big kid bed in his room instead of in Logan's room. I knew the trap of co-sleeping, so no judgments there, but since his uncle wasn't home, I was going to try to get him into his own room tonight.

"Big boys go to bed on time, in their big boy beds," I told him. I knelt down near the little bookshelf next to the bed and studied the books. "Come show me which story you want to read."

"Okay..."

He pulled out three different books and handed them to me. He climbed onto the twin mattress, and I sat next to him. He cuddled into my side, and I opened the first book to read to him. After the first book, he had fallen asleep. Kids wanted to fight you, even if they were sleepy.

I eased off the bed and put the books away. I tucked him in and quietly left the room, making sure the nightlight was on if he woke up later. I found my bag and changed into a pair of leggings and a hoodie. I shed my restrictive bra and flopped down on the couch. I turned the TV on and found the hockey game, put it on low, and took my laptop out.

I wanted nothing more than to be at home playing video games. I wanted to do that so bad. It would have been so weird if I had lugged my console over to Logan's. He'd probably think I was weird. I already dealt with 'fake gamer girl' comments from jerks in the gaming community. I wasn't sure a jock like Logan would understand my love of games.

The only good thing about not being able to play Dragonspire right now was that it forced me to focus on my business. I opened up my browser and started working on my website. I needed to get this up and running soon, but I wasn't much of a webmaster. I was using a simple program to have a basic website to get myself started. I wasn't sure starting this business was smart, but I'd been going to job interview after job interview with no luck. At least I had work booked with the tattoo shop and the bar. Hal said he'd want my help with his personal finances during tax season, too, so I was making strides.

I had only been working for twenty minutes when I heard a scream. I tossed my laptop onto the couch beside me and ran into Liam's room. The little boy was crying for his mama. I went to him and rocked him into my arms.

"You're okay, you're okay," I told him while I stroked his back and tried to get him to calm down.

"MAMA!" he cried and clung onto me for dear life.

There was nothing in the binder about this.

So I did the only thing I could think of—I crawled into the tiny bed with him and held him to my chest. I let him cry it out while I sang to him and whispered that it would be okay. I didn't know what was going on with him, but my heart hurt at hearing this little boy in so much anguish.

Eventually, he calmed down, and I wiped his tears. "You're okay, baby," I cooed. "I got you."

"I miss Mama," he sniffled.

My heart hurt for this little boy and all the emotions he couldn't contain. No wonder Logan looked overwhelmed every time I saw him. He was in over his head trying to do the single dad thing. He needed my sister's help.

"Are you my new mama?" Liam asked.

"No, baby. I'm here to help take care of you while your uncle's at work."

"Uncle Logan sad," he muttered as he buried his head in my chest.

They said kids were observant, and there was a loneliness around Logan. Was it sadness? I wasn't sure. I barely knew him. I shouldn't waste my energy worrying about someone who was a mere acquaintance. But I wanted so badly to fix everything for him.

It was the mom in me. Or it was because I was in the same boat. I knew the loneliness that set in when you were trying hard to take care of the little person in your life. Or maybe it was because when I looked into Logan's eyes, it was like I had known him my whole life. I wished I knew why I felt that way around him. The only thing I knew for sure was that I had to make sure the little boy in my arms was taken care of.

CHAPTER NINE

LOGAN

"Hell yeah, that's how we do it, boys!" TJ yelled as we walked into the locker room after another much-needed win.

I stripped my jersey off and began taking off my gear, all the while shaking my head at him.

We played a good game, but I wasn't happy with my performance. The worry over Liam and what I was going to do while we headed out on a road trip in a couple of days was a raging storm cloud over my head. I let it affect my game tonight. Coach noticed it, and so did my teammates. Blaise even said something when we were riding the pine together.

I should have cooled down on the bike before heading out, but I had to get home. Lily was already doing me a huge favor by watching Liam and finding me a nanny. I chatted with Mari earlier today and got a good impression of her, but I wanted to check her references. I needed her to meet

Liam first to see if they fit. I was hoping he'd latch onto her like he did with her sister.

"Man, you okay?" Blaise asked.

I shook my head. "I gotta get going."

"Liam's fine with Lily."

I rubbed the back of my neck. Blaise wouldn't understand the shit I was going through until after Veronica had their baby. Then he'd understand my constant state of worry.

"Come on, Cully, get your ass in the shower. We're getting drinks!" TJ yelled at me from the other side of the room.

Riley eyed the forward. "T, leave him alone."

Thank the hockey gods for Riley being the voice of reason. It was no wonder Coach gave him the 'C.'

I headed toward the shower, ignoring TJ. When I got out, Riley sat in his cubby, dressed and waiting for me. "You okay, man?"

I felt bad he stayed to chat with me, especially since he had a newborn and wife waiting for him at home. That was another reason why he had the C; he was always there for us when we needed his advice.

I sighed. "I looked bad tonight."

He nodded. "You seemed on edge."

"Still don't have a nanny."

He nodded again in understanding. "Okay, but let us know. Fi will help."

I shook my head. I couldn't do that to them, especially since they were still adjusting to parenthood. "No, it's fine. I got someone potentially."

"Okay, but you have people who will help you. Tomorrow, let's do extra drills during practice on the penalty kill. And we'll review video. Okay?"

I nodded.

That was fine with me. Riley was all about video. He wanted to study what we did wrong and analyze our next opponent for their weaknesses. That's why he was the best defenseman on the team.

He clapped me on the shoulder. "Don't worry about T. He's just busting your balls."

"He's a pain in my ass."

Riley laughed. "That's TJ! He got on my shit while Fi and I were trying to have a baby. Like sorry dude, I'd rather be with my smokeshow wife than have a beer with you assholes."

I laughed too. "I get that."

He studied me for a split second. "Do you?"

"I can imagine. All I have is hockey and Liam, and I'm fine with that. I gotta get going. A friend did me a favor by watching him tonight."

He raised an eyebrow. "She hot?"

"Yeah, but it's not like that. Plus, Blaise said she's off-limits."

"Why?"

I shrugged. "She's friends with his girl."

Riley's eyes lit up in recognition. "Oooh, V's friend Lily. She's cute. If I recall, you two looked pretty cozy at Blaise's barbecue last summer."

"Nah. Just commiserating being single parents. She's cute, but...yeah, I don't have time for that, and neither does she."

Riley seemed like he wanted to say something else, but then Blaise came back from his shower, and we both shut our traps.

I wasn't sure why Blaise said Lily was off-limits, but I respected him enough to know there had to be a reason. It was probably because Lily didn't have time for anything either. She might be a cute little blonde with a pretty smile, but I wasn't going down that road.

I left before TJ could goad me into going out with them. One beer led to three, and I didn't want Lily to wait up so late for me to get home. I didn't get home until at least midnight if I did post-game media or cooled down on the bike. I felt guilty that she'd dropped her free night to help me, so I raced out as soon as I could.

I drove back to Old City, and when I parked in the garage, I realized I should have told Lily to park down here. I'd have to ask her where she parked. After she dismissed taking payment for helping me with childcare, I was sure she wouldn't let me pay for parking. I didn't get that stubbornness. I might not be making what Blaise or Riley made, but I knew I made way more than she did.

I got out of my car and went up the elevator to my floor. When I walked inside, the TV was on in the living room, turned to the sports network, and a laptop was laid out on the couch, but there was no sign of Lily. The hair on the back of my neck raised in alarm.

I burst into Liam's room, and then my heart fluttered at the sight of Lily in the kid bed with Liam curled around her. They were both asleep and looked so peaceful.

I walked over to the bed and knelt down beside it. "Lily?" I whispered, but she didn't move an inch. "Hey, Lil, wake up."

She stirred and held Liam to her tighter. Something about the movement made my chest puff out in pride. Watching this woman I barely knew be protective of Liam got my pulse jumping.

I lightly tapped her. "Lil."

Her eyes fluttered open, and she took a minute to realize where she was. "Oh. I must have fallen asleep."

"Come on."

I helped her get out of the bed, hoping she didn't wake up Liam. He stirred a little, but I tucked him back into the bed and kissed his forehead. Lily gave me a look of adoration as she watched me with my nephew. We crept out of the bedroom and shut the door.

She ran a hand through her hair, trying to fix her bedhead. "Sorry. He woke up screaming for his mama, and it was the only way to get him to stop."

"Fuck, I forgot to tell you about that," I said. "You want a glass of wine or something? I need a beer."

"Um sure," she said as she bit her lip.

I took off my suit jacket and hung it on the back of the couch before going into the kitchen. I grabbed a beer but opened a bottle of red wine and poured her a glass. Maybe I shouldn't have asked her that. She probably wanted to get going.

I found her on the couch in my living room, furrowing her brow at her computer. I handed her the glass. "Oh, thanks," she said, but she didn't look up from her computer.

I undid my tie. "I'm sorry. I should have warned you about the screaming."

"You put everything else in the binder. What's that about?"

I took a pull off my beer. "My sister and her asshole husband died about two years ago, and I got custody of Liam. He's still having a hard time with it."

"What about his grandparents? Why you?" she asked.

"Mom died when we were in high school, and Dad's been in jail for a long time. He's never getting anywhere near Liam. His dad's parents are long dead. So it's just me," I said.

I didn't realize I had been curling my hands into fists until she touched my arm and pulled me out of it. "Are you okay?"

I shook my head. "Sorry, I'm good. I feel like an ass for asking you if you wanted a drink. You probably want to get home."

"I'm baby free this weekend, so this glass of wine's perfect. Unless you're kicking me out?"

I took another sip of my beer. "Definitely not." I eyed her computer. "What are you working on?"

"Oh, trying to get my website up and running."

"I never asked what you did for a living."

"Accountant. Well, I was until I quit my cushy corporate job because I was going to be a stay-at-home mom. Then I found out my husband was a piece of shit cheater, so I got divorced and moved back in with my mother, who's passive-aggressive as shit and likes to tell me 'I told you so' as much as she can," she rambled on in one breath.

I furrowed my brow as her words hit me. They felt so familiar to me. Like we had this conversation before, but I couldn't remember when. Maybe we had it at Blaise's barbecue, but that wasn't something you blurted out to someone you had just met.

When I glanced over at her again, her cheeks reddened, but I wasn't sure if it was from the wine or the embarrassment of her outburst.

"Sorry, that was too personal. I'm doing bookkeeping work for Blaise's dad and for the tattoo shop Veronica works at. I'm trying to go freelance while I look for something permanent."

I shook my head. "Not too personal. Have we talked about this before?"

She shook her head and closed her laptop. She curled her legs underneath her as she sipped on her wine. "I don't think so."

Hmm. I definitely heard someone else say those things to me. Maybe she forgot she told me.

"Did you watch the game?" I asked and pointed to the TV.

She shook her head. "Like one period? Then Liam started screaming. I don't want to overstep, but you should have him talk to someone."

I nodded. "I know. How was he?"

"Good. He made me play hockey with him pretty much until dinner. He was only a handful at bedtime, but I got him into the big kid bed."

"I'm amazed. He keeps on wanting to be in my bed."

"Logan! If you let him co-sleep with you, he'll get too used to it," she said, and her cheeks got pink again. "Sorry, it's not my business to tell you how to parent."

I set my beer down. "No, you're right. I hate when he cries, though. Can't help it."

She smiled. "I get it. That's why I went in there and slept with him until he calmed down. I'm a hypocrite for judging you."

I put a hand on her thigh. "I appreciate that. I really do."

She froze and stared down at my hand. Then she gulped more of her wine before setting it on the coffee table. She put a hand over mine. "You're welcome. I understand what you're going through."

The way her hazel eyes studied me made me brazen. I rubbed my thumb across the back of her palm. She didn't pull away, didn't even flinch. I saw the way she stared at me earlier when I opened the door without a shirt. That hadn't been intentional, but I had to admit I liked the way her eyes had tracked hungrily over my body. Then when she fixed my tie, a spark of electricity coursed through me at her touch. There was something pulling me toward her. I shouldn't do what I was about to do, but my dick was in charge, and he didn't care.

"Logan?" she breathed out in a shaky breath.

I pulled my hand away from her thigh, only to reach up and push her hair behind her ear. I stared into her eyes, and when she nodded, I leaned over and slanted my mouth on hers.

Fuck, her lush mouth against mine felt so good. It hadn't been that long since I last had sex, but it felt like it had been eons while I devoured her mouth. I angled her head, and she submitted to me, opening her mouth and letting me slide my tongue inside. We kissed until we were a messy tangle of hands and lips, trying desperately to be closer.

I pulled away, and she had a shocked look on her face, but then I pulled her into my lap. She straddled my legs, and we kissed again. My cock was hard as a rock, and I felt her own arousal through the thin cotton of her leggings as she ground against me. My dick strained against her pussy, wanting so badly to be deep inside her.

"Logan," she moaned.

I slid my hands up her hoodie and found her breasts bare underneath the material. I slid a thumb across one of her nipples and hissed at how it sharpened to a point at my touch. I wanted my mouth on it. I wanted to kiss and lick her to completion before I had her pinned beneath my large body as I fucked her until she screamed my name.

That's when I snapped out of it. "I'm sorry. I should—"

She shut me up with another kiss.

I didn't know how this had happened so fast, but my horny brain didn't care. There was a hot woman in my lap, kissing me and grinding on my dick. Fuck Blaise and his 'off-limits' rules. Fuck me not having time for a relationship. As long as Lily knew this was only for the night, we could have fun while she was free of her responsibilities.

"Bedroom?" she asked in between rough kisses.

I didn't even answer her. I held her to my chest and got up from the couch. This was such a bad idea, but she was into it, so who was I to say no when a woman wanted me as badly as I wanted her? So I took her into my bedroom and decided I was going to make bad decisions tonight.

CHAPTER TEN

LILY

His hands reached up to frame my face, and I felt the air leave my lungs when he leaned over and fused his lips to mine. My whole body tingled as we kissed. I hadn't been kissed or felt the weight of a man's hands on my body in so long. I melted into him and let him angle me into whatever position he wanted as he pinned me down against his bed. I never thought my night of babysitting his nephew would end like this, but I relished it.

I arched my hips against the friction of his cock. Oh God, I knew he was a big guy, but it felt like he was packing some heat down there. I pressed my hands against his chest as he kissed the breath out of me. We were both panting and our hands clung to the hems of each other's shirts when we pulled away. Looking up into his ocean-blue eyes, all I saw was white-hot heat for me.

A thought meddled in my brain at what he'd think about my post-baby body. Seth made comments about not bouncing back to my old weight. Not to mention how self-conscious I was about my stretch marks.

None of that mattered because I reared back and flinched at the blood-curdling scream from the next room. Logan didn't say anything; instead, he jumped up from the bed and ran into his nephew's room.

I lay back on his bed with a sigh. What was I doing? I couldn't be getting involved with a hockey player. Or anyone. I was a single mom who needed to focus on her career. Getting involved with Logan was a bad idea.

A BAAAAAAD idea.

It didn't stop the way his kisses made me feel alive again. Or how he made me feel cared for when he cradled me as we kissed like I was all he ever needed.

I should have left. I should have slunk out of there as soon as he got Liam, but I didn't. Just how I went to Liam when he made that same piercing scream earlier. The mama in me couldn't bear hearing the little boy cry out like that. I wanted to go in with Logan and hold Liam until he calmed down. But I didn't want to overstep.

Logan's frame filled the doorway, and I cocked my head at him, but then he walked into the bedroom with Liam in his arms. He tried to comfort the little boy, but Liam's face was scrunched up and splotchy from all his tears.

"Bring him here," I said, surprising myself.

"Miss mama!" Liam cried.

I gestured for Logan to bring him over. He walked over to the bed and put Liam down in the center. Liam crawled over to me and laid his head on my chest while he continued to cry. Logan got into the bed beside me.

I brushed Liam's hair. "I know, baby, you get it all out. Your Uncle Logan and I are here."

Logan reached out and stroked Liam's hair while I

rocked him in my arms. My heart hurt seeing this little boy in so much anguish.

"Shush, I got you." I hummed to him until his crying ceased, but the little boy clung to me, and it broke my heart.

When I glanced over at Logan, there was a deep crease in his brow.

"What's wrong?" I whispered.

"What were you humming to him?"

I hid the cringe. To a jock like Logan, telling him I was humming the theme song of the nerdy video game I played was embarrassing.

Logan stared at me. "Was that the theme of Dragonspire?"

I stared at him for a long time while he squinted at me.

"Yes. It's the only thing that gets Rosie to sleep," I muttered while I caressed Liam's head.

"You know what Dragonspire is?"

I narrowed my eyes at him. "What? Because I'm a woman, I can't be a gamer?"

He shook his head and held up his hands. "Not saying that. Just unexpected. The boys give me shit for playing that nerd shit instead of sports games like them."

I laughed. "So boring! RPGs are where it's at!"

He grinned. "Console or PC?"

A small smile tugged at my lips. "Console. You?"

"Same. I'd love to get a nice PC setup, but I don't get to play a lot with traveling all the time."

I nodded. "I got busy when I got pregnant, but it's easy to drop in, make armor, and do a dungeon crawl. I have a few people I play with, but I'm not in a guild or anything. I don't have that time on my hands."

He nodded as he stroked Liam's head soothingly. Liam hadn't gone back to sleep yet, but he calmed down once he was lying in between us. "I'm too busy with this one and playing hockey to be a serious gamer."

"I didn't pin you for a Dragonspire player."

Now it was his turn to raise an eyebrow at me. "Why? Because I'm a jock?"

I felt heat color my face, but then a smile spread across his freckled face. "Are you making fun of me?"

He held his forefinger and thumb together. "A little. Sorry about him being a handful. You probably want to get home, yeah?"

I nodded, but the little boy in my arms burrowed into my chest and clung to me. "No! Stay!"

"Buddy, Lily has to go home, okay? She has her own baby she needs to take care of."

Liam shook his little head. "No!"

Logan gave me a pained look.

"It's okay," I mouthed over Liam's head.

"Gimme a minute. I gotta change out of this monkey suit," Logan said, and he got out of bed and went into the walk-in closet.

Liam snuggled down against me again, and I couldn't be mad at him. He was so cute, and with Rosie being with Seth, I was missing my snuggly baby. I was glad I had taken off my bra and was wearing leggings and a hoodie. Sleeping in my jeans would have been uncomfortable.

It was probably good Liam had stopped Logan and me from doing something impulsive. Logan was hot, but sleeping with him was a bad idea. Even though I wanted to kiss him again.

I stroked Liam's hair as his little head lay nestled against my chest. Logan needed help with the little guy. My heart broke for them in equal measure. It was the mama in me. I wanted to dry all of Liam's tears and take the burden from Logan. I couldn't help it.

"Hey, did you get a chance to call my sister?" I called out to Logan.

"Yeah!" he called back, his voice muffled as he got changed in the closet. "I want to check her references and have her meet the little guy."

"I'm one of them! I trust Mari with Rosie's life."

"I'm still gonna check the others."

"You don't have anything to worry about. Mari doesn't like men, so she won't hit on you."

Logan walked out, and I gulped at the sight of his ridiculously fit body in only a pair of pajama pants. Was this man trying to tempt me? He got back into the bed with me and Liam and brought the comforter over us.

"She doesn't?" he asked.

"Mari's been with her girlfriend Kelly since high school. V told me about the...issues you've had with other nannies."

He sighed. "I want someone to help with him when I'm on the road. I don't have time for anything like that."

"What about the rest of this weekend? When do you travel next?"

Logan put a finger to my lips. "Relax, I have it handled. But thank you for the offer. You should enjoy the rest of your weekend free from baby duty."

I smiled at him while he hit the light, plunging us into darkness. "You know what I was going to do tonight before you asked for my help?"

"What?"

"Play Dragonspire."

He laughed. "A girl after my own gamer heart."

The smile stayed on my face. "I misjudged you, Logan."

"Well, we've only known each other in passing...but I'd like to get to know you better."

Yeah, I was sure he did. I was pretty sure his mouth and his hands and even his cock wanted to get to know me a lot better tonight. Too bad there was a little boy between us preventing that.

"Show?" Liam asked, pointing to the large flatscreen mounted on the wall.

"No, buddy, bedtime," Logan said in a stern voice.

He kissed the top of Liam's head, and I smiled at how affectionate he was with his nephew. A lot of guys weren't like that with their kids. They gave into that toxic masculinity of men never showing their emotions. I liked that Logan showed the boy he raised kindness and love. All kids needed that.

I lay beside Logan for several minutes, listening to the heavy breathing of the child in-between us.

"You can go if you want. He'll be okay," Logan whispered into the dark.

But the thing was, I didn't want to go. I should have, but the mama bear in me wanted to stay and make sure Liam was okay.

"It's okay," I whispered back.

"He's attached to you."

I wrapped my arm around Liam, a protective move as if that would keep him safe from whatever haunted him. "Logan?"

"Hmm?"

I took a breath before asking what was on my mind. It was none of my business, but the hurt across the little boy's face tonight made me nosy.

"How did she die?"

"Car crash."

"Does he understand that she's gone?"

He sighed. "We've talked about it at length. He's having a hard time coping. He cries for her all the time. I don't know what to do."

I put a hand on his arm. "You're doing amazing. You'll figure this parenting thing out."

"I hope so. You don't have to stay; you can leave if you want to get home."

"Can I tell you a secret?"

"Yeah?"

"Your bed's super comfy, so I kinda want to stay."

He tried not to laugh. "Thanks for everything tonight. I owe you. Seriously, I'll treat you to a nice dinner to thank you. Wherever you want."

"I'm an easy gal. All I want is pizza, beer, and a night to myself playing video games."

"Well, once I figure out my nanny situation, maybe I can help with that, too."

I smiled. That sounded amazing. I didn't need a fancy dinner. I was content with my controller and a night to myself in front of a video game. Or with my favorite comic book open in front of me. I never needed fancy.

It wasn't a lie that Logan's bed was comfy, but that wasn't why I wanted to stay. I couldn't stand to see his nephew so hurt. So instead of leaving like a normal person and sleeping in my own bed, I fell asleep next to a stranger.

CHAPTER ELEVEN

LOGAN

I woke up to a tiny foot against my head, not an uncommon practice when I brought Liam into my bed. I eased him into a different position, and that's when I noticed the other form in my bed.

Lily lay asleep in the bed with Liam in between us. She had one hand outstretched toward Liam protectively and the other behind her head underneath the pillow. Her blonde hair was spread across the pillowcase, and she looked so peaceful.

I hadn't expected her to stay last night. Once we got Liam back to sleep, I was sure she'd leave. That's what I would have done.

I cringed as the memory of what we had been doing before he woke up came rushing back. Dammit. I shouldn't have kissed her. I didn't regret it by any means, and she had been eager to be beneath me, but Liam cockblocking us was a sign from the hockey gods that whatever we were about to do was a bad idea. Blaise would use my nuts as practice shots if he found out.

I ran a hand down my face. I didn't want to tell her it was a mistake, but I had to nip it in the bud. Finding out she was a gamer made her a hundred times hotter in my book. And she played Dragonspire, of all the games? It was like she was my dream girl. But like a dream, it was unattainable. It was Liam and hockey for me; nothing else could take up space in my life.

Liam stirred and crawled back over to Lily. Her eyes fluttered open, and she let Liam snuggle into her side. Our eyes met, and she gave me a sleepy smile. "Hi."

"Morning. You want breakfast?"

She nodded and rubbed the sleep from her eyes. "I should get going. Crap. I never told my mom I was staying over."

She mentioned she lived with her mom, and I imagined that was annoying. If my mom was still alive, I'd have her living with me, far away from the sperm donor. Sometimes I was glad Mom never lived to see Rose end up with an asshole like our father. Although if she had, she could have warned Rose before it was too late.

"I'm hungry!" Liam piped up.

"Then come on, little man," I told him. "Let's go fix breakfast for our guest."

Liam barreled over me and ran into the kitchen. Lily laughed, and I shook my head as I went into the kitchen to find my nephew. I sat him down at the kitchen table and gave him some dry cereal while I started the coffee.

Lily walked into the living room, now dressed in jeans and a long-sleeved striped shirt. She had pulled her hair up into a ponytail, and my hand itched to pull it out and run my fingers through her silky blonde locks.

Yeah, I couldn't think about that stuff.

She went into the living room and came back with her half-drunk glass of wine and my beer from last night. She poured the wine down the drain and set the glass on the counter. She poured out the beer and searched for the recycling.

"Don't worry about that. I got it."

"Do you want help with breakfast?" she asked.

I poured two cups of coffee into mugs. "Nah. Let me make it as a thank you. Milk's in the fridge, and sugar's in the cabinet above your head."

She wrinkled her nose. "Oh, I drink it black."

I made a face back at her. "Gross."

She took her mug of coffee and sat at the table across from Liam, who immediately started chatting her ear off. It was seven a.m., and he was already running a mile a minute. When I looked back at them, the way she smiled at him and encouraged him made me want to reconsider not trying a relationship. But that was a ridiculous thought. I may have shared a heated kiss with this woman, but I barely knew her.

I busied myself with making eggs and toast, trying to drown out my heart telling me what to do. Or maybe it was my dick. Either way, it needed to shut up because my brain knew better.

I grabbed plates, sectioned our respective portions onto them, and brought them over to the table. I used the special plate for Liam because he hated when his food touched, especially at breakfast. He usually only wanted pancakes, but when Lily made a big show of taking a bite of her eggs and saying, ' Yum!' dramatically, he started eating too.

The fact she was so good with him was obviously

because she was a mom. But I had to admit, it was a huge turn-on.

"Can we talk about what happened last night?" I blurted out.

She raised an eyebrow. "Me staying over? I know you said I could leave, but I couldn't. He seemed so upset."

I shook my head. "Not that. Before."

Her eyes widened in recognition, and she shifted around in her chair uncomfortably. "We don't have to talk about it."

I rubbed my beard. "I'm not... I don't have time for a relationship."

She narrowed her eyes. "Who said I did?"

"I—"

"Forget it, Logan," she said, but in a firm voice that meant I pissed her off.

"I'm not trying to—"

But she cut me off with a glare, and Liam looked between the two of us in concern. I ruffled his hair to let him know it was okay.

Lily pushed her plate of food away. "I better get going. I'll see you around, Logan." She got up from her chair but knelt down in front of Liam. "Bye, Liam. I had fun with you last night. Don't be too hard on your uncle, okay?"

"No, don't go!" he cried and wrapped his arms around her neck.

"I gotta, baby. Be good, okay?"

He nodded enthusiastically, while I sat there silently watching her grab her things and leave.

I sighed at the sound of the door slamming behind her.

"I like Lily," Liam said.

"Me too, bud."

Because I did. What I saw of her, I liked. In the long

run, it was better if I pissed her off instead of her getting ideas that we could be something more. It didn't help the raging boner I had in my pants when I thought about her moans as we kissed last night, though. A part of me knew things were better this way, but the other part of me was kicking myself for being an asshole.

My phone beeped, and I saw a text message from her sister.

MARI: Hi! I'll be back in Philly on Sunday. I could swing by and meet Liam if you like?

That was quick. Maybe Mari needed me as much as I needed her.

ME: That would be awesome. Your sister already said she trusted you with her daughter's life.

MARI: I love Rosie! But please check my other references before you hire me.

Already Mari seemed more professional than any of the other nannies I had hired. I hoped this worked out.

"Okay, bud, we're gonna meet a new friend today," I told Liam and tried to get him excited.

"Lily?" he asked with a hopeful look in his eyes.

My nephew was attached to the woman, and he had been sulking since she left in a huff the other day. I still wasn't sure how to fix that. I hurt her feelings, but I'd rather hurt her now than later.

"No, but it's her sister, and I'm hoping she can be your new nanny."

"I'm not baby!" he pouted.

"I know, little man, but you need someone to take care of you when I have work, okay?" I bent down to his level to look him in the eye. He seemed to think it over, the gears of his tiny brain working it out. "Let's meet Mari, okay?"

He nodded, but he wasn't paying attention to me. He was more interested in playing with the new toy I got him. Did I bribe Liam to meet his new nanny? Yes. No judgments here. You do what you have to do when you're a parent.

All of Mari's references had gotten back to me and had great things to say about her. Except for the one family who joked she was terrible, but only because they wanted her back for the summer when their kids were out of school. The mother I spoke to told me she was kidding and said Mari was like Mary Poppins. That made me feel way better about hiring her. But first, I needed Liam to like her.

My phone buzzed with an alert from the front desk, and I let them know Mari was okay to send up. I'd never get used to living in a place that had a doorman, but I was grateful to Mac for letting me sublet the place. Once I felt more secure in my standing with the team, I'd look for something more permanent.

I went to the door when I heard the knock. I opened it and found a petite woman with her dirty blonde hair in a messy bun and a grin on her face. You could see the family resemblance between Mari and Lily.

"Hi!" she said to me.

"Hey, come on in," I told her and opened the door wider. She walked inside and kicked off her shoes and her jacket. I took her jacket and hung it up in the hall closet.

I didn't even need to introduce her. She got right down on the floor with Liam and started playing with him.

"Hi, Liam. I'm Mari. Can we be friends?" she asked.

Liam looked at me for guidance, and I nodded my approval at him.

He handed her a toy truck. "Let's play!"

She smiled. "Okay, little man. What are we playing?"

I watched, amazed, as he took a shine to her instantly. Maybe it was the blonde hair. My sister dyed her red locks blonde for as long as I could remember, and Liam took to blonde women well. As I watched them, though, I knew it wasn't just that. Mari seemed to be great with him. When he got cranky, she managed his emotions swiftly. Yeah, I was hiring her for sure. She was perfect.

"Okay, little man. What say I come over and play with you when your uncle has work?" Mari asked.

"Otay!" Liam agreed as he ran his truck across the carpet.

She smiled at him. "Okay, gimme a minute. I want to talk to your uncle."

She sat on the couch next to me, but her eyes were still on Liam, not leaving him out of her sight for a second. "So how did I do?"

"Awesome. You're hired!"

"Great, because I could use the work. I have to ask you something because Lil won't."

I raised an eyebrow.

"I help her out a lot, so would it be okay with you if there are some days I have both of them? Lil will never ask you that because she doesn't pay me to help with Rosie."

I didn't realize when Lily offered her sister, it affected her too. The family who didn't want to let Mari go had four kids and said she was more than capable of handling one rambunctious toddler.

"If she's good with that, I'm fine with it. I need

overnights when I travel for work and during the day when I have practice and other stuff going on. I have a binder of all the info and my schedule," I told her and gestured to the binder on the coffee table.

"Okay, perfect. And you have a game on Wednesday, so when do you travel for that?"

I eyed her carefully. I was under the assumption Lily wasn't into sports, so it surprised me her sister already knew my schedule.

She waved me away with her hand. "I checked the schedule out to be prepared."

"We fly out Tuesday. I'll be back Thursday."

She put a gentle hand on my arm. "You're doing fine. Lily told me about his nightmares and the co-sleeping. I can help with stopping that."

"She told you that?"

She nodded. "Yes...and...other things."

I groaned. "Like how I was an as—" I caught myself before I swore in front of Liam, "jerkface."

She smiled. "Yeah."

"I owe her dinner or something. She wouldn't take payment when she babysat him."

Mari shook her head. "That's her pride showing. She likes roses and authentic Mexican food."

I cocked my head at her. "Are you trying to get me together with your sister?"

She grinned. "Maybe. Look, you're hot, and my sister's been through it. She needs to relax for once."

I shook my head. "I can't give her something serious."

"That's not what I was trying to say. She's not looking for something serious either. But you could have some fun together."

"Why are you encouraging this?"

"Because..." She looked at Liam to see if he was paying attention. "She needs to get L-A-I-D. Think about it. Roses."

"Roses?"

She nodded. "Yeah, that's why she named her daughter Rose."

"I thought it was Rosie."

She nodded. "Yeah, but it's tradition in my family for the women to have flower names. I'm Marigold, she's Lily, Mom's Violet, our grandmother's name was Rose, so Lily used that as her excuse."

I rubbed the arm where I had the tattoo of a rose in honor of my sister. "Rose was my sister's name."

Mari smiled. "Too funny."

She knelt on the floor with Liam again, and I felt a weight lift from my shoulders. I was so glad I found Mari. She seemed perfect. Except for the part she was encouraging me to get with her sister. That was a bad idea. I wasn't doing that at all. But I would take her to dinner to say thanks and send her flowers to apologize for being a dick. I owed her that at least.

CHAPTER TWELVE

LILY

"Hey, you have a delivery," Veronica told me as she came into the office.

I looked up at her and gave her a funny look when she brought over a bouquet of red and white roses. "For me?"

She nodded.

I pulled out the card, my brow furrowing in thought about who could have sent them. I didn't have a regular schedule. I was back and forth between the tattoo shop and the bar. When I wasn't doing that, I was going to interview after interview. So who could have known where to find me here today? And why?

I found the card and opened it.

Lil,

Sorry for being a dick. I still owe you dinner. Name the time and place.

-Logan

I stared down at his messy handwriting. I had a feeling I knew who had a hand in this. Especially since my sister had been working for him for about a week now, and Liam adored her.

"Who's it from?" Veronica asked.

"Nosy," I teased.

She grinned. "Gimme the gossip!"

"Logan."

Her eyebrows rose high. "Oh. I'm surprised he's going against Blaise's wishes."

It was my time to raise an eyebrow at her. She clamped a hand over her mouth as she realized what she said. "V, what did Blaise say to Logan?"

"That you were off-limits."

What the heck? Is that why Logan got so weird after we kissed? Because my friend's man told him to stay away? I liked Blaise, but he had no right to tell Logan that.

"Logan says he can't have something serious because of Liam, so Blaise told him that to protect you," Veronica explained.

I sighed. "V, I don't have time for something serious either."

She eyed the flowers. "Did something happen when you watched Liam?"

"It was nothing," I said, hoping that if I brushed her off, she'd drop it.

It was nice Logan sent flowers and apologized, but I probably overreacted. It hurt that he thought I was looking for a relationship with him. I didn't have time for that either. I wasn't sure I even had time for a one-night stand. When Liam woke up and interrupted us, it was a sign that I couldn't even have one moment of pleasure.

"Tell me!" Veronica begged.

She must have been feeling better today if she was in here bothering me.

I gave her my mom look. "V, I have a lot of work to do today."

"Tell me, hoe!"

"I'm not a hoe."

"Then tell me!"

I sighed. "You're so annoying. It was nothing. We kissed and almost..." I felt my face get hot at remembering the way Logan had kissed me until I submitted to him. How his big hands lifted me up like I was a sack of groceries and he took me into his bedroom. "Liam interrupted us before it could go anywhere."

"Oh, no!"

I waved her off. "He was kinda jerky about it later when he was all 'I can't have anything serious.' I wasn't trying to propose to him. I just wanted to have sex! The flowers are him apologizing."

Veronica laughed. "Um, okay. Well, maybe you two could have some fun together."

I shook my head. "Bad idea. He already seemed to think I have ideas in my head."

She snatched the card from off the desk and read it. "Oh my god, let him take you to dinner. You deserve it. I'll babysit for you."

I glared at her, but she looked so giddy.

"V," I pleaded with her. I wanted to finish actualizing these numbers, and she was distracting me.

"Come on, Logan's wound as tight as you are. You could both use it."

I shook my head. "You're ridiculous. Go back to tattooing people and leave me in peace."

"Think about it!" she called to me on her way out.

I *had* been thinking about it. I thought about the weight of Logan's hands on me all week. I definitely shouldn't fantasize about him or where else he could put his mouth.

Damn, Veronica and Mari were right. I needed to get laid.

I glanced at the card on the desk warily. Then I picked up my phone and scrolled until I found Logan's number.

ME: Thanks for the flowers. I like Mexican food.

LOGAN: I know just the place. You free tonight?

Tonight? He had to be kidding me! My phone beeped with another message before I could answer.

LOGAN: Mari already said she'll watch both the kids.

I chewed on my lip. I should say no. I already felt bad he agreed to let Mari watch both Liam and Rosie together. Especially since I didn't pay her, and he did. I had talked to him about it when I brought over the crib from Mari's apartment. I wanted to make sure I wasn't taking advantage of his kindness.

My phone vibrated against the desk again.

LOGAN: Come on. Have dinner with me and a kid-free evening.

I stared down at my phone and mulled over the options. A kid-free evening sounded amazing. Seth flaked on me again last weekend, so it would be fun to have a night off. That made me sound horrible. I loved Rosie, but sometimes a mama needed a break. Last time I had one of those, Logan kissed me.

I couldn't let that happen again. Tonight was merely a thank you dinner for helping him out of a huge bind. That was all. We'd have a nice adult conversation with yummy food, and that was it.

I picked up my phone and texted him back.

ME: Okay, tell me when and where.

LOGAN: I'll pick you up at 7.

Hmm. That sounded an awful lot like a date. But it wasn't a date. Definitely not.

After I got the bulk of my work done, I raced home to take a shower and change for my non-date.

Mom was getting home from work while I was in the bathroom curling the ends of my hair. I was kidding myself by pretending dinner with Logan didn't seem like a date, but if I was going to go out, I wanted to make tonight count.

"Are you going out?" Mom asked when she found me sliding lipstick across my lips.

"I'm getting dinner with a friend."

She studied me for a second. "What friend?"

"The one I babysat for. The one I helped Mari get a job with."

"Mmmhmm."

I unplugged the curling iron and told myself to take a breath before saying what was really on my mind. "We're just friends."

"You said that about Seth."

I sighed. "I said that because you didn't like him, and I was trying to warm you up to him."

"Well...I was right. Where's Rosie?"

"Mari has her. She's fine."

"Mmmhmm," she said noncommittally and then walked away.

I needed to get out of this house and away from all her passive-aggressive looks and noises. It was getting on my nerves.

I put the curling iron back underneath the sink and swore silently when the doorbell rang. I checked my phone and saw he had texted, but I hadn't seen it in time. Great, now Logan had to deal with my mother.

I ran down the steps, trying to head her off, but no such luck. My jaw dropped when I saw my mom laugh at something he said. Logan's smile was infectious, and he was already charming the pants off of her.

Logan wore a cream-colored cashmere sweater and dark wash jeans that looked painted on his thick thighs. He had cleaned up his beard and styled his bright red hair to perfection. What right did he have to look that damn good for a non-date? Frankly, it was rude.

I wondered if I was dressed up enough. I assumed we'd go to whatever hole-in-the-wall Mexican place he could find and had dressed casual for the occasion in jeans, a camisole, and a loose plaid cardigan. He looked like he might take me somewhere fancy.

"Hey, you look great," he told me as he noticed me for the first time.

"Lily, I can't believe you haven't introduced me to this young man."

"Mom, this is Logan. Mari works for him now. He plays with Veronica's boyfriend on the hockey team."

Mom snapped her fingers. "That's why you look so familiar!"

Logan smiled from ear to ear. "That's me."

He was being so charming. What was happening?

I grabbed my jacket, and Logan helped me into it. He lifted my hair over the collar in a gentlemanly move I hadn't expected.

"Have fun, you two!" Mom said in a voice that made me think a changeling had replaced her. My passive-aggressive mom had just been so judgmental to me, but upon meeting Logan, she did a complete one-eighty. Logan was nice, but he wasn't that charismatic.

"I'll have her home by midnight, Ms. Mathews," Logan said to my mom.

Mom waved him off. "You have her home when you're ready. Mari's got the kids. You take all the time you need."

What the heck? Who was this woman, and where had my mom gone?

Logan led me over to the door, and we walked out together. I was still reeling from how my mom acted like a completely different person in front of him. It made little sense.

"What's wrong?" Logan asked as we walked over to his car.

"Nothing."

"You sure? Your mom seemed nicer than how you spoke about her."

I frowned. "I don't know who that woman was, but that was not my mother." I eyed him suspiciously. "You don't have secret ginger powers, do you?"

He laughed and opened the driver's side door. "Nope! Get in the car – let's roll."

I got into his car, and we drove off. "Where are we going?"

"Rittenhouse Square. Benny recommended a place that has authentic food."

"The best places are those little hole-in-the-wall places with fluorescent lighting."

He laughed and rubbed his bearded jaw. "I don't disagree with you, but I wanted to treat you to something nice. I know Liam was a handful, and you really helped me out."

"He's such a sweetheart." I reached out and put a hand on his thigh. "Whatever you think, you're doing great raising him." He nodded, and I pulled my hand away from his thigh, sensing his nerves. "Thanks for the night out, though. It's nice to get out and be kid-free once in a while."

He grinned at me but continued to drive into Center City.

When we got to Rittenhouse Square, Logan found a parking garage to park his car. We got out and walked over to the restaurant.

The exterior was a beautiful historical craftsman style-building, like most of the architecture on this side of the city. Logan held the door open for me, and we walked inside. The interior was as beautiful as the outside, but this place was fancy, and I felt underdressed.

I gasped when Logan's hand pressed against the small of my back and his lips were at my ear. "You look fine. Come on. Let's go eat."

My body vibrated from his touch, and I had to tell my libido to calm down. We were not going there. This was just dinner with a friend. An acquaintance, really. But one who had charmed the pants off my mother in two seconds flat. This had all sorts of bad ideas written over it, but when Logan gave me that smile, I stopped thinking about all the wrong things that could happen tonight.

This would be fine. We would enjoy each other's company tonight, and that was it.

Right?

CHAPTER THIRTEEN

LOGAN

I smiled from over my glass of tequila as I watched Lily pore over the menu in front of her. We had ordered drinks, and she sipped on a margarita while she tried to decide. She looked cute, with her nose wrinkling as she thought.

Stop it, Logan. This is not a date.

The place was pretty upscale, though, and the dim lights made it romantic. But it was definitely not a date. Not at all. It was hard pretending it wasn't when Lily looked so nice. She did something different with her hair tonight, and her face was done up like she was ready for a long night out. Her attire wasn't that fancy — a simple pair of jeans, tank top, and a white plaid sweater. But it made me want to peel it off her later.

Not going there.

Even if I wanted to, I had a kid to get home to, and so did she.

She glanced up from the menu. "What are you going to get?"

I peered down at the menu. "Tacos?"

She laughed. "So boring!"

"What are you getting?"

Her cute little nose wrinkled again as she perused the menu. "I'm going to get the Mole Poblano."

"I'm gonna get fish tacos. It's probably the thing my nutritionist will get the least mad at me about."

She tilted her head in question. "You have a nutritionist?"

Before I could answer, the server came over and asked if we were ready for our orders. Lily gave him a friendly smile as she ordered, and then I told him what I wanted. I'd rather have the enchiladas, but I had to be serious about my nutrition during the season. If I wanted to stay at the big show, I had to make sure I was careful with everything. That meant what I ate, what exercises I did, and my performance during games.

"So tell me about the nutritionist. I've seen Blaise wolf down a cheesesteak, so I'm confused."

I laughed. That sounded like Blaise. "He'll run five extra miles or eat those on cheat days."

"Ah."

She took a sip of her margarita, and the way the light hit her hair made her shine. Or maybe it was the smile that lit up her entire face and made her hazel eyes sparkle like amber. I had no business sitting here across the table from this gorgeous creature.

"How's work?" I asked.

She took a huge sip of her drink.

"That bad?"

She sighed. "I need to find more clients. Or get a full-time gig. It's tough. And..." she trailed off and shook her head. "You don't want to know about this."

"Sure I do."

"Seth flaked on taking Rosie again last weekend."

Red-hot anger flashed through me. "He's done that before?"

She nodded. "My mom was right. He's just like my sperm donor."

I arched an eyebrow at her phrase for her dad. "You don't talk to your dad?"

She shook her head. "Left when I was a baby. I guess mom saw him in Seth, but I was so in love I couldn't see it. I don't still love him. That went out the window when I realized he cheated on me. But I'm afraid of him not being there for Rosie."

I reached across the table and squeezed her hand. "You're an awesome mother."

"How do you know?"

"I saw you with Liam. You wouldn't do that if it wasn't the mama in you."

"Thank you," she muttered.

"Single parent life's rough!"

She pinned me with a quizzical look. "I feel like you've said that before."

I didn't think I said that to her before.

Holy fuck.

I said that to FLOWERCHILD183. And something Lily said to me sounded an awful lot like something Flower said. It had to be a coincidence. There was no way Lily was the gamer girl I'd been playing Dragonspire with since I was sixteen. No way.

"Anyway!" her voice cut through my thoughts. "Let's

talk about something less depressing than my ex-husband. How's hockey?"

"It's...okay."

"Just okay?"

I sighed. "I'm worried about not staying with the team next year. I want stability for Liam."

She nodded in understanding.

I took a sip of my tequila. Talking about my career doubts wasn't something I should do with her. She barely knew me. You didn't unload on someone like that.

"Thanks for getting me in touch with your sister," I said, changing the subject.

She beamed. "I told you Mari was perfect." Then she frowned and glanced down at her empty place set. "You don't mind if she has Rosie while she watches Liam?"

I shook my head. "Nope. Believe me, trying to find her was a nightmare. I owe you."

She pushed a strand of hair behind her ear and nodded.

"You're not taking advantage of me," I reassured her.

Mari mentioned Lily wouldn't take my money because of her pride, and I could see that now. She was too proud to ask for help, and she didn't want to make it seem like she was taking advantage of my kindness.

"Mari's working out then?" she asked.

I nodded. "She's amazing. I think it's partly because of you, but Liam hasn't slept in my bed all week."

Her eyes sparkled as she smiled. "I don't think that was because of me, but that's good. He's growing up!"

I smiled back at her, but she was wrong. Liam kept asking me when Lily would come over and play with him again. He was still having nightmares, but he wasn't sleeping in my bed every night.

Lily sipped on her margarita as she peered around the restaurant. "This place's nice."

I smirked at her. "Not a hole in the wall?"

She laughed. "Nope! But I judge a place by its food. Upscale's nice, but if it's good, I don't care about aesthetic."

I wanted to ask her what she meant by that, but then the waiter brought over our food. I took a bite of one of my tacos while Lily cut into her chicken that was smothered in a dark sauce. She closed her eyes as she chewed.

"Good?" I asked.

Her eyes popped open, and her face lit up with excitement. "Very good."

"When Mari said you liked Mexican, I asked my teammate Benny for a recommendation. He said his kitchen, but then he recommended this place."

She stared up at the ceiling like she was trying to pull something out of her memory. "He's the big guy with huge muscles, right?"

I laughed. "That describes half my teammates."

A cute rosy blush colored her face. "He's very tall. And his girlfriend's curvy with dark hair, right? I only met them once."

"Yeah, that's Rox. Benny's not wrong, though, and he's an excellent cook. He makes a mean tamale around the holidays."

She gave me another warm smile, and we made small talk while we ate. Every time I made her smile or she tipped back her head and laughed at something funny I'd said, I wanted to do it more. I was drawn to her in a way I couldn't understand. But my heart and my dick were having a hard time remembering this wasn't a date.

After we finished eating and our waiter took away our plates, I ordered a coffee while she pored over the tiny dessert menu. I wasn't one for dessert, another symptom of trying to adhere to my nutritionist's plan, but she looked excited about it.

"Ooh, they have tres leches cake!" she exclaimed.

"Order it."

"Will you eat some?" she asked. "I know you mentioned—"

"I'll run an extra mile on the treadmill tomorrow."

She bit her lip, and the action made me think of biting that plump lip with my own teeth. "You sure?"

"Lil, get the dessert."

She grinned big and ordered it when the server came back over.

Something alerted her, and she dug into her purse to find her phone. Whatever she saw on her phone made her put her hand to her mouth. "Aw."

"What's up?"

She held her screen up to me, and it was a picture of the kids from earlier playing sweetly together. I had been a little worried about Liam with other kids since he came to live with me. It was why I pulled him out of daycare and hadn't signed him up for preschool yet. After the accident, he acted out a lot. But he was so sweet on Lily's baby, and they played together with minimal fighting.

"They're so cute," she said.

I grinned. "And they know it."

She laughed. "Yeah. As much as I hate my ex for what he did, I never would have had Rosie if I'd never met him. She's my entire world. Nothing else matters."

I nodded in agreement because that was exactly how I felt about Liam. Maybe that's why I felt so drawn to Lily. She was the only person who understood being a single parent.

"She's really cute. She obviously takes after her mama," I told her.

She blushed again and took another sip of her water, not daring to look me in the eye.

The awkwardness subsided when the server brought over her dessert. She pushed the second spoon my way, then scraped hers into the cake and took a huge bite. I dug my spoon into the other side as we shared the dessert.

"This is good," I said.

"Told you!"

There was that bright smile again. I had to stop thinking about her. Stop thinking that this was anything more than a thank you dinner for helping me out with Liam. But fuck me, watching her lick the white cream off her lips was hot. My dick thickened against my leg as I imagined her licking something else off those lips.

I was way too horny to be out to dinner with this woman. Not after the kiss we shared. Especially not with the heated gaze she sent my way.

"Logan?" she asked, her voice a hushed whisper.

"Hmm?"

"Is this a date?"

"No."

She squinted at me as if she didn't believe me. "Then stop looking at me like that."

"Like what?"

"Like you want to kiss me again."

"But I do," I blurted out and wanted to kick myself for letting it slip out. I did. I wanted to kiss her again. I wanted to pin her down against my bed and have my way with her.

But then I remembered our kids were at my place with her sister. After dinner, I'd drive her back to my place where she'd pick up her baby, and they'd both go home. And then this non-date dinner would be over. I'd bang a bunny next week when I was on the road or beat off again to the memory of Lily's moans. Then these thoughts would go away.

"Then do something about it, or stop it," she demanded.

She was looking down at the tablecloth in front of her, but when she lifted her head up, and we locked eyes again, the heat inside hers matched my own.

Yeah, I was going to do something about it, and it was a horrible idea. A colossally bad idea. But my dick didn't care.

CHAPTER FOURTEEN

LILY

Why did I say that? Why, oh why, did I let my libido speak for my brain?

Okay, moment of truth — it was because Logan was hot. I wanted to run my fingers through his fiery red hair and feel his lips on mine again. Then grind against his large bulge.

And...I was sex-deprived. That was the real reason.

It wasn't because when Logan spoke, a sense of calm came over me. Or because when I looked into his eyes, I felt like I could tell him all my worries and fears. Definitely not because of the way he stared hungrily at me while I licked tres leches cake off my lips.

Totally not the reason at all.

"Let's go," he growled.

I blinked back at him. Did men actually growl at you? I thought that was something I only read in my steamy romance novels. But when I looked over at Logan, his eyes seared through me, and he looked like he was hungry for another meal — me.

I stared back at him in silence while he gestured to the waiter for the check.

This was a bad idea, but the part of me that hadn't had sex since I was pregnant craved the attention he was giving me. Craved the way he made me want to jump out of my skin.

But it wasn't just that. Logan was a good guy. He didn't seem like those asshole jocks I went to high school with. And he was a good dad. Liam might not be his son by genes, but he was the boy's parent through and through. He sacrificed his own happiness to make sure his kid was loved and protected, and that was sexy to me. A single dad who did what he had to without a thought for himself was a turn-on. With the way Seth had been flaking out on our daughter, seeing Logan do everything for Liam gave me hope that there were decent men in the world.

"Lil?" Logan's deep voice pulled me from my thoughts.

He stood next to me, with his hand outstretched toward me and my coat in his other hand. I took his offered hand and let him help me back into my coat. I hitched in a breath when he slid his hand into mine and led us outside onto the street. The early October air was chilly, and I shivered at the wind nipping at my cheeks.

Logan was a man on a mission. He took big strides back to the parking garage, and I had trouble keeping up. I wasn't very tall for a woman, but the six-foot giant had legs on him. He pinned me against the car before I could get inside.

"Tell me you don't want me."

I shook my head.

"No?"

"No. I'm not going to tell you that." I put a hand on his

chest and slid it down until my fingers grazed the top of his jeans. "I want you, Logan, so bad."

He didn't give me time to prepare before crushing his lips against mine. We kissed like we were two horny teenagers sneaking in a make-out session before one of our parents got home. I pressed against his jeans and felt his hardness arching toward me. Just wanting me to unbuckle his belt and get down on my knees and take him down my throat right here in the parking garage.

Logan yanked my hand away and pulled back from our kiss. His eyes held a fury in them that turned me on. "You don't do that here, understand?"

I nodded. I shouldn't like him ordering me around. But I did. It was sexy the way he commanded me in ways I wanted. I bet he was bossy in bed, and I needed to find out for myself.

My face crumpled when the reality of the situation set in.

His eyes widened in concern, and he cupped my face as he searched for what was wrong. "Did I do something wrong?"

"No. The kids are at your place, and I live with my mother." I made an annoyed face at the end of my sentence. There wasn't anything wrong with people my age living with their parents, but moving back in with my mother because my marriage was over made me feel like a failure.

His smile made his eyes twinkle. "Yeah, we're getting a hotel room."

I pulled back and shook my head again. "No. Absolutely not!"

"Lil, get in the car, or I'll fuck you in the backseat instead."

"Then why don't you?" I huffed out.

He brought my hand up to his lips and kissed the back of it. "Because, princess, you're a classy lady and deserve better than that. Now get in the car."

I should roll my eyes at the cheesy princess line, but secretly I liked it. Tonight had been a perfect first date. He took me to eat my favorite food and was a gentleman the whole night. He even won over my passive-aggressive mother and didn't care if I talked about my kid or my crappy ex-husband.

Logan was too good to be true. Therein lay the answer. He was unavailable. But that was okay because so was I. We could pretend for tonight. We'd give into our desires for one night, and then we'd both go back to being struggling single parents juggling it all.

He leaned down and kissed me again. I gave into it, clutching onto his chest as we kissed in that parking garage like we had all the time in the world.

His lips set fire across my skin as they traveled from my mouth down to my neck. He sucked on my flesh, and I let out a tiny mewling.

"Get in the car, princess," he whispered huskily into my ear.

I nodded, lost in a daze from the way he kissed my doubts away. He walked me around to the other side of his car and opened the door for me. He waited until I was inside, and then he shut the door. This man was so kind and gentlemanly. I wasn't sure what to make of it.

He got into the driver's seat, but before he turned on the car, he lifted my hand up and kissed it again. "You okay with this?"

"Yes."

He let go of my hand and started his engine. He drove like a madman, finding the nearest hotel and pulling into the parking garage. I jumped out of the car behind him, and we rushed into the lobby together. He slammed his credit card down on the counter as we booked the room for the night.

He slid his hand back in mine once he got the room card from the concierge, and then we headed for the elevator. Once those doors closed, he had me up against the wall, his hands in my hair and his lips bruising mine. I didn't care. I let him crowd me against the wall and kiss me. He bit my lip as his kisses got rougher, more aggressive, and I gave into that too. I wanted to be his plaything. To let him do whatever he wanted to me.

We might have undid each other's jeans right there in the elevator if it hadn't dinged, letting us know we were on our floor. Logan rushed us down the hall and toward our room. He fumbled with the room key while I ran my hands up and down his soft cashmere sweater.

He yanked open the door, and in a flash, we were behind it, and he had me up against it. I ran my hands through his hair while we kissed, and his hands inched up underneath my camisole.

We kissed until there wasn't any more air left in the room. I felt his hard length pressed against my core, especially when he lifted my legs up and wrapped them around his waist. I moaned into his mouth, urging him to move us to the bed, but he was taking his time with me. I ground myself against him, trying to tell him what I wanted.

He nipped at my ear. "Patience, princess. I'll give you what you want."

"Please?" I begged.

He kissed my neck. "Don't need to beg. I'm going to savor you tonight."

I bit my lip. When was the last time a man said that to

me? Had a man ever said that to me? Or did they just sleep with me until they got off, not caring if I got what I needed?

Logan walked us back to the bed, where he carefully laid me down on it. I shed my cardigan and watched him pull his sweater over his head, revealing the hard lines of his cut physique.

An uneasy feeling crawled up from my stomach. Logan's body was like a work of art, and I still hadn't lost my baby weight and had stretch marks. He had been so gentlemanly tonight, but I felt self-conscious about what he'd think about my body. If he was any other guy, I wouldn't care. But I saw what the hockey wives and girlfriends looked like.

I slapped at the light switch next to the bed, plunging us into darkness. I pulled my camisole off and was working on my jeans when the overhead light turned back on. I wrapped my arms around my middle. Logan was only in his boxers now, and he kneeled on the bed over me.

"I want to see all of you," he hissed and pulled my hands away from my stomach.

I shook my head. "I have stretch marks, and I'm not back to my pre-baby weight."

Logan ran a hand down my stomach and then bent to kiss the faint lines. "I don't care about that."

"Really?"

He lifted his head up, a scowl across his face. "Did you think I wouldn't want you because you have scars and curves?"

"I—" I stuttered out.

Seth didn't want me after I gave birth to our daughter. He had waited on me hand and foot when I was pregnant with Rosie, but after she was born, everything changed. He made comments about my weight here and there. I made excuses because we were so busy planning the wedding, but he really showed me who he was. I was just so blissfully in love, I ignored all the waving red flags.

Logan undid the top button of my jeans and slid down the zipper. "I want you. *All* of you. Every delicious curve I can get my hands on." He peeled my jeans off, and a sly grin materialized on his face when he plucked the string of my lacy thong. "These are sexy for a non-date, huh?"

Heat rose on my face. Yes, they were. I might have intentionally worn them because a small part of me was hoping he'd pull them off me later. Why else would I wear a matching set if I didn't think there was a tiny chance something would happen tonight?

He slid the material down my legs, and I reached behind me to remove my bra, leaving me vulnerable beneath him.

He kissed the inside of my knee, slowly making his way up my body. "So sexy."

I gestured to his boxers. "Your turn."

He shook his head, and before I could stop him, he shouldered his way between my thighs. All I could see was the top of his red hair, and then my eyes closed tight when he drug his tongue across my pussy.

I clutched at the sheets, arching my hips up as he ate me to his heart's desire. He played with me, using his tongue to explore me until he sucked my clit into his mouth. I couldn't hold back the way the sensation tossed me toward the edge.

But it surprised me to hear him moan while he did it. Seth only ever went down on me out of obligation, but Logan sounded like he was getting off on it. Like he could spend hours down there.

I gasped when he pumped two thick fingers inside my

entrance. I clenched around his fingers, and then he slammed a third one in.

"You can take it," he purred.

Then he licked and fingered me through my orgasm. I cried out and felt like I was floating up on the ceiling as the pleasure coursed through me.

When I came back down to earth, Logan was looking up at me earnestly, and his ginger-colored beard was wet with my cum. That shouldn't be sexy, but it made me want him even more.

He wiped his beard off with the back of his hand and got up to strip down. His dick bounced against his stomach, and my eyes were saucers wondering how it was going to fit inside me. I hadn't had sex in so long. Another thought blared like a warning bell in the back of my mind.

"Do you have a condom?" I asked.

He rifled through his jeans and pulled one out. "I got it covered." He frowned. "No lube, though."

"Don't care. C'mere," I growled at him, surprising even myself, but then a grin spread across his face as he got back into bed and kneed my legs apart.

I reached my hands up to his face and pulled him down for another kiss. I forgot my worries while he kissed me, that the shock wasn't as bad when he pressed himself inside me in one swift motion.

I wrapped my legs around his waist and pulled him in tightly. I broke the kiss so I could watch as he slid his dick all the way inside me and then back out, slow and gentle at first.

God, it felt *so* good.

We moved together, trying to get as close to each other as possible. The bed rocked as his thrusts got rougher, harder, like he couldn't stop himself. Like being inside me brought an animal out in him. I liked it. A lot.

His lips trailed down my jaw until he was at my ear. "Lily."

I dug my nails into his back, arching my hips up to meet him again. "Don't stop."

"I'm gonna come."

"Okay."

He pressed his thumb against my clit. "You gotta come first."

"S'okay," I slurred. I was pretty sure I'd come along with him. I'd feel sore tomorrow, but it was worth it. My walls clenched around him, and my body tingled again.

He put more pressure on my clit. "Not yet. Come for me, princess?"

I nodded. I would do anything he asked in this moment. He had me teetering toward the edge again, and I wanted him to push me over it.

The rocking of the bed got louder, and I was crying as he found that spot deep inside me.

"That's it," he purred. "You come on this dick."

"Fuck," I moaned. "Logan, fuck!"

And then my orgasm took over, and I was coming so hard, I forgot where I was, forgot that this was a one-night stand to scratch the itch we both needed.

Two seconds later, he roared out his release, a loud and guttural male sound I wanted to etch inside my brain. I wanted to remember this perfect date with this man and how he rocked my world for only one night.

I'd think about the consequences later. Right now, I melted into the bed in the aftershocks of my orgasm.

CHAPTER FIFTEEN

LOGAN

"I really needed that," Lily murmured into my chest.

She was curled around my torso, her hair spread out across my shoulder as we cuddled together post-sex. I didn't want to move. I wanted to stay here all night with her, but that wasn't an option. I might have booked this room for the night, but we both knew we weren't using it the whole night since we had kids we needed to get back to. I wanted a few more moments of fantasy with her in my arms.

"Me too." I ran my hands through her blonde hair, smoothing it down from the wild sex hair I gave her.

"Can I tell you a secret?" she whispered.

"Sure."

She blew out a breath. "I haven't had sex since I was pregnant."

I furrowed my brow as I did the math backward. Rosie was still little, but she had to be over a year old. That didn't compute to me. "How old's Rosie?"

"Sixteen months."

I winced. I hadn't had sex in a couple months, but a year and a half?

White-hot rage coursed through me because I had a good idea that her asshole ex-husband was the reason why. She didn't say, but it explained why she had hangups about her post-baby body. Hockey players might go for the supermodel type, but I wasn't one of them. I liked women of any shape or size, but I loved a woman with curves. Lily certainly had the perfect amount of those. And stretch marks? Who cared? I didn't. It bothered me she thought that shit mattered to me.

Her hand on my beard brought me out of my sour thoughts. Her eyes searched my own with a worried look on her face. "What's wrong?" she asked.

I took her hand and kissed the back of it. "Nothing. Why haven't you had sex in that long?"

She flopped back on the bed. "You don't want to hear about how naïve I was and believed everything my ex said to me."

"You can tell me. We're friends."

"Are we?"

"I like to think we are."

"I still barely know you, but...it's like we've met before. You sure you're not from Philly?"

I laughed. "Definitely not. I'm from the state of hockey."

She arched an eyebrow at me.

"Minnesota," I explained.

Her mouth formed a little 'o.' "Well, you don't want to talk about my ex. I still feel so guilty about my relationship with him."

"What do you mean?"

"I didn't know I was the other woman. I still can't believe Veronica's my friend after what I did."

I furrowed my brow. I knew that about Lily and Veronica's friendship. That was why Blaise told me to back off, but part of it reminded me of what Flower told me. She had a similar story. It was too identical to be a coincidence.

"Are you okay?" she asked.

"Yeah, why?"

"You keep on furrowing your brow like you're mad at me."

I kissed the back of her hand again and pulled her into my chest, wrapping my arm around her. She was so tiny next to my gigantic frame, but she fit so perfectly beside me. "Lost in thought, sorry."

"We should get going soon. I gotta get Rosie and get home."

I nodded.

We needed to head back to my condo to relieve Mari, but neither of us moved from our position. I had the comforter wrapped around us as we lay naked in the bed together. I hoped she didn't notice that I was hard again from the way her hand made circles absent-mindedly against my chest. I didn't have another condom, so I wasn't suggesting a round two.

She kissed my chest and slid her hand down it. I grabbed it before she could continue her motions. "What are you doing?"

She gave me a cheeky grin but continued her descent until her hand stroked my dick. "You seem like you need help with something."

"Lil, I don't have another condom."

She kicked the comforter off us and slid down in between my legs. She stroked me almost torturously.

"That's okay. I want to return the favor," she said, and then she slid my dick inside her mouth.

Fuck, that felt so good.

Her eyes were closed while she took my dick as far into her mouth as she could. I reached down and bunched her hair up above her head, so I could watch as my dick slid in and out of her mouth. She moaned around it like she was getting off as much as I was from every stroke and swirl of her tongue. That was sexy. A woman who enjoyed giving oral and didn't think it was a chore was awesome.

"Lil," I moaned, arching my hips up to press deeper inside.

I wanted to face-fuck her, to ram my dick down her throat and make her swallow it all up. But I couldn't be that rough with her. She was a lady, a princess, who should be treated with care.

I forgot about all that when her mouth worked me over, and I lost all sensation to my brain. Her wet hot mouth pulled me in, then back out, faster, more urgently, that I couldn't help as the orgasm washed over me. I didn't have time to warn her as ropes of cum spilled into her pretty little mouth. To my surprise, she didn't mind. She kept her eyes closed, and her hand stroked my cock as she swallowed all my cum. Then she popped my dick out of her mouth with a wet sound.

"Fuck," I groaned as I laid back on the bed.

She climbed up over me and kissed me again. "Thanks for the night out. I needed this."

I wished I had another condom. I wanted to savor her to every last drop and really make it count. To treat her like the princess she was. "Princess..." I breathed.

She smiled. "Why do you keep calling me that?"

I brushed her hair away from her face. "Because you deserve someone to treat you like one. I can't do that."

She cupped my face. "I don't need that. I just needed to get laid. Logan, I know how chaotic your life is; I'm probably the only person who gets that. I'm not looking for a relationship, either. But..."

I held her face in my hands and looked deep into her eyes. "But, what?"

"If you're looking for some occasional fun with no strings, let me know."

I was not opposed to that. Not like I couldn't get laid on my own. But honestly, the girls on the road who just wanted you because you were a hockey player got old. At the same time, I didn't know if a friends-with-benefits situation was a good idea. Feelings could get in the way.

"It's not a marriage proposal!" she told me with a laugh. "I gotta get going anyway."

She climbed out of bed and put her clothes back on. I lay in bed for a minute and watched her. I really liked her, but we couldn't have anything real. There was definitely something that drew me to her like a magnet, though.

She laughed. "It's funny you called me princess."

"Why?"

She pulled on her cardigan. "Because the character I play in Dragonspire wears a crown. People always ask me if she's supposed to be a wood elf princess."

I stared at her for a long time.

She played as a wood elf. That made so much sense; she was tiny like the Elves in the game.

Flower also played as a wood elf, and I made that joke about her being a princess when I saw her character wearing a silver tiara. Lily was not FlowerChild183. No way. Lots of chicks played as Elves and put on the crown decoration. Lots of them.

"You okay?" she asked.

I nodded. "Right, fine. Let's go get your baby, huh?"

She smiled. "Thanks for tonight. I needed the night out. Sometimes it's nice to let go, you know?"

I definitely knew. I wished we had more time. I would have spent more of it between her legs, pleasuring her until she tapped out from too many orgasms. But we both had responsibilities. All we could have was these few stolen hours tonight.

We left the hotel slower than when we came, and I drove us back over to Old City. "Wait, do you need me to drive you home?" I asked.

She shook her head. "Nope, my sister has a car seat for Rosie. She'll take me."

I pulled into the parking garage, and we walked together toward the elevator. An awkward silence wafted between us, and I didn't like that.

We walked down the hall to my condo together, and I opened the door. Mari smiled at us but then squinted at her sister. "Hmm. Good for you. You needed to get laid."

"Marigold!" Lily hissed at her sister.

Mari shrugged. "What? It's true. You both needed to get it in. You're wound so tight."

Lily put a hand over her face. "I'm sorry. You can fire her if you want."

"Hey!" Mari cried.

I chuckled. "Nope. Mari's perfect. Finding a nanny's hell. I'll take the razzing. How were the kids?"

Before she could answer, I heard a cry from the bedroom. Without thinking, I rushed inside. Liam was sound asleep, but Rosie was standing up in the crib crying. I didn't think about it when I picked her up and tried to soothe her. I couldn't help it. The dad in me wanted to take all her tears away.

"It's okay, little miss. I got you," I said to her, bouncing her in my arms. She was still crying but seemed to calm down the tiniest bit at my soothing voice. I turned to find Lily had entered the room, but she had a hand on her heart as she watched me. "You want your mama?" I asked Rosie.

But Rosie shook her head and laid it on my chest. "No. Da-da."

Oh, my heart.

Honestly, it was not the first time she'd said that. There had been a couple times when I came home for my pre-game nap and she said it to me while I was giving both kids cuddles. Mari tried to correct her, but little miss didn't care.

Lily frowned and walked over to me, taking Rosie out of my arms. "No, baby, that's Logan. Daddy's not here."

"Want Da-da!" the little girl cried. But she was reaching out to me, wanting me to hold her again.

Lily stroked her daughter's back while she tried to rock her back to sleep. "I know, baby. You go to Daddy's tomorrow. Let's go home. Someone needs to get to bed. Say bye-bye to Logan?"

Rosie waved at me, and I waved back. She was so cute, and it was clear Lily was such a good mom. I felt for her with all the bullshit her ex put her through. If I ever met the guy, I might want to drop the gloves with him. He straight-up sucked. But I knew violence was never the answer, no matter if that douche nugget deserved it.

"Let me walk you and Mari out," I said.

She waved me off. "We're fine. Thanks, Logan. Dinner was great. I'll see you later."

And then she was gone, leaving me scratching my head

as if tonight meant nothing. But I guess it did. She was the one who offered no strings. So why did that bother me so damn much?

CHAPTER SIXTEEN

LILY

I tapped my foot to the beat of the music as I crunched numbers for the tattoo shop. I loved working at Golden Rose, especially since Veronica's brother Alex put in a good word for me at another shop. I was crossing my fingers I turned them into a new client. Hal didn't need me as much as the tattoo shop did, so I needed to build up a client list.

"You're in a good mood," Veronica's voice pulled me out of the zone.

I held up a finger to her and finished actualizing the row of cells I was working on. "Hey! How are you?"

Veronica pushed her colorful hair out of her face. The tips were fading, and her natural mousy brown roots were coming in. She wasn't dying her hair until she was in the second trimester. I told her I thought it was fine to dye her hair, but like when I was pregnant with Rosie, she was fretting over every little thing.

She took a seat in the chair across from the desk and put

a hand on her still small stomach. "I'm feeling...okay, not great, but better than before."

"That's good."

"So, how did your date go?" she asked, and a cocky smile upturned on her lips.

"It wasn't a date," I insisted.

It was so not a date that he booked a hotel room for the night, and we only used it for two hours tops. That was so reckless. I was glad we remembered to use protection. I didn't need another oops baby.

"Are you sure?" she asked, and her grin got bigger.

I felt heat climb up my neck, so I stared at the lines on my spreadsheet, hoping she thought I was drowning in work. "We're just friends."

"Mmmhmm. Well, you seem in a great mood."

"We had a nice time," I admitted.

"Oh, my God, will you admit you got laid already?"

I stared back at her. "Excuse me?"

She cackled out a big belly laugh. "It's all over your face! Good for you — Logan's a cutie. If you like a ginge."

"Redheads are hot," I blurted out without thinking.

She pointed an accusatory finger at me. "I knew it! Good for you."

"Don't get excited. We both don't have time for that."

"Um, Blaise and I did the casual thing, and now we're having a baby," she said.

She looked down at her stomach and rubbed her hand on it. Despite the morning sickness, Veronica looked so happy that she and Blaise were starting their family together. A part of me would always feel guilty about what happened between her and Seth, even though it wasn't my fault. I was glad she got her happily ever after, despite what he did.

"Who's having a baby?" Alex asked.

Veronica and I both jumped at the sound of his voice. Alex stood in the open doorway, peering at his sister suspiciously. Veronica hadn't wanted to tell her brother or his husband that she was pregnant yet. Especially this soon in her pregnancy. I gathered he knew already with the way he stared pointedly at her stomach.

"No one," I told him. "Talking about my baby."

Alex gave Veronica an exasperated look. "V, admit Blaise knocked you up. Everyone knows."

I gave Veronica a sheepish look. I had kept that secret close to the vest. I would've never given it up. I knew how tough it was being in the early stages of your pregnancy and how you weren't supposed to tell anyone.

Veronica frowned. "How did you know?"

Alex rolled his eyes. "Blaise is constantly touching your stomach and being all cute. And you vom like every day." He pointed at me. "You totally knew."

I cringed and held up my hands. "Guilty, but I was sworn to secrecy."

Alex looked giddy. He ducked his head out of the door. "HEY BABE!" he called to his husband.

I smiled while Veronica put her head in her hands. "This is why I didn't tell them."

"Aw, they're excited."

"We're gonna be GUNCLES!" Alex yelled.

I shook my head at them. I lost all hope of getting any more work done. I saved my work and made a note in my planner on where I left off. I needed to get across town for the consultation with the tattoo shop in Manayunk.

I packed up my stuff, waved goodbye to Veronica, and walked to my car parked a couple of blocks over in one of the lots. That was the one thing I hated about the city. Too much city, not enough places to put your car. When I lived with Seth after the baby was born, we had moved out to the suburbs. I liked being a little further away from it all. Even where I grew up in the Northeast was a little more manageable than the hustle and bustle of Center City.

I drove over to Manayunk and rehearsed what I wanted to say to the client while I drove. I had a proposal ready, but they didn't discuss their needs with me. If they needed a full-time bookkeeper or someone to run their numbers monthly. Last night, I put together a plan for both options. I was prepared for anything because I needed this to be a success.

I found the shop quickly and parked my car on the street after driving around the block a couple of times. I checked my hair and makeup in the overhead mirror before I got out.

The shop was on a corner, and the exterior was painted black with a big sign above the door bearing the shop's name. When I stepped inside, it was exactly what I expected. There were tattoo designs hanging up on one wall and a large reception desk in front. A woman with purple hair and tattoos up and down her arms and even chest sat behind it.

She peered at me with a bored expression. "Can I help you?"

"Hi, I'm looking for Rich. We have an appointment."

She gazed up and down at me, assessing my white skin bereft of any ink. I wore one of my nicer designer dresses and a blazer over it with smart pumps on my feet. I couldn't turn off the corporate business attire, but I definitely looked out of place.

"Rich!" the woman called into the other room. She

looked back at me with a curious look. "Is this your first tattoo?"

I shook my head. I let Seth do a tiny rose on my wrist. It had hurt slightly less than childbirth, but I was glad I did it. Kinda wished Veronica had done it, though, since flowers were her specialty. Seth's artwork wasn't bad, but it burned the memory of his betrayal into my skin.

I pulled back my sleeve and held up my wrist. "Nope," I told her with a smile.

Before she could say anything, an older man who was round in the middle and had a big bushy greying beard came up to the front.

"Lily, right?" he asked and put out his hand.

I shook his hand firmly. "That's me."

"Come on back to the office so we can talk in private."

I followed him through the doorway where there were a few different stations with artists inking up their customers. Rich stopped to speak to an older woman around his age, tattooing the back of a burly biker dude.

"Honey, this is Lily. She's going to help us with the books."

The woman had streaks of grey in her dark brown hair that was piled high above her head, and she wore cat-eye glasses on her face. She paused shading in a dragon on her client's body to give me a small smile. "Nice to meet you. I'm Allison. Alex said good things about you."

"Good ole Alex. He and Veronica practically grew up in this shop," Rich said.

"Oh?" Veronica mentioned tattooing was a family affair, but she clamped up when I asked about her dad.

"Yeah, their dad used to run it. They both apprenticed here," Rich explained. "They're our god kids."

Allison smiled. "They're both good kids."

"Come on back," Rich told me again, and led me to his office.

Once inside, he sat behind the desk, and I took the seat on the other side. I opened my briefcase and pulled out the presentations I'd put together.

"So I want to get an assessment of your needs. If you need a regular bookkeeper or if you're just looking for someone to do your taxes. We can talk budget and plans for any of these."

Rich leaned back in his chair. "Oh, you came prepared."

I grinned. "That's me."

"Alex told me you were good. I'm getting too old for this shit, so a bookkeeper would really help us. I also need someone to do my quarterly business taxes."

I nodded. "I can do that."

We talked numbers, and he agreed to my rates. I was giddy on the ride home that I had secured yet another client. I mentally planned out my schedule with the new workload. A new client was great, but I had to start advertising about tax season.

I sat at the kitchen table and worked on applying to jobs and coming up with my plan to get all this work done. I felt much better about the state of my career, but not one hundred percent happy. That was okay. I'd get there.

I had been working so long, I didn't hear my mom come home. I jumped and held my hand to my chest when her high heels click-clacked against the tile floor.

"You scared me!"

"Sorry, hon. I'm surprised to see you home. Thought you'd be out with Logan again."

I pinned her with a confused look. That was a jump to a conclusion. She had warmed up to Logan immediately, but we had only gone on one date. One that wasn't supposed to be real despite the fact that we ended up tangled in the sheets together.

"We're just friends," I told her.

"But he took you to dinner?" she asked and crossed her arms over her chest as she stared me down.

I gritted my teeth. "Yes. He's the one who asked me to babysit, and Mari's his nanny now."

"Right, you mentioned that. I like him."

"I like him, too."

"I like him better than Seth."

I sighed. Yeah, me too. If only I had listened to my mom about him... But I couldn't dwell on the past. I closed my laptop. "It's not like that, Mom. Why do you like him, anyway? You met him for like thirty seconds."

"Because he came in and introduced himself and then was a gentleman who helped you with your coat. Seth only ever honked his horn and dragged you out of my house before you were ready."

I closed my eyes and tried not to feel like a teenager again. Moving back in with my mom felt like a step backward. The fact my career still wasn't together didn't help.

"You don't have to keep throwing it in my face about how much of a failure I am," I muttered.

Mom's face fell. "Oh, honey, is that what you think?"

I furrowed my brow as I stared at her. "Are you serious? Every chance you get, you throw all my mistakes back at me. Like I don't know that I messed up when I got pregnant or when I married Seth. Like I don't know how much my life is in shambles right now."

"I don't want you to be me. Pining over the man who left you high and dry."

"Who said I was pining over Seth? I'm the one who left. I don't regret having Rosie. She's the best thing that ever happened to me. But you telling me how much of a fuckup I am doesn't help."

"I don't want you to struggle like I did. I only want the best for you."

"You have a real funny way of showing it."

Mom sighed and ran a hand through her blonde hair. "Lily pad, I struggled so much after your father left, I didn't want that for you, and now the cycle's repeating itself. I'm so proud of you for starting your own business and working at it, but I hate seeing you struggle like I did."

"Mom, you were a badass single mom."

She gave me a hard look. "That's because you didn't see the hard stuff. I don't want you or your sister to deal with that."

"I'm figuring it out. I met with a new client today, and I have another interview this week," I insisted.

If I convinced her I was getting my life together, maybe I could convince myself too.

"Honey, that's great! I'm sorry if you feel like I'm being hard on you. I want a better life for you. You have to understand that now that you're a parent."

I nodded. Yeah, I understood that, but she didn't have to be so mean about it. I let the argument drop and had dinner with my mom. I should have enjoyed my child-free night while Rosie was with Seth, but after dinner, I went upstairs and worked. I applied for more jobs, set up my services on different self-employed work sites, and updated my website.

It was late by the time I got done, and I should have gone to bed, but I eyed my game controller. Maybe one little quest in Dragonspire before bed.

I logged in, and a smile spread across my face when I got a chat invite from GINGERPOWER33. I put my headset over my ears and plugged it into my controller.

"You're up late!" he said into my ear. He sounded energetic, like he had been running circles around his room or something.

"I could say the same to you."

"I'm always wired after a game."

Something in the back of my mind tickled at that. Ginge and I talked little about personal stuff. I didn't even know what state he lived in. Me telling him about my ex and him telling me about his nephew was the closest we got to personal.

Wait. Nephew. That was too much of a coincidence. But it couldn't be. There was no way Ginge was Logan. That would be like something out of a romcom. Not real life.

"Game?" I asked after a few minutes of awkward silence.

"Yeah, um..." He trailed off like he didn't know what to say. "I don't think you'll believe me, but I'm a professional athlete."

"Like eSports?" I asked.

"No. Um...what do you know about hockey?"

My heartbeat was loud in my ears at his answer. There was no way. There were lots of hockey teams, and professional hockey didn't mean the national league. There were other pro leagues. And it wasn't like he lived in PA, let alone Philly. He could be on the West Coast for all I knew. But he wouldn't have made that comment about it being late if he was in a different time zone.

"My ex was a huge Bulldogs fan, so I know a little, but not much."

On the other end of my headset, Ginge was quiet.

I cringed when I realized my mistake. I shouldn't have name-dropped the Bulldogs.

"Yeah, I'm familiar with the Bulldogs."

Hmm, that was an empty response, but I didn't press him on it. "Cool. Want to do a quest together?"

"Come on, elven princess, let's do it."

Elven princess. I wouldn't have thought anything of that joke if not for the conversation I had with Logan after we had sex. Could it be? Was Logan GingerPower33?

While we waited for the area to load, I searched Logan's name on my phone. His number was 33. That couldn't be a coincidence. If Logan was the man I had been playing Dragonspire with since I was a teenager, it made sense. It explained why when I first met him, I felt like I had known him forever and why his voice calmed me. But that couldn't be right.

When the screen loaded, we started our quest, and I tried to forget all the questions swirling around in my brain. I didn't want to think too hard about the possibility that Logan was my long-time internet friend. Probably my best friend.

CHAPTER SEVENTEEN

LOGAN

"Come on, one more drink!" TJ goaded me.

I sighed and put my empty beer bottle down on the bar. TJ was being needy right now. Probably because Noah didn't come to the bar after the game since when he wasn't being an absolute beauty on the ice, he was busy planning his wedding.

"Man, get off his dick," Benny came to my rescue.

"You're all boring!" TJ exclaimed and took another swig of his beer.

Cally and I shared a look and shook our heads at TJ's antics. After a week-long road trip, we were back home and had a much-needed home win. I told TJ I'd have one beer at Eileen's, and then I had to go home.

"I thought the nanny was working out?" Benny asked.

"She is, but I don't want her to work twenty-four-seven. I owe Lily so much for getting me in touch with Mari."

At the thought of Lily, I felt a tightening in my pants.

Thinking about her made all the memories of our night together flash into my mind.

I couldn't go there again. She said she was down for some no-strings fun, but I knew how that ended. She was a nice girl, and I didn't want to hurt her.

"Lily, huh?" Blaise asked with an arched eyebrow.

Cally got a giddy look on his face. "Yeah, that's the cute blonde, right? She single?"

"She's my fiancée's best friend, so you better back off," Blaise warned the rookie.

I cringed. Blaise's over-protectiveness of Lily made sense, especially after what she said about her ex.

"Um, excuse you, Blaise. I don't remember when I asked you to protect my honor," an annoyed feminine voice said from behind me.

My dick kicked against my zipper at the sound of her voice. I turned around and saw Veronica and Lily standing in front of us. The latter of the two had her hands on her hips and a sour look on her face.

My eyes trailed up Lily's body, even though I shouldn't have. She wore a nice dress that fit her perfectly and a blazer over it. Almost as if she was still in work attire.

Blaise gave her a sheepish look. "Sorry, Lil, you know..."

She pinned him with the 'mom look.' "Blaise, I'm not looking for an overprotective older brother."

Veronica went over to Blaise, and I watched as he put a hand over her stomach and kissed her sweetly. Veronica smiled up at him. "Sorry, Lil, he can't help it. But he'll stay out of it for now. Right, babe?" Veronica gave him a look that told him he was in trouble, and he nodded.

"Sorry, sweets, can't turn it off. Ready to go?" Blaise asked Veronica.

She nodded. "Yeah, I want to throw up again, and you all smell."

Lily let out a loud laugh and shook her head. Veronica and Blaise left shortly after, and I ended up standing with Lily at the bar. Ayden noticed her from behind the bar and brought her a drink.

"I'm surprised to see you here," I told her.

She sipped on her wine. "I had to shift around my hours because I had a job interview today. I was working late in the office tonight."

"Ahh."

She peered at her drink. "I really needed this drink. Are you going to hang for a minute?"

"I was going to relieve Mari."

She waved me away. "Oh, go on then. I don't want to keep you."

But I could see the number of men looking for an in with her. One was across the bar checking her out, and something territorial crawled up inside me. I didn't like the way they looked at her.

So I ordered another beer instead.

"Don't stay on my account," she said and looked down into her glass of wine.

"I'll stay for one drink. How's Rosie?"

She beamed. "She's good. She's at her dad's again tonight."

"So things are better, then? He didn't flake on you again?"

She shook her head. "Nope. How's Liam doing? He's still having nightmares?"

I blew out a breath. "Better. Your sister has been helping with that. He adores Rosie."

The corner of her lips curled up into a smile. "Mari

sends me photos of them playing together. He's so sweet with her."

"I think he has a thing for blondes," I joked and gave her a grin.

Her hair fell into her face, and before I could tell my brain to stop, I reached a hand up and pushed it behind her ear. God, I wanted to kiss her right here in this bar. When I stared into her gold-flecked eyes, the sounds of the bar melted away, and all I saw was the gorgeous creature in front of me.

"Logan?" she whispered, pulling me from my distracted thoughts.

"Hmm?"

I should have stayed far away from her, but something pulled me to her. I had to resist it, but it was a losing battle as I stared at those plump lips, just waiting for my kiss.

She planted a hand flat on my chest, and electricity sparked through the material of my dress shirt. When she reached up on her tiptoes, I bent down and took her mouth. I dropped my guard and kissed the woman who had been invading my thoughts all week long. Until my hands were in her hair and my tongue was in her mouth.

What the fuck am I doing?

I wrenched myself from her mouth, and when I pulled back, her lips were bruised and her face flushed. Like a woman who had been well-kissed and ready for more.

"Logan?" she whispered again.

My dick answered for me, even though my brain knew it was a bad idea. "Go out with me again?"

She cocked her head at me in an unasked question. I shouldn't want to take her out again. I should fuck her in the backseat of my car and be done with it. Or better yet, leave her alone altogether. But my horny brain was on overdrive all week long, remembering the sound of her moans and the way her lithe body fit together with mine.

"My offer was no strings," she explained, staring at me, so I understood what she meant. "If you need something casual, you don't have to take me out again. Hell, if all you want is someone to game with when you have thirty minutes to do a quest in Dragonspire, I'm down for that too. Or if you need a fellow single parent to bitch to, I got you there."

"No."

"No?"

"If you're going to spend your precious time with a guy who can't give you what you deserve, I'm gonna make it worth your while."

She gave me a small smile. "I'm a simple Philly gal who likes pizza and playing video games all night long."

A grin spread across my face. "I love that you're my dream gamer girl, but I still want to show you a good time. Even if whatever this is—"

She leaned up and kissed me again, cutting off my sentence. I let her take the lead, but soon I was angling her head again, and I knew we were drawing attention to ourselves. We must have looked like two horny teenagers.

I pulled away and loved how she looked out of breath. Her lips were bruised from too many of my kisses like I had branded her with my mouth.

"Logan, we're two friends enjoying each other's company, nothing more."

I cupped her jaw and rubbed the pad of my thumb against her cheek. "Then you'll have no problem letting me take you out again."

She sighed. "Okay, you win, but only because you're cute and you have good taste in dinner."

"I have a game in Jersey tomorrow, but when I get back, I'm taking you out again."

"Okay."

"And then I'm going to fuck you all over the place. Multiple times," I growled.

She gulped, and her cheeks went pink at my horny admittance. "Is that a promise?"

"Promise, princess."

She put a hand on my chest. "Wait, when?"

"Let me check my schedule and get back to you, okay? We'll figure it out. If you have Rosie, I'll take care of everything so we have a night to ourselves."

She nodded.

"You want a ride home?"

She shook her head. "No, I'm good. Call me later?"

"You bet your sweet ass, I will."

Her eyes twinkled when she looked at me, and it hit me right in the chest. I reminded myself going out with her was to scratch that itch again and nothing more. We just needed each other for comfort in our loneliness.

The real reason I wanted to take her out? I felt like a creep if all I was doing was calling her up for a booty call. Plus, I enjoyed her company. So going out on dates together and having adult time afterward would be exactly what we needed.

I waited for her to finish her wine and walked her to her car. I wanted to kiss her goodbye — my dick kicking against the zipper of my jeans wanted to do even more, but I held myself back. I watched her drive off, making sure she was safe.

I didn't bother saying goodbye to my teammates. If I did, TJ would've pressured me into another drink or a round of shots, and I didn't have time for that. I walked to my car and drove home.

When I walked through the door, Mari was sitting on the couch where she always was, watching a trashy reality TV show I teased her about. I slumped on the couch next to her.

"Sorry, I'm late," I told her.

She waved me off. "You're fine."

"How was he?"

"Good," she said. "Can I ask you something?"

"Sure."

"Why don't you have him in preschool yet? I've been working with him on sight words and stuff, so I know he's ready, but..." she trailed off and clamped her mouth shut. "Sorry, that was rude of me. You don't have to explain your parenting choices. Some kids skip preschool altogether or start late."

I rubbed the back of my neck. "He was in daycare, but he acted out a lot after he came to live with me. He missed his mom, and I didn't know how to handle it. You're so good with him. I'm afraid of that happening again."

She put a hand on my arm. "Logan, you're doing fine. I can help you look for preschools or a tutor to help prepare him for kindergarten."

I leaned back on the couch and undid my tie. "Mari, that would be amazing."

She beamed. "It's my job. I'll get on it tomorrow."

I scrolled through my phone and looked at my schedule, trying to figure out a day that would work to take Lily out again.

"What's with the brooding face?" she asked.

"I think I have a date?"

Her eyes widened, and then she gave me a playful slap on the arm. "Are you going out with my sister again?"

I rubbed my beard. "Am I foolish for doing that? I can't give her what she deserves."

Mari rolled her eyes. "It bothers me that you think you don't deserve happiness. You're a good man, Logan. Go out with my sister, but if you hurt her, I might have to quit."

She smiled, so I knew she was joking, but that was what I was afraid of. Lily understood my need for something casual, but I didn't want her to get ideas we could ever be something more. Even though I couldn't stop thinking about her. Or the fact I was pretty sure Lily and Flower were one and the same. I wasn't sure how to bring that up to her yet.

"Just because you're a single dad doesn't mean you need to give up everything. You can still have a love life," Mari said.

I shook my head. "I'm too busy with hockey."

Mari chewed on her lip and looked like she wanted to say something more, but she shut her mouth.

"Uncle Logan?" a tiny voice came from behind me.

"What are you doing up?" I asked my nephew.

Liam rubbed his sleepy eyes. "Can you read me a story?"

"All right, bud. Say goodnight to Mari."

He ran over to her and hugged her. Mari took his hand and guided him back to his bedroom. She got him settled down into his bed when I walked in. Mari hugged him to her chest and sang to him.

She ruffled his hair. "I'll see you tomorrow, okay?"

He didn't seem to want to let her go.

"Liam, Mari has to go home now. Say goodnight."

"Night, Mari," he said through a yawn.

Mari pulled the blankets up and tucked him in. "Night, buddy. See you tomorrow."

I walked her to the front door. Liam was still awake when I came back in. I sat in the chair next to him and pulled out his favorite book.

"Uncle Logan?" he asked.

"Yeah, bud?"

"Why do you go?"

That made my heart hurt. I tried to explain that I traveled a lot for work, but it wasn't clicking for him.

"Because, bud, I have to travel to other cities to play hockey against them. If you want to be a hockey player, you'll have to do that."

He shook his head. "No."

"No you won't?"

"I don't want to play hockey."

That was new. Liam tried to emulate me so much. "What do you want to be when you grow up?"

"Firetruck."

"You mean firefighter?"

He shook his head, furrowing his little brow like I was the one who wasn't getting it. "Firetruck!"

So much about parenting was not wanting to laugh in your kid's face. What did he mean he wanted to be a firetruck? What did that even mean? Maybe I let him watch too many cartoons.

I ruffled his hair instead of laughing. "Okay, bud, time for you to get back to bed."

"Story!"

I tickled his belly. "You're lucky you're cute, little man. Okay, one story, then bedtime."

He simmered down and fell asleep when I got to page

two of his book. I left his room, leaving the night light on, and went into my bedroom.

Mari stayed over when I traveled, but she felt weird about sleeping in my room, so she made the couch her bed. I felt bad about that, especially since she took it upon herself to do my housework.

I peeled my suit off and changed into a pair of pajama pants. I took off my shirt before slumping down on my bed. I checked my schedule and shot a text off to Lily.

ME: How about Wednesday?

LILY: Ooh! Seth has Rosie again then. It's perfect!

Me: It's a date!

It was supposed to be Mari's off day then, so I didn't feel comfortable asking her for more childcare. She'd do it, but she needed a break every once in a while too. Veronica had no issues doing it, so I texted her next.

ME: Can you do me a favor and watch Liam at your place next Wednesday? I have a date.

V: YES!!

I shouldn't be giddy like a virgin before prom, but I was. I should have known then how utterly fucked I was when it came to Lily. I was kidding myself about it only being casual with my dream girl.

CHAPTER EIGHTEEN

LILY

"What do you mean you can't take her?" I asked Seth.

I put my head in my hands as he rattled off some excuse about a work convention he had this week that I didn't believe for a second. The last time he had one of those, I found out he had been cheating on me months later.

"Are you done?" I asked into the phone.

"Come on, Lily Pad, gimme a break."

I sighed. "This isn't about me. It's about your daughter."

"It's for work!"

Yeah, I didn't believe that for a single second. I understood how Seth lied now. The way his voice went up an octave and how defensive he got. It wasn't about me or how he did me wrong, though; it was about Rosie. I didn't want her to grow up and figure out her dad was a deadbeat.

I didn't bother responding. I clicked end on my phone and tossed it onto my bed. I sighed as I stared at the date outfits I had laid on the bed and resigned myself to putting them back in my closet. Logan would understand, but this sucked.

I put the outfits away and shot off a text to him.

ME: Sorry. I have to cancel.

LOGAN: Why?

ME: Seth has a work thing and can't take Rosie now.

He didn't respond, so I tossed my phone back onto my bed and went to wake up Rosie from her nap. My sister had watched her while I worked today, but I couldn't ask her to do an overnight, especially when it was her day off. That wasn't fair to her.

Rosie was up and awake in her crib. She wasn't taking long naps anymore, but she stayed in her crib until I got her.

"Okay, Rosie, change of plans. We're not going to Daddy's today."

"Da-da!"

"Daddy has work. Okay? You get to hang out with Mommy tonight."

I picked her up and changed her diaper. I walked with her in my arms into my room, where I heard my phone vibrating on the bed. I grabbed it, angling my head to hold the phone against my shoulder while Rosie was in my arms.

The person on the other line didn't wait for me to answer. "Bring that sweet little baby to my place," Veronica's voice rang in my ear.

"What?"

"You and Logan deserve a night without the kids, so Blaise and I are gonna take them."

I didn't know what to say. Logan said he'd take care of everything, but I hadn't expected this from a guy who only wanted me for sex. It was nice, though. Seth never would have done that.

"Girl, you need this. You and Logan could be good for each other," Veronica said.

I don't think Veronica got how much Logan and I just needed each other to scratch that itch. "It's not like that," I argued and jostled Rosie in my arms.

"Sure it's not," she said, and I could imagine her rolling her eyes at me.

Veronica confided in me that after Seth left, she had a ton of meaningless hookups. Blaise was the first man that made her want to love again. She was hopelessly in love with her blonde giant, and now she wanted everyone else in love too.

"V, we just need grown-up time. Nothing more," I explained.

"That sounds fake, but okay!" she exclaimed. "I'm coming over to grab Rosie. Get ready for your date, okay?"

"Thanks, V. I don't know what I'd do without you."

"Have a really boring life."

I laughed. I hung up with her and got Rosie ready. "Okay, baby, you're going to Uncle Blaise's and Aunt V's tonight! You're gonna have so much fun with them."

I got her dressed and put her on the floor with one of her toys while I packed an overnight bag for her. Blaise had already built a crib for their baby, so I didn't have to worry about sending her over with the pack-and-play. Thank God Veronica and Blaise were prepared to take her overnight.

After packing everything up, the doorbell rang. That was quick.

I lifted Rosie in my arms and went downstairs. I opened the door and found Veronica behind it. Rosie shyly hid her face in my neck.

"Aw, baby, it's just Aunt V!"

"Come on, sweet thing. We're gonna have a sleepover with Liam tonight," Veronica told her.

Rosie's head lifted up at Liam's name. The two spent so much time together that they were attached at the hip. It was so cute. "Liam?" she asked.

I nodded. "You'll have so much fun tonight. Give Mommy a kiss."

Rosie gave me a big sloppy kiss, and I laughed as I handed her off to Veronica. I helped her get all the stuff into her car, making sure the car seat was secured and Rosie was in there nice and tightly.

I kissed Rosie's forehead. "Be good, okay, baby?"

I shut the car door and walked over to the driver's side, where Veronica was behind the wheel. "Call me if there are any issues. I'm serious."

"We're fine. Now go get ready and wear something sexy!"

I shook my head. "Why are you such an instigator?"

"Because you and Logan are cute together."

"V, I told you, it's just fun."

She grinned. "Well, make it count then."

I waved to them as Veronica drove off with my daughter, giving me the time to get ready for my date with Logan. I went back inside and pulled out the date outfits again. They were nice, but were they sexy enough for the hunky hockey player? He hadn't told me where we were going yet.

I pulled out my phone and texted him.

ME: Where are we going?

LOGAN: Secret. Dress casual again.

I chewed on my lip and looked at my outfit choices

again. I ended up going with the black skirt and chunky sweater with my thigh-high boots. The boots would be sexy. I laid my clothes out on the bed and then took a shower. After showering, shaving, and plucking my eyebrows, I was almost ready. Maybe it was a mistake to go on another date with Logan, but there was something about him that made me want to give in to my desires. Even if it was only for a temporary fix.

I was also eighty percent sure Logan might be my gamer friend. I wasn't sure how to bring that up to him. Like, 'hey, I know you also play Dragonspire. What's your gamertag so I can find out if you're my friend I've been playing with since high school?' What a weird question. How could I even go about asking him that? Unless I was a creep and started his console up to see what username it logged him in as. That was ridiculous. I wasn't doing that.

I heard the front door open while I was putting the finishing touches on my makeup. Footsteps came up the steps, and it surprised me when my mom leaned against the bathroom doorway.

"Are you going out with Logan again?" she asked and had a giddy look on her face. What spell had Logan cast on her to make her like him so much after one meeting?

I nodded. "Yup. Don't wait up for me."

"Did Seth pick up Rosie like he said?"

I cringed. I was hoping she wouldn't ask about that. "He had a work thing. Veronica took her for the night."

Mom's mouth was a thin line. "Are you sure he really had a work thing?"

I shook my head. "Mom, can you drop it?"

She crossed her arms over her chest. "This is exactly what your father did. I don't want Rosie to grow up without her dad."

I sighed. "Mom, can we talk about this later?"

She looked like she wanted to argue more, but I was saved by the bell. Literally.

"I'll get it," Mom offered, and I didn't stop her as I did one final swipe of my lipstick.

Downstairs, their voices floated up the steps, and I tried to remember what else I needed for tonight. Logan was charming the pants off my mom, but I didn't want her to get any ideas. Logan was well-mannered, so I could see why my mom immediately took a liking to him. I had to admit, she had a point about Seth never coming to the door but rather honking his horn and waiting for me to come out. Logan wasn't even my boyfriend, and he made more of an effort than Seth ever had.

I grabbed my purse from my room but paused before going downstairs. I found a small overnight bag in my closet and shoved spare clothes inside. I checked my face in the mirror once more, and then I walked downstairs.

It was unseasonably warm for October, so tonight Logan wore a black t-shirt that contoured to his rippling muscles and a leather jacket over top of it. He wore a pair of dark jeans and sneakers that I was sure cost a lot of money. I looked down at my outfit and contemplated changing. I wasn't too dressed up, but he was dressed a little more casually.

He looked up at the sound of my heeled boots hitting the hardwood. A smile spread across his freckled face when his gaze came across mine. His eyes were dark with want as they walked down my body, like he was peeling back all my layers in his mind. I didn't hate the way he looked at me like I was something he wanted to feast on. I liked that he desired me. That he wasn't an asshole jock who only liked women who sported the so-called perfect figure.

"Wow, you look great!"

Mom beamed. "You do, sweetheart. Have fun, you two. It was so good to see you again, Logan."

"Likewise, Ms. Mathews," Logan said and gave my mom a wink.

Logan helped me with my light jacket, and then we walked out the door together. I tried not to think about the mixed signals he gave me as I slid into the passenger side of his car.

"So, where are we going?" I asked as he drove off.

He rubbed his beard, and that naughty smile came across his face again. "Well...my little gamer girl, what do you think about Player Won?"

My face broke out into a smile at his suggestion. Player Won was a bar arcade in Fishtown that catered to old-school cabinet arcade games and craft beer. I wasn't that big of a beer drinker, but I loved the suggestion of us getting our game on together. It was the perfect date for my little gamer heart.

"That sounds awesome."

"I knew you'd like it, my little wood elf princess."

I paused at his words. I mentioned I played as a wood elf, but Ginge had said those same words. Was I hearing what I wanted to hear? Or was I grasping at straws? Was Logan my gamer friend? It was too weird to be a coincidence.

"You okay?"

I shook my thoughts away. "Yes, let's do it!"

"Atta girl. Let's get our game on."

"I could have brought my console over, and we could have played Dragonspire together tonight instead."

He furrowed his brow. "Oh my God! Why didn't I

think about that? I'm turning around. Let's go get your console."

I laughed and put a hand on his arm to stop him. If Logan wasn't Ginge, I was going to look foolish, but I had a good feeling about this. "Maybe later, Ginge. Let's get food and drinks and play some old-school video games."

CHAPTER NINETEEN

LOGAN

A great whooshing sound rang in my ears, and it took me a minute to realize it was my heart beating fast inside my head.

No, she didn't. She didn't say what I thought she said. Did Lily know I was GingerPower33?

"I—" I stuttered. I was focusing on driving, so I couldn't look at her. I was ninety percent sure Lily was FlowerChild183, but I had no clue she suspected I was Ginge.

"Because that's who you are, right? You're GingerPower33?" she asked.

"Flower?"

"Yup, that's me."

How the fuck did she figure it out? I thought I was going to be the one to make the big announcement.

After circling the block a few times, I found a spot to park the car. I cut the engine and turned to her.

She gave me a sheepish look. "It's you, isn't it?"

I nodded. "How did you know?"

"Certain things you said were familiar, and then the other night, you said you were a hockey player. I kept trying to convince myself it wasn't true, that it was all a coincidence. I still wasn't sure."

"What sold it?"

She gave me an annoyed look. "Wood elf princess, really?"

I laughed. "Caught! I was going to make a show of asking you for your gamertag."

She laughed with me. "Is that why you said for me to get my console?"

I grinned. "Maybe."

She shook her head. "I can't believe you're Ginge! We've been playing together since high school."

"It makes sense, though, huh?"

"How so?"

I rubbed a hand down my beard. "When I met you at Blaise's last summer, it was like I already knew you. I didn't understand why, but now it all makes sense."

Her lush mouth turned up into a smile. "It does."

"Come on, wood elf princess. Let's game!"

"Okay, ginger warrior."

I ran a hand through my red hair. She was totally teasing me about my redheaded warrior character I played in Dragonspire. Now that we knew, it couldn't have been more obvious. I played as a tall, hulking giant with bright red hair, and she played as a tiny blonde elf.

Lily hopped out of the car, and I'd be lying if I didn't notice how her skirt flipped up, giving me a flash of black fabric underneath. Her legs were bare, but those boots on her feet made me imagine the heels of them over my shoulder as I railed into her.

Focus, Logan!

I got out of my car, locked it, and followed her inside the bar. The interior of the bar was all brick walls and wooden beams, with rows upon rows of old-school arcade cabinets along the back wall. The place lit up in bright lights from the machines, and Lily's eyes sparkled as she spied a popular fighter game.

"Game or eat first?" I asked.

"Game!" she cheered.

God, she was so damn cute. With that bright smile and cute outfit, I couldn't help but want to give in to her every desire. "Want to grab a drink first?"

"Oh, yes, please!"

I tried not to bite my fist at that sentence. I'd definitely have her saying that again later. We walked over to the bar, and she scanned the long line of taps against the wall. "Oh, they have MacGregor Brothers Brewing Company here."

"What's that?" I asked.

"Oh, it's a local brewery. Well, sorta, they're out in the suburbs. Veronica used to live in the town where they're located. She got me hooked."

The bartender came over and asked what we wanted. I gestured for Lily to start. "I'll take the Drakesville Lager."

"I'll do the Area 267," I said after scanning the board and reading it was a hoppy IPA. I was all for local beer. I handed the bartender my card and asked him to keep my tab open while Lily dragged me over to one of the cabinets.

She gave me a daring look. "You ready for this, Ginge?"

I barked out a laugh. "Oh, it's on Flower!"

I went over to exchange cash for the weird bar tokens the machine took instead of quarters, and we each put tokens in and started up Street Fighter. We were total nerds picking our characters, her going with one of the few female playable characters and me going with the most popular male one. When the infamous music came on for our first round, it was on.

At first, I went a little easy on her until I noticed her fingers flying across the buttons in time with her other hand jostling the joystick. Her tongue stuck out, and she glued her eyes onto the screen, calculating my every move. It was when her character slammed mine on the ground and knocked me out to win the first round that I realized I had to step up my game. She was kicking my ass and had a gleeful look on her face while doing it.

And she had never looked more beautiful to me. Where had this sexy and smart gamer girl been all my life? Oh, right, staying home playing a nerdy fantasy RPG with me on the other end.

"You're good at this," I muttered as I tried a combo move but missed her.

"What, you think I'm a fake gamer girl?"

I shook my head. "Def not. Didn't know you'd kick my ass in an arcade game, though."

"Ha! Arcade was how I got my start," she explained. Her hands flew over the controls as we jabbed and punched at each other in the game. "Spent the summers at my grandparents' place down the shore. My sister would bathe in the sun, but my nerdy butt was in the arcade until I ran out of quarters."

"Damn, where have you been all my life?"

"What do you mean?"

"You're my dream girl."

She laughed, but then the little sneak knocked me out and won the round. She turned and took a big sip of her beer, giving me a shy smile behind it. "Too busy sitting at home playing video games."

"Rematch?"

She shook her head. "Pinball?"

"Hell yeah!"

We moved from game to game, some to play together, some to watch each other kick ass. Like right now, while I watched her take down a bunch of aliens in Space Invaders. Watching her play almost made me forget all the reasons I couldn't make her mine. I had to remember that we were just two single parents desperate for a night out.

She groaned when her eight-bit spaceship blew up. "That's some bullshit. Hey, are you hungry now?"

I rattled my empty beer bottle. "I could use a refill. Let's eat."

We ordered at the bar and found a table to sit at. I smirked at the fact we both ordered tacos. She daintily ate her al pastor tacos while I almost swallowed my chicken ones whole.

"Good tacos?" I asked, and took a swig of my beer. This beer was good; I'd have to pick up more from this brewery later.

She raised her hand and waved it back and forth like a scale. "They're okay."

"Just okay?"

"It's a fine pub version of tacos, but the other place was better."

"I'll have to remember for next time."

She took a drink of her beer. "It's been a fun evening. I almost forgot all the things weighing me down."

I nodded in agreement. I had a good time with her, and I wanted to keep the night going. Now I understood why I was drawn toward her. I had known this woman for a long time.

"Thanks for taking care of everything so I didn't have to cancel," she said and looked down at the table.

I clenched my teeth together. Her ex seemed like such a douche. Of course I'd begged Veronica to take Rosie for the night. Lily needed another night out as bad as I did.

I curled my hand around my beer bottle as I wondered what else that douchebag had done to Lily. If I found out he ever laid a hand on her...

I wrenched away when I felt her hand on my arm. Her eyes searched my own, and I realized I must have been stuck in my head for far too long.

"Logan. Are you okay?" she asked in a low voice.

I nodded. "Sorry. Lost in thought."

She pulled her hand away, but she didn't try to get me to open up. I let it slip about my dad being in jail, but I never told her the reason. Chicks didn't want to know about my awful childhood. It wasn't something you brought up in pleasant conversation, especially not on a date.

"About what?" she asked.

I sighed and ran a hand through my beard. "I hate your ex."

A smile tugged at her lips. "Me too."

"I hate that he keeps leaving you in a lurch."

She nodded. "I don't want Rosie to grow up without a dad. He said he had a work thing, but I don't believe him. I found out he was cheating on me because he lied about a work convention. When I saw the receipts, I realized what a fool I had been. I didn't see that he was exactly like my dad. My mom loves to rub that into my face."

"She just wants to protect you."

"I know. Some days I wished I'd never met him, but then other days, I get to snuggle with my baby, and I remember there's a little life counting on me. It's hard sometimes."

I raised my beer bottle, and she clinked hers against mine. "I feel you on that. I wasn't supposed to be a dad."

"Do you regret becoming his guardian?"

I shook my head. "Not regret. It's frustrating some days. I was a single guy living it up with my dream career as a hockey player, and then I got a kid dropped on me."

She nodded.

I rubbed the back of my neck. That made me sound like such an asshole. "It wasn't a life I chose, so yeah, some days I'm frustrated that I have responsibilities while my teammates are off partying. But that little boy is my whole world, and I love him to pieces — tantrums and all."

She reached out and squeezed my hand. "I can tell. Being a parent's hard, but you're doing a great job."

I gave her a small smile. I never admitted any of those frustrations to anyone else, but of course, she understood. It was my understanding her pregnancy wasn't planned, so we both became parents before we were ready.

She pushed her finished plate aside. "Anyway, no more talking about the kids. You wanna get out of here?"

I gave her a naughty smile. "And do what?"

She arched an eyebrow at me. "How about you make good on your promise, huh?"

"That's what I like to hear."

As soon as we got into my condo, I was on her in a flash. We were all tangled limbs and desperate kisses as we clawed at each other's clothes. She angled her head for me and submitted to my dominance just the way I liked. She yelped when I hiked her up into my arms and led her into my bedroom.

She put her hands on my chest, trying to rid me of my jacket, while I slid my hands up her soft sweater and pulled it over her head. Beneath her sweater, she wore a sexy lacy bra, and I wanted to know if she wore matching panties. I deposited her on the bed, tore my jacket off, and pulled my t-shirt over my head.

Her eyes scanned across my chest. "God, that's so unfair."

I smirked at her and pulled her boots off. As much as I wanted to fuck her in them, I didn't love the idea of shoes on my bed. "What is?"

She shimmed out of the skirt, and I pulled the material down her legs, kissing them as I did. She gestured to my six-pack. "You look like a work of art."

"I work pretty hard on my body."

"I want you to work hard on mine," she muttered, and then her cheeks grew pink as she realized what she had said.

I looked down at her, lying in my bed with her blonde hair fanning around her head like a halo. She was indeed wearing matching underwear, and if I could get harder than I already was, the image of her right now would have done it.

I undid my jeans and slid them down my thick thighs. "Don't you worry, princess. I'm going to take care of you tonight."

I shoved off my jeans and boxers and slid into the bed beside her. I attacked her mouth, kissing her roughly while my hands roamed down to cup her breasts. I slid her bra strap down her shoulder and kissed her pale skin, marking a trail of my lips as I made my way down to the valley of her breasts.

She reached behind her and undid her bra for me. I helped her out of it and made my way toward one of her nipples. She arched her back when I licked at her, sliding my tongue around the bud until I pulled it into my mouth. I hadn't done that last time. I went straight into oral, not giving her time to warm up. Usually, I loved getting a woman all hot and bothered until she was crying for my cock.

I switched to her other breast, giving it the same treatment, and made my descent down her stomach. I kissed the lines that made her self-conscious, letting her know I didn't care about her scars. My elven princess had battle scars from bringing her daughter into the world, and I didn't care one iota about them.

"Logan, please," she begged.

I curled my finger around the waistband of her lacy bikini-style panties, toying with her. "Please what, princess?"

She squirmed on the bed. "I need you, please."

"You'll get me," I purred and pulled her underwear down her legs. "After I feast on this pretty little pussy."

She bit her lip, but then it turned into a moan as I took that first lick. She tasted as good as I remembered. I put her legs on my shoulders and opened her up, stroking her slowly with my tongue. I ate her to my heart's desire, exploring her until she was panting. She was so close, but when I wrapped my lips around her clit, she was done for.

"LOGAN!" she cried and gripped my hair in between her delicate fingers.

I sucked harder, giving her more pressure while she rode out the wave of her orgasm on my face. I licked her through her orgasm until she flopped back on the bed with a sigh of contentment.

I lifted my head from between her thighs, and my cock stirred at the sight of her laid out in front of me. She was spread eagle for me, her body limp from my mouth working her over. Damn, did she look gorgeous after she came.

"C'mere, my warrior," she purred and crooked a finger at me.

I kinda liked her calling me that in bed.

"I'm your warrior, huh?" I asked. I opened the bedside table drawer. I pulled out a condom and slid it on my cock.

She nodded. "C'mere and show me just how strong you can be, my warrior hero."

"Patience, little wood elf princess, want to make it good for you."

I pulled out a bottle of lube and spread a liberal amount down my cock.

She didn't wait and pulled me down for another rough kiss. Her hand threaded through my hair while we kissed like we were starved for each other. I didn't stop kissing her when I settled myself between her legs. She moaned into my mouth when I teased her by dragging the head of my cock along her clit.

She wrenched her head away and dug her nails into my back. "Please take me."

"That's what you want, huh? To be taken by your warrior, little princess?"

"Please. Need my big, strong warrior to fuck me into submission."

Hell yes.

I didn't wait for more permission and instead found her entrance. We groaned together as I moved inside her. I slid all the way out and then slammed back in, watching my dick sliding in and out of her perfect pussy over and over again. She met my every downward stroke by arching up and grinding her hips against mine.

I liked that she wanted to call me her warrior, almost as

if we were role-playing as the characters we played in Dragonspire. That was hot. I never had a woman try that in bed with me. I had one pull out whips and chains, which was not my thing, but this I could get into.

I pressed her knees to her chest and drove deeper, forcing her inner walls to squeeze around my dick. I groaned at the sensation. She felt so tight and perfect that I wouldn't last long. Her cries egged me on, forcing me to slam into her harder and faster, taking her as rough as I could. The sounds of pleasure she made beneath me told me how much she loved it.

I squeezed my eyes shut, trying to hold off my orgasm before she came again. "Princess," I moaned as if begging her to let me come already.

"Do it," she moaned back, understanding my pained non-question.

I put her legs over my shoulders, giving me better access to bury myself inside her as deep as I could until I bottomed out. I looked into her eyes as I gave her what she wanted, driving into her until she cried out. And I mean literally cried. She moaned uncontrollably as she came. Then I rutted on top of her like the animal I was, fucking her hard and rough until I spilled out my release into the condom.

I took a second to catch my breath and slid her legs off my shoulders. We were both breathing heavily as we stared at each other in the aftershocks of our orgasms. Her hazel eyes looked like amber in the dim light of my bedroom. A man could get lost in them.

I reluctantly slid out of her and got up to get rid of the condom in the bathroom. When I got back into bed, she had a big smile on her face. I pulled her across my chest, and she sprawled across my large body.

I kissed the top of her head. "You like me being your warrior, huh?"

She buried her face in my chest, and I chuckled at her embarrassment. "Oh my God! I kinda made you role-play with me, sorry. I don't know what came over me."

I tilted her head up. "Don't apologize. I liked it."

"It wasn't weird?"

I shook my head. "Nope. I'll be whatever you want me in bed. I'll get you a crown, and you can really be my elven princess."

She bit her lip.

My eyebrow shot up at the shy look that came across her face."Wait, do you already have one?"

She nodded sheepishly. "I'll show you my cosplay sometime later."

Fuck, that was so hot.

Cosplay girls were so fucking hot. One of my ultimate weaknesses.

"Please don't tell me you also read comics. Then you'd be the complete nerd girl package."

She cringed.

"Oh my God, Lily, you're killing me!"

She smiled. "I'm surprised that for being a jock, you like such nerdy things."

I laughed. "Yeah, the boys give me shit for it, but being a nerd and being good at hockey aren't mutually exclusive. I can contain multitudes."

She chuckled and kissed my chest. I played with her hair while we basked in the afterglow of post-sex. Her lips traveled down my chest until she kissed each of my ribs. My dick lifted in interest, ready for round two already.

"What you doing down there, princess?"

She kissed my hip bone and gave me a sultry look. "Giving my warrior what he needs."

And then she took my cock in her mouth, and it was game over for me. She had finished me.

If I had time for a relationship, I'd seriously think about how I could keep her forever. Because Lily Mathews was, without a doubt, my ultimate dream girl. Smart, kind, kicked my ass in video games, and sucked my cock like nobody else.

Why did my life have to be so complicated?

But I stopped thinking about all that when I was fucking her face and coming down her throat.

CHAPTER TWENTY

LILY

This bed was so comfortable, but I should leave.

Last night, Logan made good on his promise of taking care of me all night. My legs felt like jelly by the time we called it quits after taking a shower together. Where he fucked me against the tile wall. He had to hike me up against it due to our size difference, but it was so hot. He might be a complete nerd, but his athletic stamina made for interesting sex.

I should get up and go get Rosie, but Logan's muscular arm was wrapped tight around me protectively, and I didn't want to leave the warmth of his embrace.

"Princess," he growled into my ear, startling me. "You better stop."

"What?"

He held my hip down with his big hand. "Stop rubbing up against my morning wood."

I didn't know I was doing that. "Oh. Sorry."

He pressed a kiss on my neck. His hand danced across

my skin, edging closer to my center. "You're not sorry," That growly tone had returned to his voice, and I shivered at it.

I wanted to buck against him again. That deep growling voice of his turned me on. Last night was amazing. He hadn't even blinked when I slipped up and called him my warrior, pretending like he was his character in Dragonspire. Instead, he called me his wood elf princess and went with it.

That had surprised me. I tried once, ONCE, to get Seth to role-play with me, but he wasn't interested. The most he would do was push my face into the mattress and fuck me from behind. But I didn't love doggy style; I loved being face-to-face with the person I was having sex with. He never got what I wanted.

But last night, Logan did. He took me like he was wild, like if he didn't fuck me as deep and rough as possible, he wouldn't be able to come. When he finally came, it was the hottest thing I ever saw.

"You're bad news for me," Logan whispered in my ear.

I wanted to ask what he meant, or why he wasn't touching me yet, but then his alarm blared on the bedside table, and he pulled away from me.

I snuggled down into the bed, trying to get back the warmth that his big body had provided me. He swung his legs over the side of the bed and sat up, rubbing the sleep from his eyes.

"I gotta get to morning skate," he told me.

"Oh. I should go get Rosie from Veronica and Blaise's then."

He turned around, leaned over, and kissed my forehead. "Stay as long as you like. I asked Mari to do it."

"No, I should go."

He got out of the bed and went to his dresser to pull out

clothes to wear. I wasn't sure what morning skate was, but I was pretty sure he had a game tonight. I wasn't sure what that all entailed. We talked little about hockey when we were together.

"Stay in my comfy bed if you want."

"Logan?"

"Yeah, princess?"

I grinned at the nickname. "Thanks for last night. I had a lot of fun."

He grinned back at me. "Me too. I can't believe you kicked my ass."

"Are you sure you didn't let me win?"

He shook his head. "A little at first, and then you hit me with that combo move and KO'd me."

"Ha! That's a classic move. I couldn't believe you didn't see it coming."

I shamelessly watched him get dressed. He came back around to my side of the bed and kissed me again. "Seriously, stay."

"I better get up. I have to go to Manayunk today for a client."

"Whatever you want, princess. I'll be back later."

I flopped back on the bed and watched his cute butt leave. Logan was so hot that it surprised me he was as big of a nerd as I was. I should have left with him, but he must have tired me out last night because I fell back asleep.

When I woke up again, it was to the sound of the front door opening and two yelling little kids.

A knock sounded on the closed bedroom door. "You decent?" my sister's voice asked through the wood.

"Yeah!" I called back, and before I could ask her why, the door flung open, and two pairs of tiny feet ran into the room. Liam crawled on the bed, cuddling up against my side, while Rosie stood next to me with her arms up.

"Up? Mommy up?" she asked.

I pulled her up into the bed with me and gave her a kiss. "Hi, baby. Did you have fun at Aunt V's and Uncle Blaise's?"

"Da-da?" she asked.

"Not here, baby. Give Mommy a kiss?"

She gave me a wet, sloppy kiss and giggled when I tickled her little belly.

"Lily! Lily! Guess what?" Liam asked me excitedly.

I held Rosie to my chest on one side while he bounced around the bed on my other. I gave him a patient smile. "What's up, bud?"

He gave me a conspiratorial look. "Uncle Blaise and Aunt V are having a baby," he whispered and then put a finger to his lips. "But it's a secret."

I mimed zipping my lips. "I'll keep that a secret. You better too, okay, bud?"

"Okay!" he said, and then he leaned his head on the other side of my chest. I ran a hand through his hair and looked up to see my sister leaning against the bedroom door with her phone out.

"Aw, so cute! I'll send that one to Logan," Mari told me. "Come on, kids, and help me with breakfast."

Liam raced over to her, and Mari laughed as she led him out of the room. My sister was magic with these kids, and even though she hadn't been his nanny for all that long, Liam was attached to her already. Rosie didn't want to budge. I should get to Rich's tattoo shop, but I would never get this time back with Rosie, so I'd rather be cuddling up in bed with her.

"Come on, baby. Aunt Mari's gonna make breakfast," I told her.

I got up from the bed and took her into the kitchen, where I placed her in her highchair while Mari sat Liam down at the kitchen table with his coloring book. Mari raised an eyebrow at my attire, and I realized I was still only wearing Logan's t-shirt. I sprinted back into the bedroom, shutting the door behind me and changing into the clothes I shoved into my overnight bag. In my haste, I only packed a t-shirt and some leggings. I definitely had to run home before going to the shop.

I swiped at my phone on the bedside table and checked my email. My face fell when I saw an email from Rich, but then I saw it wasn't something bad.

Hey, Lil. Love your work. I forwarded your name to a friend. See you later today!

I scrolled through my emails, seeing a couple of job requests from the freelance site until I found one from an unfamiliar name.

Hey, Lily. Both Rich and Alex spoke highly of your work. Would love to set up a meeting to talk business.

~Adam, Heart of Ink Tattoo

All the blood rushed to my head. Heart of Ink was where Seth worked. He was working at Golden Rose for a while until I made a scene there when I found out he was cheating on me. Alex kicked him to the curb right after that. I felt bad about that, but not really, because Seth sucked.

"Did you get lost?" Mari yelled from the other side of the door.

I walked back out into the kitchen and took the offered mug of coffee my sister handed me. She flipped pancakes on the stove and raised her eyebrow at me. "What's wrong?"

I took a sip of coffee. "I got an offer from a new client."

She gave me a confused look. "Okay...but that's good, though, right?"

I frowned. "It's for the shop where Seth works."

She wrinkled her nose. "Okay...but you need the work, right?"

I nodded and set my coffee cup down. I took out plates and divided up the finished pancakes. Mari continued to cook while I gave Liam his food and tousled his hair. "Here you go, bud."

I cut up the pieces smaller for Rosie and started feeding her. "Here, baby." She could be a fussy eater, but she was being good this morning.

"Lily?" Liam asked.

"What's wrong, Liam?"

"Are you and Uncle Logan gonna get married?"

Mari and I looked at each other in horror. I tried not to let Liam see the shocked look on my face. I set down the fork I was using to feed Rosie, but she happily grabbed a bite of pancake in her tiny fist.

"Liam, why did you ask me that?"

His little brow furrowed. "You slept in Uncle Logan's bed. Aunt V said only people who love each other do that."

I cringed. I had a feeling Veronica said that for a particular reason, but it wasn't helping me.

"No. I'm not gonna marry your uncle," I told him gently.

He frowned. "Why not?"

"Liam," Mari interjected, "how about we finish those pancakes, okay? And then, we can play mini sticks?"

"Okay!" Liam cheered and ate his pancakes in rapid succession. Kids could be so easily distracted. Thank God for that. I mouthed 'thank you' to my sister.

I turned back to my daughter, who looked more interested in playing with her food than eating it. I sighed. "Rosie, you have to eat!"

She thought that was funny, as indicated by her giggling. Liam laughed too.

Mari sighed. "They're rambunctious today. I think Aunt V fed them too many C-O-O-K-I-E-S last night."

A smile spread across my face. Liam and Rosie were too damn cute; I'd give them all the cookies too. That was the hardest thing about being a parent — you wanted to be gentle yet firm with them. Hard enough to do that with a partner, even harder when you did it by yourself.

Mari eyed me with a raised eyebrow. "So, how was last night?"

I felt myself flush. "Good."

Mari rolled her eyes. "Good, that's it?"

"Really good?"

"What did you do?"

I looked between the kids. "I'm not telling you in front of the kids."

"Not that! Where did he take you?"

"Oh," I said, feeling foolish that the first thought I had when it came to Logan was how he had me spread-eagle on his bed pretty much all night. "He took me to this bar that had a bunch of old-school arcade games."

She laughed. "Wait, is he a nerd like you?"

I nodded. "Mari, you have no idea."

She squinted at me. "What does that mean?"

"You know that guy I game with?"

Mari made a grossed-out face. "The one who's probably a creepy forty-year-old man?"

"Mari," I whispered. "He's Logan."

Her mouth dropped open. "Wait, are you serious?"

I nodded. "Isn't that wild?"

Her eyes lit up. "Oh my God, it's fate. You two are great together. Logan's a good man, but he feels like he needs to be a martyr and sacrifice everything."

I shook my head. "We both don't have time."

Mari rolled her eyes again. "That's BS, and you both know it. Do you like Logan?"

"Yeah..." I whispered and thought about how kind he was and how generous he was in bed. He didn't need to take me out if we wanted a casual thing. I could be a booty call, but he wanted to give me a good time. I liked that he wanted to pamper me and called me a princess. "I really do."

"Then make time! That's why I'm here, to help you both out when you need a mommy and daddy date night."

This time, it was my turn to roll my eyes at her. I checked the time on the stove and realized I had to get going. I might make my own hours, but I liked to keep a normal nine-to-five schedule when I could.

I stood up, cleaned up Rosie's dish, and put it in the sink.

"Eat before you leave!" Mari scolded me.

I waved her off. "I have a protein bar in my purse. I have to stop home before going to Manayunk and then maybe to Kensington later."

She sighed. "Sis, please eat. You're gonna run yourself ragged."

Too late for that.

I walked back over to the table and bent down to give Rosie a kiss on her head. "Okay, baby, be good for Aunt Mari. Mommy's gotta go to work."

"No, don't go!" Liam cried.

I walked over and gave him a big hug. "Aw, bud, I'll see you later, okay? You be good for my sister too, okay?"

"No!"

"Liam," Mari said in a warning tone. "Lily has to go to work. She'll be over to play again. Let's get cleaned up, and then we can play, okay?"

He seemed to be okay with that, but he still clutched at me. I smoothed down his hair and hugged him back. My heart ached at leaving Rosie and Liam, but this mama had to pay the bills. I called a rideshare to take me back to the Northeast, so I could get ready for my work day.

On the way over, I emailed Adam back, asking if we could arrange a meet. Did I want to work for the tattoo shop where my ex worked? Nope. But I couldn't afford to turn down any work. I was getting some small jobs on the freelance site too, so things looked like they were going my way.

I tried not to think about what my sister said about me and Logan. But I really liked him, and the fact he was the man of my dreams made it hard to tell my heart to stop thinking about it.

CHAPTER TWENTY-ONE

LOGAN

I was all smiles at morning skate. I was usually salty about having to get up early and on the ice before a game. But today, I skated around the rink with Riley and Blaise with a grin plastered across my face.

I didn't bitch about the team meeting either or when I had to talk to the media. I was even cracking a bunch of jokes with them. I wasn't a dick to the media, but I wasn't usually in such high spirits.

It wasn't just because I got laid last night. It was because of Lily. I was playing a dangerous game with her, telling her and myself that this could only be casual. When I was already trying to figure out when we could go out again. Or when she could come over for a kid-free gaming session.

Fuck, I wanted her to dress up in her character's cosplay for me, and then we could really role-play. Did I search for cosplay ideas for the warrior class I played as? Yes, I did. Was that weird? Probably. But she'd be into it. Wasn't a bad idea for Halloween in a few weeks.

"You're all smiles today," Blaise commented when we were sitting at his dad's booth having our ritual game day lunch.

I nodded.

Blaise cocked an eyebrow at me. "So you and Lily, huh?"

"It's just some fun."

"Hmm."

I narrowed my eyes at him. "What does 'hmm' mean? I thought you wanted me to stay away from her?"

Blaise ran a hand over his tattooed arm. "Look, man, Lil's been through some shit. I was trying to protect her. Don't fuck it up."

"Blaise, she's my dream girl."

"How so?"

"You know how you guys make fun of me for being into nerd shit like video games and comics?"

Blaise laughed. "Ha! Yeah, you nerd!"

I rolled my eyes. "Well...we found out we have been playing an online game together since high school. Last night I took her to this bar that has old-school arcade games, and she kicked my ass!"

Blaise squinted at me.

We hockey players were ultra-competitive, so to him, getting my ass handed to me was a bad thing. I'd kick her ass if we played ping-pong or air hockey, but that wasn't the type of game she was into. The fact she hit some high scores last night was sexy to me. Blaise wasn't a gamer, so he wouldn't understand.

"Okay...then I don't get your hang-up about dating her because this is the second time you went out with her, and stress isn't weighing you down anymore. Which means you'll play better tonight."

I shoved food in my face, hoping he'd drop the conversation. He wouldn't understand until he had his baby.

My phone vibrated in my pocket, and I pulled it out, realizing I hadn't checked it in a while. My chest felt warm when I saw Mari had sent a photo of Lily in my bed with the kids on either side of her. Liam cuddled against her side while she held Rosie to her chest and kissed her little head. Something stirred inside me, nagging at me to listen to Blaise. To take a shot with Lily for real, and not just in a casual sense.

Blaise kicked my foot. "Bro, do you want to date this chick or not?"

"I do," I admitted.

"Then date her and stop moping about how you can't or you're too busy. You can make it work."

He took a bite of his cheesesteak and shrugged, ending the conversation.

I ate the rest of my lunch in silence, mulling over his words. I wanted Blaise to be right, but I still wasn't convinced. It wasn't like Lily was looking for anything more, either. She had been firm that she only had time for something casual.

Blaise talked my ear off about the baby and his fears about not being a good father. I gave him the ear he needed and assured him he was going to be fine.

We parted ways, and I headed back to my condo to take my pregame nap. I smiled when I walked inside and saw Mari sitting on the floor with Liam and Rosie while they played beside each other. Rosie was playing with blocks while Liam drove his firetruck around Mari.

"Uncle Logan!" Liam cheered and jumped up when he saw me.

I tousled his hair. "Hey, bud! Have you been good for Mari today?"

"No," he said honestly.

Mari laughed. "He's very energetic today. They both are. It's time for a nap."

"No!" Rosie said indignantly. "No. No. No."

"Yes, little troublemaker," Mari told her niece. She picked Rosie up and took her into the bedroom.

I listened to Liam talk my ear off as I plopped him down on the couch.

"Uncle Logan?" he asked, his big eyes looking up at me in wonder.

"Yeah, bud?"

"I like Lily."

"I like her too."

"Can she be my new mommy?"

Oh boy. I let out a breath as I thought of the best way to explain it to him.

"Liam, your mommy's always gonna be your mommy." I put my hand to his heart. "She loved you very much, and she'll always be in your heart, okay? She might be gone, but I'm always gonna be here for you."

He rubbed his eyes. He was growing out of nap time, but he still was getting sleepy around now. "I miss her."

"Me too."

"But I don't miss Daddy. He was mean and made Mommy cry."

I cringed. I never knew how much Liam saw. It took me a long time to figure out my sister was in a bad way. I'd regret that for the rest of my life.

Mari walked out of the bedroom, and we shared an uneasy look.

I kissed Liam's forehead. "I know, bud. I have to go take

my nap. When I wake up, you can help me pick out my tie for the game."

"Can I come?"

"To take a nap with me?"

"Game!"

I looked toward Mari for reassurance. "I'll bring him. Lily usually picks up Rosie by then."

A thought crossed my mind, but I had to ask Mari if it was a bad idea or not. Liam lost interest in me, running over to one of his toys on the floor while Mari crossed the room and sunk into the spot on the couch next to me.

She grinned at me. "So, you and my sister had a good time, huh?"

"Yeah. Hey, would your sister want to come to the game? I know she has Rosie tonight, so maybe not."

Her eyes lit up. "Oh, that would be amazing. Are you going to really give it a go?"

I shook my head. "It's just a little fun."

Her lips were a thin line. "Uh-huh."

"I've been very upfront about that with her, and she agrees."

Mari frowned. "Look, it's not my business as your employee, but I don't understand why you don't want to date her. You're a good guy, Logan. I see that every day with how you are with Liam — Rosie too, and she's not even yours. Lily needs someone good in her life. She chooses men like our dad."

"You're right; it's not your business. My schedule's bananas. That's too much to ask someone to deal with. Hers isn't any better. Factor that with us both being single parents... A relationship isn't in the cards."

Mari gave me a hard look. "But you could make the time if you really wanted."

"Not gonna happen, Mari, okay?"

She nodded, but by the way she pursed her lips, I knew she had more to say. That was one thing I liked about Mari. She wasn't afraid to speak her mind. I appreciated that, but right now, I wanted her to drop it.

"I gotta take my nap," I said with an air of finality.

"I'll wake you up later. Go on."

I walked into my bedroom, shutting the door behind me. The bed was made-up neatly. I wasn't sure if that was Mari's or Lily's doing. Mari kept doing housework for me, even though I told her it wasn't her job. That's how good she was. She saw what I needed, even when I refused the help. If I had never met Lily, I never would've found Mari, who was the perfect nanny to take care of Liam. Almost like the hockey gods were clicking everything in place for me.

I got changed and slid into my sheets in just my boxers. But before I took my nap, I shot off a text to Benny's girlfriend, Rox, who was a sales manager for the team.

ME: Any chance I can get extra tickets for tonight's game?

She immediately texted me back.

ROX: Oooh, you're bringing that cute blonde, eh?

This team was nosy as fuck.

ME: Maybe and her baby. And my nanny's bringing my nephew.

ROX: Done. I got you! Good for you, she's really cute.

I shook my head and texted Lily. Probably should have

texted her first, but I'd rather be prepared. No matter what, I'd need a ticket for Mari, anyway.

> ME: Hey, princess. Liam wants to come to the game tonight, so Mari's bringing him. Wanna come too?

CHAPTER TWENTY-TWO

LILY

My phone vibrated in my briefcase, but I ignored it while I finished my speech to Adam. I hadn't been looking at my phone all day since I worked a few hours at Rich's shop and then made the trek to Kensington. Seth was nowhere in sight, so maybe there was some truth to the work convention thing.

Adam was younger than I expected. He had dark brown skin and tattoos that ran up and down his arms. He had colorful pieces on his neck as well. I didn't intend for most of my clientele to be tattoo shops, but I'd take whatever work I could find. The word of mouth was definitely helping me.

"You don't have to dress that formal here." He motioned to my charcoal grey pantsuit. Then he held up a hand. "Sorry, that's not supposed to be an insult. You look great, but we're a little casual here."

I laughed. "I'm not insulted. It's a force of habit."

"Rich said you did good work. I talked to Veronica too, and she talked you up. I'm surprised she took my call since I hired her ex after Golden Rose kicked him to the curb."

I cringed.

His eyebrow shot up. "Wait, do you know Seth? I hate that weasel, but he does good work. My step-daughter's dating him now, and I don't trust him. He called out sick the past couple of days, too," he told me with a shake of his head.

I stared at him unblinking.

Out sick.

Not at a conference.

He was doing it again. The asshole was doing it again, but not to me, to our daughter. Red-hot rage spread through me at the thought he was lying to do God knows what and miss out on time with our daughter.

"Seth's my ex-husband."

"Ohhh. Is that going to be a problem for you?"

I shook my head. "Absolutely not. Especially if you don't need me all that much. We co-parent, so I'm used to being civil."

He nodded, and we negotiated my rates and expectations. He agreed to my rates, and I made plans to come back in to meet the first quarter deadline for him to file his taxes. On my way out, I checked my phone and was glad it was only a text from Logan and nothing important.

> LOGAN: Hey, princess. Liam wants to come to the game tonight, so Mari's bringing him. Wanna come too?

I chewed on my lip as I thought about it. I had a good time at the last Bulldogs game I went to with Veronica. If

Mari was bringing Liam, that meant I could bring Rosie too. But if I went, it felt like that was a mixed signal. Logan said he didn't have time for a relationship, but coming to his game sounded like something you'd ask a girlfriend to do. Not your casual fuck buddy.

"Hey, are you Lily?" an unfamiliar feminine voice asked me, pulling me away from my phone.

I turned and saw one of the tattoo artists from the shop standing in front of me. She had long black hair and colorful traditional-styled tattoos. I saw her when I walked in to meet Adam, but I hadn't paid her any mind.

"Um, yeah, that's me."

"I don't want to get in between you, but can I ask you why you're keeping Seth from his daughter?"

I raised an eyebrow at her.

Hold up. What was she talking about? I was keeping Rosie from Seth? I had a feeling I knew who this woman was, and I knew then that Seth was doing it again. This poor woman didn't have a clue.

"Excuse me?" I stuttered out.

"Seth said you have an arrangement, but you keep flaking on him and not letting him see her. I know you guys broke up, but she's his daughter."

I pressed my lips into a thin line. The truth was a different story than what he was feeding her.

"Are you Katie?" I asked.

She nodded. "Yeah. I'm sorry, I know it's not my business, but I grew up with a deadbeat dad, and I don't—"

I interrupted her by holding up my hand. "Where's Seth?"

"Well, see, that's the thing I don't get. You say he can't see her, but then you'll drop her off without notice so he has to call out sick."

I rubbed my forefinger and thumb on the bridge of my nose. What an asshole.

"That's funny because Seth keeps calling to cancel on me. This time, he said he couldn't take her because he had a tattoo convention. He was supposed to have Rosie last night and through the weekend. I'd never keep him from his daughter."

"No. It can't... He's not..." She trailed off, shaking her head like that could make his lies true.

"Are you okay?"

"I think he's cheating on me."

I frowned. I wanted to say it served her right, but I got the distinct feeling that Seth had done her wrong too.

"When did you and Seth start dating?" I asked.

"Last September. Like last year, not last month."

We didn't get married until last November. How could I have been such a fool?

"What did he tell you about me?"

"That you had a baby together, but it was over."

I closed my eyes and tried to calm myself down. This poor girl was as clueless as I had been. "Honey, I'm gonna be real honest with you. Ditch Seth. We got married two months after you started dating."

Her mouth dropped open. "No. No way. Why would he do that?"

"Because he's a selfish asshole. I'm sorry, hun, but he did it to me too. I didn't know I was the other woman either. Don't beat yourself up about it. It's not your fault."

Her eyes were shiny with tears. "I thought he was a good guy. I'm so sorry. You should hate me!"

I shook my head. "I'm sorry, Katie. And I don't hate you. Wish he didn't do you dirty, too." I pulled out my card and handed it to her. "Gimme a call if you need to talk."

She wiped her eyes and took my offered card. "Oh my God, I feel like such an asshole. I was all ready to give you a piece of my mind. I'm so sorry."

"It's not your fault. I'm sorry too. But I have to get going."

I needed to get out of there. I felt so bad about what happened with her and Seth, but I wasn't surprised. He was such a sneaky asshole. A part of me didn't even want him to have a relationship with Rosie anymore. That was selfish of me, though; I'd never keep my daughter from her father. No matter how terrible of a person he was.

I handed Katie a tissue from my briefcase because I was a mom and I always had supplies of everything in my bag. I gave her a sad smile and booked it out of there.

When I got into my car, I made my decision. I was going to the hockey game.

I texted Logan back.

ME: Can't wait to see my warrior in action!

I drove home, determined to finish up my freelance work and go to the hockey game with my sister and the kids.

"Wait, are you serious?" my sister cried over the story I told her about meeting Seth's new girl.

Liam stood in front of her, his hands pressed to the glass as we waited for the players to come out on the ice for warmups. Veronica was holding Rosie and making her laugh.

"That's why I didn't hate you," Veronica said. "As soon

as I figured it out, I knew you had no clue. You wouldn't have invited us to your wedding if you had known. But what a fu—" She stopped herself when she realized there were little ears around. "Jerk face."

"What are you going to do?" Mari asked.

I shrugged and made sure Rosie's headphones were on securely. I handed her a plushie of the Bulldogs mascot to keep her entertained. So far, she was doing good, but I wasn't sure we'd stay for the whole game.

"Nothing. I gave her my card in case she wants to talk. I feel bad for her."

"Forget him!" Veronica cheered. "You got the hockey hottie now."

Mari nudged me. "Yeah!"

I wrinkled my nose. "We're not serious." But as soon as I said it, the players came out on the ice, and all I could pay attention to was the redheaded giant skating on the ice beside Blaise.

God, why did he look so hot on the ice, helmet-less, showing off his fiery locks? The ones I sunk my fingers into last night while he spent a long time between my legs. I felt my face get heated at the memory. Definitely shouldn't have been thinking about that right now.

I watched the players skating around the ice while Liam banged on the glass and yelled for his uncle. A smile spread across my face when Logan skated over to us. He waved to Liam, who excitedly waved back. Logan's blue eyes lit up when he saw me. I mouthed, 'Good luck,' and my heart went pitter-patter at how he winked at me before he skated off.

Mari shook her head as she put Liam in her lap again. "You two are fooling each other. It's not casual at all."

"He said it has to be," I argued.

She gave me a face. "Yeah, no. You need to talk after the game."

I didn't know what she meant by that, but I got distracted when the announcer called out the starting players. I didn't hear Logan's name, and once the puck dropped, I had a hard time keeping track of all the guys going from the ice to behind the bench for their shifts.

"Uncle Logan!" Liam cried and pointed to a player on the ice. The little boy was quicker than I was. "Go, Uncle Logan!"

"Go Lo-lo!" Rosie parroted. The way she imitated Liam was so cute.

We all watched with bated breath as Logan had the puck and raced up the ice, trying to score. He passed it back to one of his teammates, who seemed to hold it for a bit, and I didn't understand why he wasn't shooting it.

"Why aren't they trying to score?" I asked.

A woman behind me laughed. "They're trying to set up the play. Just watch."

I turned around and came face-to-face with a petite brunette woman. I wracked my brain for her name. I knew I met her at Blaise and Veronica's barbecue last summer.

"Dinah," she offered. "I'm Noah Kennedy's fiancée."

"Sorry, Mom brain."

The sound of the crowd pulled me back to the action on the ice. I watched Logan skate down the other side of the ice, but the team lost their chance at scoring a goal.

Rosie had a tantrum because she wanted to lick the glass and Veronica wouldn't let her, so I took her off Veronica's hands and tried to distract her with the Bulldogs mascot plushie. She didn't like that.

I excused myself and walked her around the concourse,

bouncing her in my arms. We definitely weren't staying the whole game, but I thought we'd at least last through the first period. She calmed down eventually, and I went back into the stands.

"She okay?" Mari asked.

I sighed. "She's being fussy. I'm not sure how long I can stay."

"Logan will understand," she reassured me.

I rocked Rosie in my arms, but I knew another tantrum was on the rise. Toddlerdom was really going to test me soon.

I only knew what to pay attention to during the game when Liam was jumping up and down, yelling for Logan. The game was scoreless, but the Bulldogs had the puck again. I noticed Logan was on the ice again, mostly because Liam was yelling his little head off and because I saw the name CULLEN on the back of one of the player's jerseys who skated by.

"Oh my God, he's got the puck again!" Mari cheered.

"Oh my God, go!" I screamed.

"Go! Go!" Rosie yelled with me, repeating my words.

And then, as if he heard us, Logan knocked back his stick and aimed for the net. The red lamp behind the goaltender lit up, a loud horn blared, and everyone in the crowd cheered. The jumbotron flashed big, and the announcer yelled over the PA, 'GOAL SCORED BY LOGAN CULLEN!'

"UNCLE LOGAN!" Liam cheered and jumped up and down.

Even Rosie was shaking her plushie like it was a pompom. I kissed the top of her head and couldn't help the smile from plastering itself across my face. I watched Logan hug it out with one of his teammates, and then he skated around to us. My heart melted when he fist-bumped Liam through the glass and then blew me a kiss.

The excitement must have energized the kids because they were extra good throughout the rest of the period. During the first intermission, I felt a tap on my shoulder. I turned around and saw it was Dinah again.

"Hey, I heard you're an accountant," she said.

"I am."

Her green eyes lit up. "Okay, awesome! Because mine retired and I need a new one. I'm self-employed, so I need to do it quarterly."

I pulled a card out of my wallet and handed it to her. "That I can do. What's your industry?"

"I'm an author. I need someone who understands royalties. Oh, and my friend Fi, Riley's wife, might want your card too."

I pretended I knew who she was talking about. One of the other wives, obviously, but I couldn't remember who they were.

"I can definitely do your taxes."

She smiled. "That would be awesome. I'm a writer. I don't do numbers."

I pointed at myself. "I'm the numbers girl!"

Dinah laughed. "I'll call you later so we can go over the details."

"Sounds good."

Mari nudged me happily when I turned back around. The only reason I was building up my client list was that Veronica and Blaise kept recommending me. I didn't care how people found out about me, though, as long as I got the work.

I wanted to stay longer and see Logan after the game, but Rosie was getting too sleepy and cranky, so I had to get her home. I sent him a message congratulating him on the game and headed home. I didn't want to leave, but that was what it was like when you were a mom. Sometimes your kids made the plans, not you. If anyone understood that, it was Logan.

CHAPTER TWENTY-THREE

LOGAN

The locker room was on fire after another successful win. I shook my head at TJ as he was dancing around toward his cubby.

Riley stood in the center of the room, holding the silver helmet we gave to the MVP of the game. He held his hands up, trying to get us all to calm down. "Alright, you assholes, pipe down! You all know who earned this one tonight."

I wiped the sweat off my brow with a towel and realized all eyes were on me. Blaise nudged me, and Riley gave me a big grin. "Come on, Cully! You know it's you!"

"CULLY! CULLY! CULLY!" the guys cheered.

I stood up and took the helmet from Riley, and put it on my head.

"For starting it off and assisting Kennedy with the game-winner, it's yours, buddy," Riley told me.

"Alright, boys! Let's do it again on our road trip this week!" I yelled.

All the boys cheered while I posed for photos for PR.

Then I handed the helmet back to our equipment manager. Coach nodded at me. "Good job tonight, Cully."

"Thanks, Coach."

Coach said his last remarks and told us to celebrate, but not too much since we had to be up early to catch the jet. I jumped into the shower, but after I changed, I had to do media availability. I was in good spirits by the time I was back in the locker room and changing back into my suit.

I pulled out my phone and saw a text from Lily.

> LILY: Hey, awesome goal! Rosie got fussy, so I had to leave early. I hope you understand.

Of course I understood. Rosie would always come first, the same way Liam would come first for me. But I'd be lying if I said I wasn't disappointed she wasn't waiting for me after the game.

I shouldn't be disappointed. She was just my casual fuck buddy. Even if she was my ultimate dream girl.

"Before you all head out," Mac called out. "RSVP to the Halloween party, or my wife will have my ass."

"Are you going?" I asked Blaise.

He shrugged. "Depends on how V feels. You?"

I shrugged.

"Bring, Lil."

TJ's ears perked up. "Oh, was that the cute blonde watching tonight? That your girl?"

I shook my head. "It's not serious."

TJ snorted. "Dude, I was the king of 'not serious,' and then I fell for Max."

"Yeah, someone has to keep you in line!" Benny yelled from across the locker room.

I shook my head at them. They bickered so much, a lot of us were glad they didn't live together anymore.

Mac eyed me. "Dude, you're coming."

"I can't. I got—"

Blaise cut a glare at me. "One, you have a nanny now. Two, you need to blow off some steam. So does Lil. Invite her, bro."

"Fine, you fucking dicks," I grumbled.

They all cackled like the assholes they were, and I walked out of the locker room, giving them the two-finger salute.

Blaise confused me with his flip-flopping about Lily. First, he told me to stay away, but now he was pushing me into a relationship. Lily understood the difficulties of being a parent. How you'd drop everything for your kid. I really liked her, and if things were different, maybe I'd consider making time for her, but a relationship wasn't in the cards for either of us.

I tried not to think about it too much as I drove home. Mari was up watching TV on my couch when I quietly opened the door to my condo.

"Hey, how was he?" I asked as I took off my jacket and walked inside.

She made a face. "Rambunctious. I just got him to bed."

I cringed. "Sorry. He gets that way when he watches me play."

She grinned. "It's cute. He loves you."

I sat back on the couch beside her, slumping down on it as I thought about my schedule for the week. We were in Pittsburgh tomorrow and Columbus on Friday, and then we didn't have another game until next Tuesday, but that was back home. I checked my calendar. Mac and his wife

Natalia had planned their annual Halloween party so it didn't fall on a game day.

"Do you have plans next weekend? My teammate's having a Halloween party."

"Oh!" she said with a hint of surprise. "Yes, of course, I can do that. Let me add it to my calendar now."

I rubbed the back of my neck. "Mari, if you have plans, it's okay. I'm not sure if I'm gonna go."

She waved me off. "You should go and have fun. I know hockey and Liam are your life, but today you seemed looser, like a weight had been lifted. You're gonna take my sister, right?"

I shrugged.

"Why not? You're basically dating."

I sighed. "Mari, we're not... It's casual."

"Hmm. Whatever you say, boss man. Either way, I'll take both of the kids if need be." She stood up from the couch and put on her coat. "I'll be back in the morning before you head out. I got you."

"What would I do without you?"

"Cry!" she teased before she walked out the door.

I laughed and walked into my bedroom. I changed for bed, but then I peeked into Liam's room. He was curled up in his bed, with his arms wrapped around his stuffed plushie of the Bulldogs mascot, Bruiser.

Seeing him safe in bed was all I needed to know. Liam was safe and loved, and I'd never make him feel afraid like I had been when I was a kid. I still wondered how much he saw between Rose and her dickhead husband, but the thought of knowing he was in a dangerous situation broke my heart. I was glad he was out and I could protect him. Even if it made my life complicated.

He stirred, and his eyes fluttered open. "Uncle Logan?"

I pulled the blanket over him and tucked him back in. "Shush. Go back to sleep, bud."

"Not tired," he insisted and screwed up his little face in annoyance.

I bent down and kissed his forehead. "Yes, you are. Sleep, little man, okay? I'll see you tomorrow before I leave. You'll pick out my tie for me."

"Otay," he murmured. "I miss baby."

"Rosie?"

He nodded.

"You'll see her later, okay?"

He shook his head.

"Yes, little man."

He shook his head again, and I felt a cranky tantrum coming on.

I smoothed down his hair. "Go back to sleep. You're cranky."

"Sleep with you?" he asked and held his arms out toward me.

I should have been firm and told him to sleep in his bed, but when he looked at me with that sad little face, I caved. I was a pushover, but one day, he wouldn't want to cuddle beside me.

I picked him up and brought him into my room, where he settled down once I had us in my bed. Little man had me wrapped around his finger, and he knew it. I put the sports channel on and watched highlights with the volume on low.

I realized I'd never texted Lily back, so I chanced it even if it was late.

ME: I totally get it. Hope you had fun.

I snapped a picture of Liam cuddling up beside me, holding his Bulldog plushie, and sent it to her.

ME: This one's attached to Rosie already and misses her.

I saw the three dots come up on my screen and then a text from her. A smile broke out across my face when she sent a photo of her in a mirror position with Rosie against her chest as she lay in bed. Rosie had a similar Bulldogs plushie.

LILY: Um, this one too.

ME: Aw. She's got a little Bruiser.

LILY: ??

ME: Our mascot.

LILY: Oooh. She cheered you on with it tonight.

I shouldn't like that. Definitely should not.

Another text came through from her, this time another photo. It was of her holding Rosie and Liam in her lap. Mari must have taken it at the game. I couldn't help but notice how Lily held Liam like he was her own.

I shook the thought away. Lily was just a mom. It didn't mean anything else.

ME: Cute! Glad you could make it.

LILY: Me too. I better get to sleep. I have a meeting with a potential client tomorrow. I'll see you around, Logan!

I set my phone down and put it on the charger, making

sure to set my alarm. 'I'll see you around' was code for her setting a boundary. What we did together was fun between two single parents who didn't have time for something more. And that was perfectly fine with me. It was nice she was on the same page. I wished her sister and our mutual friends would understand that.

I turned off the TV and flicked off the lights, engulfing Liam and me in darkness. This little boy was my entire world. I had to remember that. All the sacrifices I made weren't in vain because it was all for him.

CHAPTER TWENTY-FOUR

LILY

My phone kept buzzing on the desk, but I ignored it while I finished up this line of expenses. I had been so busy the past few weeks, taking on more clients and getting more freelance work since I opened my website. I was still struggling, but after meeting with Dinah, three more of her author friends became clients, and I had a list of people needing annual tax filing.

I could do this. I'd hustle my way to owning my business, and then I'd give Rosie everything she ever wanted. Lord knew her dad wasn't doing it.

The sounds of the bar behind the office door rang through every once in a while, and it penetrated my thoughts as I worked. I was almost done, and I was debating grabbing a drink afterward. Hal offered me one when he brought me dinner while I worked through the expenses, but I needed to focus.

I sighed when my phone buzzed again, and I picked it up. I gnashed my teeth at the text message on my screen.

SETH: Can't get Rosie tomorrow.

ME: K.

Was it passive-aggressive? Yes, but there wasn't a point in asking for excuses anymore. I hated more than anything that Rosie would grow up without a father. Or rather, one who only wanted to be in her life when it was convenient for him. I hated that my mom was right.

Seth put me in a foul mood, and I was at a good stopping point, so I shut down for the night. I swore when I saw what time it was. My sister had Rosie and Liam all day today since the Bulldogs had played tonight. As much as I wanted a drink, I had to go get my kid and relieve my sister.

Logan and I had been texting a lot, and we played Dragonspire last night, but we mostly saw each other in passing. We were both so busy that it didn't bother me. He was one of the few people in my life that understood how hard it was being a single parent. If he was someone I found comfort in here and there, I'd take it.

I shrugged on my light jacket over my blazer and walked out to the bar. It was packed, as it should be on a Friday night, especially since the game was over. I wrestled through the crowd, but as I was making my way out the door, I heard someone call out my name.

I turned around, finding Logan staring me down like he was trying to tell me something. He had a beer in his hand, and there was an attractive dark-haired woman beside him drinking a cosmopolitan and looking at Logan like she wanted to eat him up.

Oh.

A spike of jealousy shouldn't have clawed up from my

stomach. He could see whomever he wanted to see. We never made promises to each other.

But before I could even say hi back, he reached out, pulled me flush against his chest, and kissed me. Instead of shock, I let him angle my head to kiss me better, letting him devour me like I was his. Heat pooled between my legs as the kiss went on for far too long.

I had to push him away to catch my breath, and by the time I did, the brunette was long gone.

Logan brushed my hair behind my ear. "Sorry, princess."

I narrowed my eyes at him. "For kissing me like that?"

He chuckled. "For ambushing you. That chick wouldn't leave me alone."

"Ooh. So I was your excuse?"

A guilty look spread across his face. "Sorry. Let me buy you a drink."

I pulled away and shook my head.

God, that kiss had been an amazing toe-curling reminder of how he could work my body. Kinda nice to have his lips on mine again, even if it was just so that woman left him alone.

"No worries. I gotta go get Rosie."

Logan frowned. "Sorry, that was a dick move. I shouldn't have used you like that."

I held my thumb and forefinger together. "Little bit. But...I get it."

He muttered something under his breath and then set his beer bottle down at the bar. "Let me give you a ride."

"That's okay."

"Lil, we're going to the same place. Unless you have your car."

"No, Mari's car is in the shop, so we're sharing," I explained.

"Then let me drive."

"Okay," I relented.

He settled his bill with Hal, who smiled at me and told me not to work too hard. Hal was so nice, and I loved working for him. I loved Veronica, but she was awful at keeping her receipts together. Hal was very organized, telling me that my assumptions that he only hired me as a favor were correct.

Logan put his hand on the small of my back and guided me out of the bar. We got into his car, and he sped off toward Old City.

"How was the game?" I asked.

He frowned.

"Bad?"

"We lost."

"Sorry."

He shook his head. "Not your fault, princess."

"Still sucks."

"Mmmhmm," he murmured. "Were you working late tonight?"

"Yeah. I had that interview this morning, so I had to shift my hours."

Last night, he'd talked me down from my nerves. Worrying about the interview kept me up, so I'd turned on Dragonspire to calm me down. Fighting dragons with him in our game had been the only solution to quiet my anxiety.

I shrugged. "I don't think I got it. Been busy building my client list."

"That's good. Noah said D hired you to help with her author stuff."

I nodded. Not only did Dinah hire me to do her author

quarterly taxes, but the annual filing for her and Noah. I'd be really busy in the months to come if this kept up.

Logan put a hand on my thigh. "That's great."

"It's a slow build, but I have to..."

"For her," he answered.

I blew out a breath. "It's nice to talk to someone who gets it. Veronica and Blaise try to be helpful, but they don't get how much I work my ass off and struggle. And then fucking Seth!" I clamped my mouth closed. Logan didn't want to hear me complain about my ex again.

Logan pulled his car into the garage of his building and put it in park. "Did he flake on you again?"

I nodded, fighting the tears that were brimming. Being a single mother was the hardest thing I ever had to do. There were days I wasn't sure I'd manage it much longer. If I didn't have my sister, if my mom didn't let me live at home rent-free, I wasn't sure I could handle it.

He squeezed my hand. "I completely understand. If you never recommended your sister, I'd be fucked."

"Mari's amazing with the kids. I love that they get along."

He grinned. "Me too. Hey, are you doing anything next weekend?"

I chewed on my lip. "I'll have Rosie. Why?"

"My teammate's having a Halloween party next Saturday. I already asked Mari to watch Liam. You should come with me."

"If you want me to."

"I do. It'll be fun. We could blow off some much-needed steam. I know it's been like we're two ships passing in the night, but..."

I held up a hand to stop him. "I'm just as busy. I totally get it. Okay, I'll talk to Mari."

"She'll do it. She'll already have Liam."

"Okay," I relented.

He turned off his car, and we walked over to the elevator to go up to his floor. I hadn't realized how late it was. Hal tried to get me to go home earlier, but I had been in the zone.

Logan led me to his door and held it open for me to enter. My sister was sitting up watching TV, waiting for us. She gave me a big smile. "Hey, you're out late."

"Working," I told her and walked into Liam's bedroom. Logan followed me as he checked on Liam while I gently took Rosie out of the crib. She stirred while I held her to my chest and got her things.

"You want help?" Logan whispered.

I shook my head and padded out of the room. He closed the door behind him, and Mari got her things together. We'd pick up her car tomorrow morning, so no more sharing. That had been annoying this week, but it was okay because she did so much for me with Rosie that I didn't mind.

"Ready?" I asked my sister.

"Yup. See ya, Logan!"

"I'll pick you up next Saturday," he called out to me.

I waved a hand at him to acknowledge that while trying to ignore the curious glance my sister gave me.

"Ooh, are you going to the Halloween party with him?" she asked once we were in the hallway.

"Yeah. Can you watch Rosie with Liam?"

She nodded. "Of course I can."

I frowned. "It's my weekend, but Seth flaked again, so not like it matters."

"Lil, I love you, but you need to file for custody."

"It's fine. Let's get you home, okay?"

She frowned at me but didn't argue further. Thank God

for that. I didn't have the energy to start with her. I already heard it enough from Mom.

"What are you going to wear for the party?"

I grinned. I knew exactly what to wear to impress Logan. I might give him a heart attack, but if he wanted a fun night together, I'd give him his gamer fantasy.

"Is this ridiculous?" I asked Veronica as she stood behind me in her bathroom doing my hair. I had a 'mom-bob,' so I couldn't do that much with my hair, but she'd pulled the front pieces back and made an intricate braid behind my head.

Veronica gave me a giddy smile. "No, you look great. Plus, it's Halloween. Who cares?" She stood back and put a hand on her stomach. "Do I look pregnant yet?"

I shook my head. "Not quite."

Veronica and I got dressed together for the Halloween party, while we waited for Logan to get here. I dropped Rosie off at Logan's, but he refused to come out of his room to say anything to me, just that he'd pick me up later. I kept nagging him about his costume, but he said it was a secret.

Veronica put on her witch hat and did a twirl in her black dress. "How do I look?"

"Awesome!"

She beamed. "I'm feeling okay today, but I don't know how long we'll stay." She eyed me up and down. "Logan's jaw will drop to the floor when he sees you. I don't get the elf ears, though."

There was no way I was telling her my costume was my cosplay of the character I played in Dragonspire. It would take too long to explain. I was still self-conscious about it because it was the first time I wore something that revealed my mid-drift since Rosie was born.

I wrapped my arms around my bare middle. "You think I look okay, though? Seth kept saying I still hadn't lost my baby weight."

Veronica's eyes flashed in anger. "BLAISE!" she yelled out, startling me, and then I heard the thunderous footsteps of her fiancé running up the steps like something was on fire.

When Blaise got into their massive en suite bathroom, his chest was heaving, and an anguished look was across his face. The cape of his devil costume was askew as he stared at his pregnant fiancée with worry. "What's wrong?" he asked.

"Nothing. Tell Lily she's hot."

Blaise raised an eyebrow and stood up straight, adjusting his cape. "Is this a test?"

"No!" Veronica laughed. "She's feeling self-conscious."

That was when Blaise finally looked at me and took a step back. "Whoa. Wait, are you an elf from that nerd game Logan plays?"

Shit.

Veronica whipped her head around. "Is that true?"

"Maybe," I muttered.

"Well yeah, he said you play it together," Blaise said.

Veronica cocked her head at me. "What?"

"We play online together," I explained. "We have for a long time. We didn't realize that until the last time we went out."

Blaise laughed. "Sweets, I told you, they're perfect for each other. Total nerds!"

I shook my head. "It's not like that, Blaise."

Blaise rolled his eyes. "Okay...well, V and I said it was

only 'temporary' until we went to your wedding, and now we're having a baby." He put a meaty hand on Veronica's stomach protectively, and she beamed. They were so cute, but he was wrong. It didn't matter what they thought because Logan and I knew we were just having some occasional fun.

"I wish I'd never married Seth, but I'm glad it brought you together," I told them.

"Sorry, Lil, I should have told you," Veronica offered.

"It is what it is," I muttered.

I'd never stop feeling guilty about what happened with Veronica and Seth, even though it wasn't my fault. And she'd never stop feeling guilty that she never told me I was the unwilling other woman.

Blaise tilted his head to the side and stared at me. "Logan won't want to go to the party."

Panic coursed through me.

"Why? Do I look that bad?" I asked.

Maybe this was a bad idea and Seth had been right about my body not looking the way it used to.

"He means because he'll want to take you home and fuck you," Veronica explained.

"Oh," I breathed out in relief.

"What did you think I meant?" Blaise asked. A creased formed between his brow as the gears in his brain turned.

I sighed. "Nothing. Don't worry about it."

He peered at me, but he didn't press me because the doorbell rang, signaling Logan was here, and Blaise went downstairs to let him in. My heart beat loud in my chest, and my body tingled with anticipation.

Veronica gave me a side hug. "You look hot. He'll love it. And we'll talk about the secret you kept from me later."

"Wasn't a secret," I explained. "Didn't put two-and-two together until recently."

"Well, it makes sense. Even at the housewarming party, you two seemed so..." She chewed on her lip as she searched for the words. "Comfortable together. Like you'd known each other for a long time. I guess you did, huh?"

"Sorta," I admitted.

I wasn't sure how to explain to Veronica that being gaming friends was different from being friends in real life. You could play a game with someone for years and call them a friend, but half the time, you didn't even know their real name or what they looked like.

I picked up the archery prop because I was nothing if not a huge nerd and put it over my shoulder. I took another look at myself in the mirror. Staring back at me was the sexy, take no prisoners wood elf princess — crown and all.

"Let's go!" Veronica cheered.

We walked down the stairs together, and I froze in my tracks at my warrior standing at the front door shooting the shit with Blaise.

Anyone who didn't play the game probably thought he was dressed like a Viking. He wore a brown tunic and a fur-lined belt. Beneath the belt, he had fur-lined leather faulds over a pair of dark jeans, giving him that warrior Viking look. But what really put the whole thing together was the horned helmet on his head.

"Holy shit!" I exclaimed before I could stop myself.

Meanwhile, Logan looked at me like he'd never be able to pick his jaw up from the floor again.

Oh, hell yeah. Tonight was going to be fun.

CHAPTER TWENTY-FIVE

LOGAN

Fuck me, she was like all my gaming fantasies come true. I used to make fun of her for that bikini top she wore as armor, but when she stood in front of me looking like a sexy wood elf princess, I was grateful for it. She even had the circlet and elf ears to complete the outfit.

"Wow," I breathed out after I picked my jaw off the floor and told my dick to be quiet. "You look great."

She beamed at me. "Really?"

"Yes, really." I scanned her body, taking in every last delicious curve.

Something nagged at me, remembering her ex said something about her weight. Fuck that guy. I didn't know what he was talking about because she looked amazing. She might have some scars from bringing Rosie into the world, but that wasn't what I paid attention to.

Blaise snapped his fingers in front of my face. "Are you two horndogs coming?"

I nodded. "Yeah. I'm good. How about you, princess?"

"Great! Let's roll."

"I don't want to Uber since we have to drive out to the Main Line," Blaise said. "I figured we'd all go together."

I nodded. "Good idea. I'll drive."

Mac and Natalia moved out to the Main Line to be closer to the practice facility a couple of seasons ago. It was better for us to drive together.

"V needs to be up front," Lily said.

"That's fine. Let's go."

We went down to the street where my car was parked. Blaise opened the door for Veronica so she could get in, and I did the same for Lily as she got in the back with Blaise. Before long, we got on the road with Veronica's Halloween playlist playing from my stereo.

"You know we're gonna hear this all when we get there, right?" I asked.

"Don't be a party pooper, Logan!" Veronica exclaimed.

"Sweets," Blaise warned.

I shook my head at them.

It wasn't too long of a drive to our destination, and I listened to the girls chat along the way while Blaise poked at his phone. We pulled up to the long driveway of Mac's massive four-bedroom home, already littered with cars. Spooky decorations filled the lawn leading up to the front door, and the party looked like it was already underway.

We got out of the car and walked up the drive. When I knocked on the door, Natalia answered with a big smile on her face. Natalia was a tall Black woman with natural curls, and tonight she was dressed like a vampire, complete with a cape and fake blood painted down her chin.

"Hey, you made it," she said. "Come on in. Mac's around here somewhere."

Natalia scanned our costumes, and when her eyes landed on Lily, she turned to me with a questioning look.

"Tali, this is my friend Lily. Lily, this is Mac's wife, Natalia," I introduced them.

Lily stuck out her hand, and the two women shook hands and introduced themselves.

"Friend, huh?" Natalia teased. "Is that what they're calling it these days?"

Underneath the dark lights of the party, Lily's cheeks reddened.

Natalia laughed. "I'm joking. Come on in and enjoy the party."

"You have a lovely home," Lily told her.

Natalia beamed. "Thank you. Enjoy, seriously. Mac loves Halloween, so he went all out. We even have a smoke machine."

At that moment, a popular Halloween song came on the stereo, and Natalia turned around, laughing at her husband leading the charge of a dance in the center of her living room.

Blaise and Veronica had wandered off during the conversation. "You want a drink?" I asked Lily.

"Sure."

I put a hand around her waist and bent my lips to her ear. "I'm very glad I got to see your cosplay."

She grinned. "It's not too much, right?"

"Princess," I growled into her ear. "I want to see you wear it in the bedroom. You're killing me."

She gave me a naughty smile and turned around to face me. She put a hand against the ridiculous helmet on my head. "You really went all out."

I grabbed her hand and kissed the back of it. "Gotta show my princess I'm her warrior."

She fanned herself. "I need a drink. You in that costume is dangerous."

I gave her a cocky grin. "I'm trying so hard to keep it in my pants tonight."

"Who said you needed to do that?" she teased.

Fuck me.

Before I could give her a witty comeback, she dragged me by the hand into the kitchen.

That's where we found my teammate Benny drinking a beer with his girlfriend Rox. She wore a floor-length black dress, and he wore a black suit. It took me a beat to realize what their costume was, and I only figured it out because he had shaved his beard, leaving only a small mustache. Next to him, Noah and Dinah were chatting with them. I was confused about Noah and Dinah's costumes. They looked like hikers?

"Oh!" Lily exclaimed. "That's so clever."

"What is?"

"They're Lara Croft and Nathan Drake."

Dinah turned around and pointed at Lily. "See, babe, I told you someone would get it."

I laughed. "Wow, okay, that took me a bit. Have you guys met Lily?"

Dinah nodded. "I'm hiring her to do my taxes. I'm a writer; I don't do numbers."

"We met at Blaise's housewarming party and again at one of your games," Lily explained to me.

"Right." I grabbed a beer from the fridge and gestured to Lily if that's what she wanted, but she was already pouring herself a drink of the spiced punch sitting on the counter. "I'd be careful with that. Mac has a heavy hand."

Rox, who could drink the entire team under the table, shrugged. "Eh. It's okay."

Lily smiled at them. "Oh, how cute. Morticia and Gomez! I love it."

Dinah tilted her head and squinted at me. "Oh! You two are from Dragonspire."

Lily beamed. "Yes. We play online together."

"I'm a gamer too, but I've only played their single-player games. You like the online version?" Dinah asked.

I nodded. "It's fun to just drop in and do a dungeon crawl."

Noah poked Dinah. "No gaming until you meet your deadline."

She rolled her eyes at him. "So strict, this one."

I grinned. We all knew that was not the case. Dinah definitely was in charge of that relationship.

We chatted a little with the other couples until Lily asked me if I wanted to get out on the dance floor. We joined the other couples, and I laughed when I saw Riley and his wife dressed up like Beauty and the Beast. He was hamming it up by flexing his muscles, but Fi seemed to love it. I was surprised to see them out so soon after Fi gave birth to their daughter, but maybe she needed to get out for a night.

Lily and I danced together, grinding against each other, making it harder for me to contain my boner. Damn, was she hot in that little outfit. Nerd fantasy came to life, and she was grinding her ass against me like she knew it.

I pressed a kiss against her neck. "You're killing me, princess."

She didn't stop. "What are you gonna do about it, big tough warrior?"

"Take you," I growled.

"Uh huh. Where?"

I groaned. That was a good question. The kids were at

my place, and we drove here with Blaise and Veronica. It would have been a dick move to abandon them.

She spun around, dancing in my arms, and had a glimmer in her eyes. She got up on her tiptoes and pressed her lips against my ear. "Car. Now."

My eyebrows shot up.

"You got a condom?" she asked.

I nodded.

"We can't abandon V and Blaise. Plus, I'm not taking you to my mom's to have quiet sex in my childhood bedroom. Car or nothing, warrior."

She didn't have to ask me twice. We crept out of the party and toward my car. I paused, pressed her up against the door, and slanted my mouth on hers. She kissed me like she was desperate, like she had been waiting for me to do it all night. She was pliable as I licked inside her mouth, holding her firm in my grip, dominating her. I only pulled away so no one spotted us outside.

We got inside the car, her sliding into the passenger's seat while I leaned back in the driver's seat. Before I could say anything, she climbed into my lap. Her nimble fingers made quick work of the costume belt, tossing it aside as she undid my jeans. When she released my cock, I groaned at her hand stroking me toward my full length.

I reached into my jeans for my wallet and fished out a condom. She stopped stroking me while I slid the condom onto my cock. She didn't wait for me to touch her before she pounced, nudging my dick at her entrance and sliding down on it until I was buried to the hilt. God, she felt so good. We kissed as she rode me, her inner walls tightening around me with each downward stroke.

I felt like an asshole fucking her in my car, not treating her like the treasure she was. But when she kissed me and held her hands on the roof of the car to give herself more leverage, I didn't care. I watched her as she closed her eyes and took her pleasure with me. It was dark in my car, but the moonlight and the floodlights from the garage shone off her face, making her look angelic.

I reached down between us to finger her clit, and I hissed when I realized she didn't have to maneuver too much because she hadn't been wearing underwear.

"Take me," she begged, and she gripped onto my helmet.

I arched up into her. "I am, princess. You love riding this warrior dick?"

She nodded and ground down on me further, sliding up and then back down, making my eyes roll into the back of my head. I pressed my thumb against her clit, and she slapped a hand over her mouth, muffling her cries.

She slammed down on me, over and over, burying her head in my neck until her climax took her away. It was only then I could let myself go.

"Kiss me, little elf," I growled. "Do what your warrior captor wants."

Captor? Was that what we were roleplaying as? I didn't know, but I'd be whatever she wanted me to be in bed. I didn't care when she cried out once more, and I swallowed the noise with a kiss while I exploded inside her.

She pressed a hand against my chest as we both came back down to earth. Her chest was heaving in the top that barely contained her breasts.

"God, that was so worth it. Do you think anyone noticed we were gone?" she asked.

"Don't give a fuck," I muttered. I held the condom at the base while she slid off me and sat back in the passenger seat. I tied the condom off and threw it in the plastic bag trashcan I kept in my car.

As if unspoken, we got out of the car together. I fixed her hair while she helped me get part of my costume back on.

"No panties...really?" I growled and grabbed her around the waist.

She gave me a sly smile. "What, you mad?"

"Fuck no, you sexy little wood elf."

"I figured you'd like it. Let's get back to the party before anyone notices we're gone."

This woman was a lot of fun, but I had to tell my heart she wasn't permanent.

CHAPTER TWENTY-SIX

LILY

I was a little tipsy by the time Veronica and Blaise caught up to us in the kitchen. I stared down at the drink in my hand. This punch was delicious, but I was more drunk than I thought.

"Hey, where have you two been?" Veronica asked.

"Around," Logan told her with an air of finality.

Nope, not gonna tell her I was grinding my ass on his dick until he couldn't contain it anymore, and then we fucked in his car like two horny teenagers. I wouldn't apologize for that. Logan might not be my boyfriend, but he sure gave in to my desires. God, when he said he was my warrior captor, I came undone. That was exactly what I wanted. He knew every part of me, every perfect word to set me ablaze. I never had that before.

And my heart needed to shut up and listen to my pussy saying it was only sex. Good sex, but not a relationship. My brain kept reminding both of them we didn't have time for that.

Veronica crossed her arms over her chest and peered at us suspiciously. "Uh huh."

"V's not feeling good. You mind if we head out?" Blaise asked.

I held up a finger and downed the rest of my drink.

Logan laughed. "I think we're ready now."

I stumbled as we walked out of the kitchen and said our goodbyes to our host. I had chatted with Natalia after Logan and I came in from the car. The house was lovely, and the school district was great. That was something I was thinking about for when Rosie got older. Because I was a mom, and even on a night out, all I did was think of my child.

Logan helped me into the backseat of his car while Veronica sat up front again. She looked a little green. Logan started the car, and we drove back to the city. I was going to need to ask my sister to drive me home. No way was I taking the bus with Rosie, especially in my state. I might have drunk a little too much, but I had been having such a good time. Sometimes I needed these nights to let go.

We dropped off our friends with little fanfare, and then I hopped into the passenger's seat. Logan put a hand on my thigh as he drove over to his condo. It was much later than I thought it was, so the kids would be asleep when we got there.

"Tonight was fun," I said.

He grinned. "We both needed that. Almost home, princess."

Home. But not quite. He meant almost to his place, and then I'd get my kid and make my final trek home.

Once we got to his place, we tiptoed inside, trying not to make a noise and wake the kids. Mari was asleep on the couch, and she woke up when she heard us creep in. She groaned. "They finally went back to sleep. Rosie's cranky tonight."

I frowned. "Aw. I don't want to wake her up and move her."

Mari arched an eyebrow as Logan took off his helmet and put it on the kitchen island. His hair was messed up, and he ran a hand through it.

"Is that your old cosplay? You nerd!" she teased me.

"She looks good in it," Logan said with a grin, doing nothing to disguise the way he stared at my exposed skin.

Mari rolled her eyes. "You two are drunk."

"I'm not," Logan protested.

That was true; he had one light beer when we first got to his teammate's house because he was driving.

Mari stood up from the couch and shook her head at me. "Glad you had a good time. You deserve that, Lil."

"She does," Logan agreed.

"Just stay here," Mari told me. "I have to bring Rosie back in the morning, anyway. Make my life easier."

I bit my lip. I didn't want to invite myself over, but Logan snaked an arm around my waist. "Stay. It's okay."

"Okay," I whispered.

Mari left without a second word, and as soon as the door closed behind her, Logan spun me around and planted his lips on mine. I pressed a hand on his chest and leaned into the kiss.

When he pulled away, he framed my face with his hands. "Come on. Let's go to bed."

I pouted. I didn't want to go to bed; I wanted to have sex again. That might have been the alcohol talking. I followed Logan into his bedroom, where he laid out a t-shirt and a pair of boxers for me, and he stripped off his costume.

"Do you not want to have sex again?" I asked as I tried

to get off my top. Veronica had to help me get it on in the first place.

Logan pulled on a pair of pajama pants. "Lily, of course I want to have sex with you, but you're drunk, and I'm sober."

I frowned. "Sorry."

He walked over to me and cupped my face. "Don't say sorry. I had a good time tonight, okay?"

I nodded.

"Let's get you out of this, okay?"

He reached around behind me and helped me undo my top, letting it fall to the floor. I slid the skirt off and took off my boots. He gave me a knowing look when I stumbled into the bed and changed into the clothes he laid out. Okay, maybe he had a point. I was a little drunk.

"I'm gonna check on the kids," he said and stepped out into the other room.

I lay back on his bed, sighing at how comfortable it was. It was so much nicer than my shitty full-size mattress at my mom's. I could languish in this thing forever.

Logan slipped back into the room and quietly shut the door. He held two glasses of water in his hands, and he set one on the bedside table next to me. "Drink this so you don't have a hangover tomorrow."

I sat up and did as he asked while he took his tablet out and started watching hockey on it.

"Sorry, I gotta review some game tape for tomorrow. I'm on the road again."

I lay back on the bed. "That's okay. I'm probably going to pass out."

He bent down and pressed a kiss to my temple. "Sleep well, princess. I'm right here."

I should have been concerned by how his words

comforted me. How it felt like we were slipping into a relationship. But instead, I let the drunken sleep take hold of me.

I jolted awake to the sound of my baby's cries. I sat up in bed, but before I could run to her, Logan sprinted out of the room.

I groaned and lay back on his bed, my head pounding from the impending hangover I'd have when I woke up again. On the baby monitor, I heard Logan trying to soothe my daughter. I should have run in there, not him, but my chest felt warm when I heard him talking to her.

A few moments later, the shadow of his figure blocked the doorway. He walked in with my daughter in his arms and Liam holding his hand. I sat up on the bed and held my arms out to my crying baby. Logan walked over and put her in my arms.

"Shush, Mommy's got you," I soothed her while I kissed her chubby little cheeks.

Logan got back into the bed and lifted Liam up in between us.

Liam patted Rosie's head. "It's okay, Rosie," he told her.

Oh, my heart. The way he was so sweet with her made me want to squeeze the little boy in my arms.

Rosie was not letting up, though. She cried her heart out. I rocked her and tried to get her to settle, but she reached her little arms out for Logan.

"She wants you."

Logan took her, and she immediately grabbed hold of his beard. "Hey, little miss. None of that, okay?"

Liam snuggled down against me, and I lay back in bed

with him by my side. I ran my hand through his hair, hoping at least he could fall asleep while we tried to soothe Rosie.

"I'm sorry," I sobbed through frustrated tears. I felt like she was regressing, like she knew Seth wanted nothing to do with her.

"She just wants to grab my beard," Logan said as he tried to pry her tiny hands off his beard. I gave him an apologetic look, but he smiled at me in return.

My heart did backflips while I watched him bounce my baby and hum the Dragonspire theme song to her. Because he remembered I said it was the only thing that got her asleep.

Unlike my ex-husband, Logan was a decent man. How was it that this man who I was barely friends with was a better dad to my child than her own father? And why was it so sexy to watch him soothe my crying baby, caring for her like she could be his own?

"Okay, little miss. Time to go back to bed," Logan whispered.

Liam shook his head against me. "We want to sleep with you."

I kissed the top of his head. "Oh, do you now? Did Rosie tell you that?"

Liam nodded vigorously.

Liar. But a cute one.

I gave Logan a questioning glance over the top of Liam's head, but he put Rosie next to Liam in the center of the bed. My heart squeezed in my chest when he kissed the top of her head and then did the same to his nephew.

As I stared into the eyes of this man who wasn't even my boyfriend, I realized this was what I pictured when I thought I was getting my happily ever after with Seth. I thought I had a partner who would do the hard stuff with me and help me take care of the kids.

I couldn't think those thoughts about Logan. We were struggling single parents juggling kids and careers. We couldn't add a relationship into the mix. Hell, that was why I'd only seen him in passing for the last two weeks. It had only been a random happenstance that he invited me to the Halloween party.

I had fun with Logan, but that was all it could be — fun. My heart needed to stop getting big ideas.

I chalked it up to my drunken thoughts, even though I knew damn well these were the sober dreams I never let simmer to the surface.

"Go back to sleep, princess," Logan whispered in the dark of his bedroom. He reached out for my hand and squeezed. "I got you and the kids. Everything's okay."

I closed my eyes and let sleep take hold, but it didn't shrug off the thoughts swirling around in my brain.

CHAPTER TWENTY-SEVEN

LOGAN

Being a parent meant you woke up on one tiny sliver of a bed because, somehow, these little beings star-fished across the whole thing. Or with a foot on your head. Sometimes two feet when you were six-foot-two, and you and your girlfriend had two needy kids in-between you.

Not girlfriend. Casual fuck buddy. Lily was not my girlfriend.

But when I looked over at her sleeping form, her arm protectively across both kids, something tugged at my heart-strings. Waking up with them in between us made it feel like we were our own little family, if only for a moment. I felt like I could tell her anything. Maybe that was because she was Flower, and we already had an intense connection. Or it was my broken shell of a heart trying to tell me something.

Rosie stirred beside me, and she crawled onto my chest. "Da-da?" she asked.

I stroked her tiny head. "No, little miss. Logan."

"Lo-lo!"

I grinned. "Yeah, that's me."

She tilted her head at me. "Mommy wake?"

I put a finger against my lips. "Shush. Mommy's sleeping."

She rested her head on my chest, and I held her against me. She was such a sweet baby that it broke my heart last night, hearing her cries. The parent in me wanted to kiss all her tears away. It also bothered me that her mama had cried in frustration last night.

Lily reached out and placed her hand on Rosie's chest.

"She's okay," I reassured Lily and turned toward her.

"Hey," she whispered.

"How do you feel?"

She groaned and put her hand on her head. "Like I drank way too much last night."

I laughed. "I had a good time. I warned you Mac has a heavy hand."

She shook her head and cringed, jostling Liam, who snuggled up against her chest in his sleep.

"Are you okay, though?" I asked. "When they woke up, you started crying too."

She dragged her hand down her face and groaned again. "I'm sorry. This is so hard. And I'm afraid..."

"What?"

She sighed. "That I've repeated the cycle."

I raised an eyebrow.

"My dad left before Mari was born. I was a baby, and I've never met him. Seth keeps flaking on me, and I don't want Rosie to grow up without a father. Doing this all on my own's exhausting. I'm working so hard at my business, but it's not enough. *I'm* not enough. I can't even provide for my daughter. I feel like such a failure as a mother," she huffed out, tears springing from her eyes.

I reached out and brushed them away. "Hey, you're an amazing mom, and your business is gonna thrive. I understand how hard being a single parent is. You're doing great."

"I'm not."

"You are. Your ex sucks."

She sighed again. "He didn't use to be that way. Or not until I found out he was a lying cheater. I met his new girlfriend at one of my jobs, and she reamed me out for not letting him see Rosie. He lied to her. Just like he lied to me. I felt awful for her. But at least she doesn't have a kid with him."

I clenched my jaw.

What an asshole.

If I ever met her ex...I wasn't sure what I'd do. I made a promise that violence wasn't the answer. I didn't even fight on the ice because of that. I'd push a guy when he deserved it, sure, but I didn't drop the gloves. I wasn't my father. I didn't want Liam to see that shit and think hitting someone solved his problems.

"I know what it's like to have a bad dad," I whispered.

She reached out and grabbed my hand. "You don't have to tell me."

But I did. I kept everything buried, and I wanted her to know I understood her plight. That I knew all about terrible fathers. When I stared into her eyes, I knew I could tell her whatever was on my mind.

"When he wasn't belittling my mom, he knocked her around. I couldn't stand up to him until I started getting serious with hockey. Until I was bigger than him and fought back."

"Is that why he's in jail?"

"Manslaughter. He was drunk and crashed his car. My mom was with him, and then my sister died the same way. The same fucking way! I didn't recognize the signs until too late because I was too busy trying to build my hockey career."

She let out a gasp and put her hand over her mouth. "Oh, Logan. I'm so sorry."

I fingered the tattoo on my upper arm. "That's why I got this. To remind myself I couldn't get Rose out in time. To show Liam real men don't hit their partners. I don't want my family history to repeat itself."

"Logan, I'm so sorry you went through that, but it's not your fault what happened to her. She'd be so happy that Liam's with you."

"I couldn't get her away from him in time," I muttered.

I was repeating myself, but the guilt was washing over me this morning. Reminding me that if I had only paid attention, she wouldn't have ended up like Mom.

She looked down at the little boy snuggled up beside her. "Was Liam there?"

I shook my head. "He was with me. I'm all he has now."

"He knows how much you love him, how you'd do anything for him. You're a good dad. You might not be his biological dad, but sometimes blood means nothing. Kids need love, and as long as they have that, it doesn't matter what type of family they have."

I rubbed the back of my neck. "Sorry, that got dark. I don't know why I unloaded on you."

She gave me a sad smile. "I told you I'm here to talk if you ever need it."

I was going to say something else, but then my alarm went off. Rosie fussed at the noise, and Liam woke up to her cranky noises. He put an arm around her and tried to tell her it was okay. A grin spread across my face at my sweet nephew comforting little Rosie.

I slipped out of bed while Lily kissed the kids good morning, and they climbed all over her. I stretched my arms above my head and tried to pretend I didn't notice her stare at my muscles, open-mouthed.

"Okay, kiddos, let's get breakfast before I have to head out," I said.

"No!" Liam cried.

I laughed and ushered him out of the bed. "I gotta travel for hockey today, bud. Mari'll be here while I'm gone to take care of you."

"And Lily?" he asked with hope in his eyes.

I gave her a 'help me' look.

"Maybe, but no promises," Lily told him. "I have a lot of work to do this week."

Liam's nightmares and crying for his mama had subsided, but he developed separation anxiety when I left. Mari had been trying to help with that, even researching a good child psychologist to have him talk to someone.

Lily got out of bed and took Rosie into Liam's room while I set Liam up at the kitchen table with his paper and crayons. He drew while I made coffee and got breakfast ready. By the time Lily came into the kitchen and put Rosie into her highchair, Mari walked through the door.

She ruffled Liam's hair. "Whatcha drawing, bud?"

"Family," he said and continued to color, not even looking up from his paper.

Lily peered over, and a smile spread across her pretty features. "Liam, that's a very nice picture."

Mari gave me a look that I couldn't decipher and shoved me away from the stove so she could finish the eggs and toast. Mari was only supposed to be my nanny, but she'd become part-housekeeper and cook along the way. I stopped arguing with her about it, and instead gave her a raise.

I brought Lily a coffee and sat next to my nephew. I peered over his shoulder at his drawing. On the paper, he had drawn two big stick figures. I guessed the one with the yellow hair and triangle skirt was Lily and the big one with red hair was me. The figures held hands, and there was a heart over their heads. He was such a little romantic. The Lily stick figure was holding hands with a tiny figure on her other side, and the stick figure me held onto the hand of a small figure with red hair.

Lily and I shared a concerned look. He was getting far too attached to both Lily and her daughter. Lily wasn't even my girlfriend, and already my nephew was drawing pictures like we were his parents.

Shit. I didn't know how to handle this part of parenting.

Lily put a hand over my palm and mouthed, 'It's okay.'

"Who's that?" I asked and pointed at the face he drew at the top.

"Mommy."

"Mommy?" I asked.

"She's in heaven," he told me matter-of-factly.

I ruffled his hair. "Your mommy loved you so much."

"I miss her."

"I know, bud."

"But Lily and Aunt Mari love me too."

Lily's eyes widened. "Liam, you know Mari's not your aunt, right? She's your nanny; she helps your uncle when he's at work."

"I know!"

I narrowed my eyes at him, but I saw Mari snickering as she plated our breakfast and brought it over to us. She gave

Lily one of the kid plates for Rosie, and Lily tried to convince Rosie to not eat with her hands.

"Come on, baby, use your fork," Lily coaxed Rosie. The little girl picked up the utensil and ate.

Lily kissed the top of her daughter's head. "That's my girl."

"Lil, don't let your eggs get cold," I told her.

She waved me off, all her attention on her baby. That was the type of mom she was, so focused on her baby. I was glad she let loose last night. She really needed it, but now we were both back to our responsibilities.

"Lil, I got her. Please eat something," Mari urged.

Lily grumbled and turned around to eat her breakfast and sipped on her coffee. I gulped mine down and cleaned up in the kitchen while the sisters chatted.

I went back into my room and surveyed my suits in the walk-in closet. I didn't have that many suits, and the boys roasted me for rotating the same three all the time. It startled me when Lily came into the room, shutting the door behind her and getting dressed in clothes that appeared from nowhere.

"Mari brought me a change of clothes."

"Help me pick out my suit?"

She changed into a pair of leggings that hugged the gorgeous curves of her ass and a soft-looking sweater before she entered the closet. She fingered the navy blue suit that was my go-to. "I like this one. It brings out your eyes. Plus, you look sexy in it."

I tipped her head up to me and kissed her. I wasn't sure why I did it. I shouldn't have. I shouldn't have let her stay over last night or had the kids sleep between us. I was blurring the lines of our casual agreement, but I couldn't help myself.

Her hands snaked into my hair as we deepened the kiss. Her lips on mine felt perfect, like her lush mouth had been made for kissing.

I pulled away and pressed my forehead against hers. "I'm sorry, I have to go."

"I know."

"How bad is it if I tell you I'll miss you?"

A surprised smile spread across her face. "You will?"

"Of course, princess. I can't take my console. Who else will game with me?"

She let out a light-hearted laugh. "Nobody. I'm your gamer girl."

I grinned. "Damn right."

I turned around and dressed in my suit, pretending I didn't notice her watching me. I opened the drawer in the center of the room where I kept my ties and cufflinks. "Which one?" I asked.

"Doesn't Liam always pick?"

"He does, but help me narrow it down."

She peered into the drawer, and I grinned when she picked the Pac-Man one.

"That's gimmicky!" I teased.

"You asked."

I picked up that tie and a boring solid colored one, and we walked out of the bedroom. We found Mari with the kids playing on the living room floor. I bent down in front of Liam. "Which one, bud?"

He pointed at Pac-Man. "This one!"

"Okay, bud."

"THIS!" Rosie imitated and pointed too.

I felt my lips curl up at her being so cute.

I stood up, and Lily surprised me by taking the tie out of my hand. She flipped the collar of my dress shirt up and knotted the tie for me. She smoothed down my collar, and something about her gentle touch made my heart beat faster.

"Hey, when I get back, we should have a gaming night," I suggested.

She cocked her head at me in question.

"Bring your console over, and we'll get take out. We'll get the kids to bed and play Dragonspire together."

Her eyes lit up. "Oh, Logan, I'd love that. That sounds like a perfect date for my little gamer heart."

I swore I heard Mari mutter 'nerds' under her breath, but I ignored it when her sister smiled at me.

I lifted Lily's chin and planted a slow, lingering kiss on her lips.

Should I have done that when we were just casual? Nope. But when she melted into the kiss, I forgot all about our arrangement. If she didn't want that, she'd have pulled away.

I ended the kiss, despite her hands clinging to my lapels, making me want to kiss her until her lips were bruised and wanting.

I walked over to Liam again and squatted down to his height. "Okay, bud, I gotta go. Be good for Mari, okay?"

He hugged me, not wanting to let go. Rosie waddled over to me and hugged me, too. "Oh, hey, little miss. Will you miss me too?"

"Say, bye-bye, Rosie," Lily told her.

"Bye-bye!" Rosie told me.

I kissed both of their cheeks, and Mari distracted them with toys while I got up and walked out of the door. I loved playing hockey, but I felt a pang in my heart whenever I had to leave Liam. Now Lily and her daughter, too.

My phone buzzed in my pocket when I walked down

the hall and toward the elevator. Blaise had been blowing me up because I was running late. I took the elevator down to the garage and found Blaise's car idling for me. I slid into the passenger seat while he sped off toward the landing strip where we'd get the jet.

He laughed as soon as he saw my tie. "Boys are gonna roast you for that nerd shit."

I shrugged. "Don't care. The kids and Lily liked it."

Blaise rubbed a hand across his jaw. "You two serious, huh?"

I shook my head. "Nah."

He raised an eyebrow but kept his mouth shut.

"Say what you gotta say, bro."

"I get you're both busy, but...are you sure you can't make it work?"

"You were the one who told me she was off-limits."

"I wanted to protect her," he explained. "Look, I'm just saying, last night you looked happy together. You seem perfect for each other. Veronica wants Lil to be happy, to find what we have."

"We don't have time for that. Casual's all we'll ever be."

But when I said it, I wasn't sure I even believed that.

You weren't supposed to kiss your fuck buddy goodbye. Or reveal your tortured childhood to her. Or miss her as much as I already did. I was barely out the door, and I couldn't wait to see her smiling face again.

I was so totally fucked.

CHAPTER TWENTY-EIGHT

LILY

You weren't supposed to miss your friends with benefits. Or get giddy when he texted you asking how your day was. Your heart wasn't supposed to do backflips when you saw him again, even if it felt like it was for a minute before he was back on the road again. You certainly weren't supposed to long for his touch.

Shit.

I fell for Logan, and I was so totally screwed.

We had been texting and chatting every day since the Halloween party. He was bummed he couldn't take Liam out trick or treating on the actual Halloween, but Mari and I took the kids out and snapped pictures while Logan was in Raleigh. The day he got back, we ate takeout lunch on his couch, and I reenacted Liam roaring like the dinosaur we'd dressed him up as. He cooed when I showed him the picture of Rosie as a little pumpkin. She looked so damn cute.

Veronica had lamented that she only had Blaise for a

few hours, and then he was gone again. I understood that now. I felt a deep pang in my chest when I only got stolen moments with Logan. I saw him for dinner, and then he was right back on the road for another couple of days.

It had been like this for the past couple of weeks, where we saw each other a few times a week, and sometimes only for a few minutes. I missed his kisses, his loud laugh, and how he held my daughter to his chest and called her little miss while he soothed her tears.

None of this had been part of the plan. I didn't have time for a relationship, and I didn't want to jump into anything this soon after my divorce. Maybe it was because Logan was Ginger, and I'd known him so much longer than I realized. That bond had cemented our future together, but I was pretty sure Logan didn't feel the same way.

My phone buzzed on the desk, and a sly smile spread across my face at a text from the man in question.

LOGAN: Hey, princess, we just got back in.
Got practice and team meetings today.
Takeout and gaming sesh tonight?

We hadn't had a chance to do that gaming session he suggested yet, and my little gamer heart had been waiting for it. Bringing my console over so we could sit next to each other while we played Dragonspire together sounded awesome.

I texted Logan back immediately.

ME: YES! I'm so game for that.

The sound of footsteps distracted me, and Alex walked into the office where I had been doing the bookkeeping for the tattoo shop.

"Hey, you got a minute?" he asked.

I set my phone down and saved my place in my work. "Sure. What's up?"

"I'd like to use more of your accountant skills versus straight bookkeeping."

The tattoo shop was my number one client right now since I was working the most here. Alex had talked about me doing their tax preparation already, which I had negotiated a different rate because it was a different set of skills.

"I hate figuring out the business side of shit, and you're great with our numbers," he explained.

"Okay, but my rate for accounting versus bookkeeping differs."

"That's fine. We're already paying you below industry rate, so I want to talk numbers with you."

I stared at Alex for a second. Since I was just starting out, I charged at a lower rate to drum up more business. So far, it had been working, and I was getting a lot of new clients and work coming off the freelance sites.

Alex smiled at me. "I looked it up, but I'm willing to negotiate pay."

We talked through numbers until we agreed, and then he left so I could finish my current task. I loved working for the shop, and they were so relaxed and let me be flexible with my schedule. It made it so much easier to juggle all my clients and childcare.

I worked for a couple more hours before I went home. Rosie was already at Logan's since Mari was watching her again. I wasn't supposed to have her, but Seth kept making excuses about why he couldn't take her. More and more, I thought my mom and sister were right about filing for custody. I basically had sole custody if he didn't want to be a father, but I needed help with her. I was seeing more money coming in, but kids were expensive, and I needed child support. If he was going to skirt his fatherly duties, the least he could do was help me financially.

I got in the shower, but since we were doing a night in of gaming and takeout, I dressed casually in lounge pants and a Mario hoodie. Logan would get a kick out of it.

I grabbed a backpack and laid a towel out on my bed. I unhooked my console and undid the cords. I put my console on the towel and wrapped the towel around it to protect it before putting it in my backpack. I put the cords in on top, chucked my wireless controller in the bag, and then I remembered I needed an extra pack of batteries. I found some in my nightstand and shoved them in my bag as well. I eyed my laptop on my bed and slid that into my bag as well. I might have time to get some work done later if need be.

I went into Rosie's room and put an overnight bag together for her. She had things at Logan's, but I wanted to be prepared.

Mom found me lugging all my stuff downstairs when she walked in the door. She pinned me with a curious look. "What's going on?"

"Nothing," I protested. "I'm going to Logan's for the night."

"Uh huh."

I rolled my eyes. "Say what ya gotta say, Mom."

"Is he your boyfriend yet?"

I shook my head. "Mom, it's not like that. We both—"

"Don't have time for that," she finished the sentence I kept repeating to her. She crossed her arms over her chest. "I don't get why you keep saying that. Because since he first took you out, it seems like whenever you go out, it's with him."

"We're just friends," I insisted.

"Uh huh."

"Mom, he's busy with hockey, and I'm busy building up my client list."

"You're so busy, but you're making time for each other when you can. Sounds like you're dating, honey!"

I shook my head. "No. We're just friends. And he's the only one I can talk to about being a single parent."

She still didn't seem convinced. "Well, have a fun time. Tell Logan I said hi."

I rolled my eyes and got out the door before she could make any other passive-aggressive remarks. There was a part of me that was thinking about her argument a lot, though. That tiny part of my heart that was hopeful. Veronica found her happily ever after with Blaise after Seth destroyed her world. Maybe I could find that too. A part of me wanted Logan to be that man, but he had been firm on not having time for a relationship, and I respected that.

I shook those thoughts away when I parked in the visitor's space at his condo building. I grabbed my bags and shot him a text that I was on my way up. Mari opened the door with a look that told me I was in for it tonight. And then I heard the wail of a tantrum.

I cringed as I stepped inside. I set my bags down in the living room and found Liam and Logan locked in a battle of wills. Logan was trying to get Liam to eat his dinner, which looked like mini burritos and Mexican rice. That explained why Rosie was being a perfect angel in the high chair. She loved her Mexican food, just like her mama.

Logan looked to be at his wit's end with his nephew, though.

"NO! You're mean!" Liam yelled.

"Buddy, please, you gotta eat," Logan pleaded.

I looked at Mari, and she shrugged. Logan gave me a

pained look, as if he was screaming at me, 'Please, help me.' Tears were streaming down Liam's face, and my mama heart wrenched inside my chest.

"He's cranky today. I can't figure out why," Mari said with a shrug.

I knelt in front of Liam and wiped his tears away. "Liam, how about you take a couple of bites, okay?" I smoothed down his hair. "For me?"

He shook his head. "No!"

"Liam," Logan scolded. "We don't yell, okay, bud?"

I mouthed, 'It's okay,' to Logan, and sat Liam in his chair. "Logan, it's fine. If he doesn't want to eat, he doesn't want to eat. Come sit down and eat with me."

I gestured to the takeout boxes he had set on the table waiting for us while I slid in the seat next to Liam. Rosie was still eating, but I eyed her carefully while I opened my takeout box. I couldn't contain the grin when I saw Logan ordered me the Mole Poblano.

Defeated, he sat across from me and dug into his enchiladas. Liam had his arms crossed over his little chest, and Mari gave him a warning look as she milled about the kitchen, cleaning up.

"Mmm, so good," I said exaggeratedly to Logan as I took my first bite of my chicken and rice.

Logan's eyebrow raised, and I glared at him, hoping he'd figure out what I was playing at.

His lips formed an 'O' when it finally clicked. "Mmm, this is really good," he agreed.

"Rosie ate what I put on her plate already," Mari told me. She walked over to my daughter and kissed her head. "She's been a little angel today. I'm going to get out of here. Bye, Liam. I'll see you tomorrow."

My sister was out the door before I could even say goodbye.

Liam took an interest in what I was eating. "What's that?" he asked.

"It's called Mole Poblano. It's chicken in a sweet sauce."

"I like chicken."

"You might not like it," Logan warned.

I cut off a tiny piece and scooped rice and beans onto his plate. I made sure they didn't touch, because I know he hated that. "You can try it, but it's okay if you don't like it."

He picked up his fork and took a bite. His face lit up when he tasted the chicken. "I like this."

"Good. If you promise to eat some of your dinner, I'll give you a little more."

That seemed to do the trick, and after prodding him, I offered to deconstruct his burrito since he made a face every time he took a bite. Once I had the burrito unwrapped and his food spread out, not touching, he happily ate more of it. How a kid didn't like burritos was beyond me, but kids were weird. Sometimes, these little people dealt with such big emotions, and they didn't know how to tell us.

Logan looked at me in relief, and I gave him a small smile in response. Whew. I didn't think I'd walk into a tantrum tonight. Rosie was getting like that, and I was dreading the oncoming terrible twos.

I only ate a little of dinner before Rosie got fussy, and I got up to get her out of her high chair. Logan and I put dinner away and gave both kids a bath. While our kids splashed in the bath together, I realized how domestic it all was. And natural. Like this was our life every night.

I couldn't stop thinking about it. Not when we dried them off and laid Rosie down in her crib, or when Liam crawled in my lap while Logan read him a bedtime story.

Especially not after we kissed both kids goodnight and shut the bedroom door.

This was how I had imagined my life with Seth. When I got pregnant, he reassured me he'd take care of everything. Then he wanted me to quit my job, urging me to take the time with the baby. I thought that meant he'd be my partner.

Logan stopped me before I headed into the living room. I gave him a questioning look, but then he cupped my face and captured me in a passionate kiss. A kiss that made my heart yell at me. I let myself get lost in him, in the feelings bubbling up inside me. If only for tonight.

After breaking the kiss, he pressed his forehead against mine. "I'm sorry."

"It's okay. Kids don't know how to tell us what's wrong."

"I was losing it. He's been fighting me on everything lately."

"He's pushing boundaries. God, not looking forward to Rosie and the terrible twos."

He shook his head. "She's a little angel."

I scoffed. "Not always."

"Alright, gamer girl. Now that the kids are in bed, let's break out Dragonspire."

I couldn't help the way he made me feel all warm and fuzzy inside at the joking comment. I was so down for a night of playing Dragonspire with my gaming buddy.

CHAPTER TWENTY-NINE

LOGAN

"YES! YES! YES!" Lily exclaimed. Her hands flew across her game controller as we took down the dragon we had been working on for weeks.

She sat next to me on the couch, her console hooked up to an old TV I brought from my last place while I had mine hooked up to the bigger TV in the living room. On my screen, I watched our avatars take one last final blow to the dragon, then it flopped onto the ground, and we collected our loot.

After we got the kids to bed, we ate the rest of our dinner and chatted before setting up our consoles. Lily looked so cute in her Mario hoodie and leggings that hugged her perfect ass. I liked the casual look and how we felt so natural next to each other. It was so weird that she was Flower, and now she was playing beside me, like we did this all the time.

She set her controller down and frowned. "Shit. I hope I didn't wake up the kids."

I laughed and checked the baby monitor, but if Liam was up, he would have walked out here asking me to watch TV. So far, no sound from Rosie. "I think we're okay."

"This was fun. I needed a gaming sesh tonight."

I grinned. "Me too. Not a boring date? You came over and helped me with childcare."

She saved my ass with Liam tonight. He had been fighting me at mealtimes lately. Mari said he was testing my boundaries, that kids had a hard time communicating their needs. Sometimes I didn't fight him and made the chicken nuggets he wanted instead. I was a pushover.

She shook her head. "It pains me to see him in tears."

"I think he has us wrapped around his little finger."

She laughed. "They both do."

"We should go to Player Won again," I suggested as I set my controller down and put a hand on her thigh.

Her face lit up with a smile. "We should! That was the best date."

"Really?"

She nodded. "Yeah, because I got to kick your ass."

"Oh, the girl's got jokes!"

She gave me a sly smile. "Mmmhmm."

I slid my hand up her thigh, and she gasped when I pulled her over into my lap. But then, the little minx ground against me before leaning down and capturing my lips in a kiss.

For the past couple of weeks since the Halloween party, we only had time to see each other here or there. I'd steal a kiss when she picked up Rosie, or we'd grab a quick meal together before I was back on the road again. We made this plan for a gaming night in because I was about to go on a long Western Canada road trip.

Fuck, I had missed her. Missed the taste of her lips, and how she smiled like it was just for me. We texted while I was on the road, but it wasn't the same as when she was right in front of me, all soft curves and an ass to die for.

Her hands snaked through my hair as we deepened the kiss, our tongues waging war with each other. My hands danced up underneath her hoodie, and I growled when I found her breasts encased by a cotton bra. I slipped a hand beneath one of the cups and gently caressed her nipple between my thumb. She arched against me, pressing her breast into my hand and grinding her legging-clad pussy against my hard-on.

I kissed my way down her jaw until I trailed my lips down the side of her neck. "I missed you," I blurted out.

Fuuuck.

I wasn't supposed to tell her that. Even if it was the truth.

Instead of pulling back and reminding me we were just friends who occasionally slept together, she angled her head to give me better access. "I missed you, too," she breathed out, and then she laughed at the ominous sounds coming from our game. "Shit. The dragon respawned, and we're both dead."

"Don't care," I growled, ignoring the indistinct sound of the music from both of our TVs. Instead, I slid my hands down her ass and got up off the couch. She grabbed the baby monitor off the couch and wrapped her legs around me.

We clawed at each other's clothes as I walked us to my bedroom. I kicked the door shut behind me and set her on the bed. As much as I wanted to lay her out and make love to her all night long, we had two kids in the other room, so this had to be quick. I needed to be buried deep inside her, and by the way she had stripped herself of her clothes and lay naked in my bed waiting for me, I knew she needed something quick and dirty too.

"C'mere," she purred.

I threw my t-shirt across the room and yanked my sweatpants down my legs. I crawled into bed, hovering over her as I balanced myself on my forearms. I caged her head in and gave her another mind-melting kiss. Her nails raked through my hair, and she pulled me closer.

"Please," she moaned when I left her lips to trail kisses down the valley of her breasts.

"What you need, princess?"

My fingers danced between her thighs to find her slick with arousal already.

"Need you now, please, Logan. Take me."

"Hold on," I muttered and opened the bedside table.

"I can't. Please."

"Are you on the pill?" I asked.

She shook her head. "No. It gives me migraines."

"Then hold on, princess. I need to grab a condom."

Her face colored. "Oh God. I need you so bad, I forgot about protection."

I fumbled for a condom in the drawer and had it down my length in seconds. I slicked my cock through her wetness, teasing her before entering her.

We groaned in unison as I filled her up all the way and then slid back out. She wrapped her legs around my waist, pulling me deeper as we became one. She had my brain spinning as I buried myself inside her, kissing her to muffle her soft cries as she came apart beneath me.

I pulled back to watch her as she squeezed her eyes shut

and the orgasm coursed through her. She was so beautiful as she came. For a second, I wanted to remember how she made me feel. Like I was the only man in the entire universe. Like I was her world. I kept going after she came, taking her as hard as I could until my body tingled, and I groaned out my release.

I kissed her neck waiting for my brain to come back online. She pulled me back to her lips, kissing me hard, like she was desperate for our connection again. I reluctantly pulled out and got up to get rid of the condom.

I came back to bed and smiled when she snuggled into my side. I pretended not to wince when she jostled my bruised side. Her gasp filled the room. "Oh my God, Logan. Are you okay?" She sat up and stared down at my bruised ribs, concern creasing her brow.

"Princess, I'm fine," I reassured her.

She opened her mouth, but then we heard a commotion from the baby monitor.

Saved by the cranky baby!

I slid out of bed and found my sweatpants, yanking them on. "I'll get her."

Liam was asleep, but Rosie was awake, her tiny hands grabbing onto the top of the crib. She looked like a little prisoner, trying to make a break for it. "Little miss, what you doing up?"

"Want Mommy!"

"Sleeping," I lied. "Just like you should be."

"Mommy!"

But I picked her up anyway because I couldn't help myself. I took her over to the changing table to check her diaper, but she was all good, and then I set her back down into her crib. I hummed the Dragonspire theme song to her while I took her Bruiser plushie and danced it around her tiny body. She giggled, and by the time I was done, her eyes had drifted shut, and she was back to sleep.

I shut the door behind me and realized we'd never turned off our consoles. I powered them down and turned off the TVs before going into my bedroom.

Lily was washing up at the sink in my bathroom. She had changed into a pair of Space Invaders pajamas pants and a matching top. She was such a little nerdy gamer girl, and I couldn't get enough of it.

I leaned against the doorway while she brushed her teeth and smiled at me through the mirror. Her toiletry bag was strewn across the sink, and I liked the signs of her in my condo.

"Did she go back to sleep?" she asked.

"All good."

"I heard you singing to her. Thank you, I could have gotten her. Did Liam wake up?"

I shook my head. "Nope. Must be luck. He's been fighting me on everything. I hate that I have a long road trip next week."

Her mouth formed an 'o' and it was like a light switch went off in her head. "Ooh. That's why. He's having trouble with you leaving, right?"

I nodded.

"He's having separation anxiety, so he's acting out."

I sighed. "Your sister said the same thing."

"We're right."

"I have the day off tomorrow. I was gonna take him ice skating again. He's been begging me for weeks."

"That sounds fun. He just needs attention from you. Believe me, I get it. You work your fingers to the bone to provide for that little life, but you have to be there for him too."

She wasn't talking about me. From the way her face contorted into a frown, she spoke from experience. Veronica let it slip that Lily wasn't getting any child support from her ex. Lily was working so hard, but she needed all the help she could get. I understood that more than anyone.

I grabbed my toothbrush and brushed my teeth while she walked over toward the bed. We chatted while I washed up like it was a normal night for us. I offered a night in because I knew it was easier with the kids, but it felt almost like the four of us were our own little family tonight.

I slid into bed beside her, killing the lights, and brought the comforter over top of us. "You should come."

"Hmm?" she muttered, half-asleep.

"Tomorrow. To the rink with me and Liam. Probably too early to get Rosie on skates, but I can skate her around the rink."

She opened her eyes and looked like she was considering it.

"Unless you have to work."

"I do, but..." She trailed off. "I can shift around my hours. I want to spend time with you before your next road trip."

My heart felt full at her words. Like she'd missed me as much as I missed her.

"Good. I want that, too. This is a week-long stretch. I want to spend as much time with Liam as I can before I go."

In the dark of my bedroom, I saw the look of adoration painted across her face. "Logan, that's so sweet. You really care about him."

"Of course I do."

"You're a good parent is all I'm saying."

My chest puffed out in pride at her kind words. When my sister died and I got custody of Liam, I had no freaking clue what I was doing. I still felt like parenting was a struggle. I almost hung up my skates to have a more stable job for Liam. I never thought I'd be twenty-four and already a parent. I thought all that was far ahead of me. But I was all Liam had, and I wanted to give him the childhood I never had.

"Thank you," I whispered. "I never know if I'm doing this parenting thing right."

"Me neither," she admitted. "But we just have to be there for them."

I slid to my side and wrapped my arm around her waist. Then I bent my head to kiss her goodnight, not caring that it was something you didn't do with your casual fuck buddy. I didn't care when my dream girl was in my arms.

CHAPTER THIRTY

LILY

A smile spread across my face as I watched Logan skating around the rink with Rosie in his arms. She was giggling as I held Liam's hand, and we skated to a crawl together on the other end.

Logan had taken us to the practice facility on the Main Line for an open skate. Families and older teens skated around the rink, with a lot of parents teaching their kids for the first time. A part of me imagined Logan teaching Rosie when she was old enough, like he had Liam. I had to shake that thought away. That wasn't something happening soon.

Liam hung onto my hand. "Lily?"

"Yeah, bud?"

"Can we go faster?"

"Oh, am I too slow for you?" I teased.

I picked up the pace on my skates. I wasn't a good skater; Liam was more skilled than I was. No wonder since his hockey-playing uncle taught him. Logan was still skating around the other end with Rosie while we tried to catch up to them.

"Yours?" a brunette woman asked as she pointed to the pair of them.

I nodded with a smile.

"Aw, your son looks just like him. You have a beautiful family," she told me before skating off.

I blinked back at her, trying to process the interaction. Liam and Logan looked a lot alike, but mostly because of that red hair. The way he was with Rosie from the outside, I'd assume the same thing. Logan skated back around toward us, and I took Rosie out of his arms.

"Did you have fun with Logan?" I asked her and nuzzled her nose against mine.

"Da-da!" she cried excitedly.

I cringed. She had been doing that a lot, no matter how much I corrected her that he was Logan.

"Logan, baby. Not daddy, okay?"

She shook her head. "DA-DA!"

"Logan," I corrected again. "Mommy's friend Logan. Lo-lo, baby."

"LO-LO!" she squealed.

I sighed.

Maybe if Seth actually picked up his phone and saw his daughter, I wouldn't be trying to convince her the man who picked her up when she cried wasn't her daddy. Even if Logan was a far superior parent than Seth ever would be.

Liam tugged on Logan's arm. "Can we go fast?"

Logan grinned. "Okay, bud."

I rocked Rosie in my arms. She was getting a little fussy —that was why Logan took her around the rink, to try to calm her down. Logan gave Mari the day off, but she had been texting me, reminding me to stick to their routines. We had been having such a great day out, I didn't want to tell Logan we had to leave soon because Rosie needed a nap.

I took Rosie out of the rink and sat her down on the bench while I put my skate guards on. I held out my hand to her, and she walked with me while I returned the skates for my shoes. I tried to distract her from running off when I slipped my shoes on. We went back to spy on Liam and Logan as they skated around each other. Rosie wanted to be pressed up against the glass. She started having a meltdown when I wouldn't let her lick it.

I shifted her against my hip and started humming the Dragonspire theme song. "Don't lick. Yucky. Ick!"

"Ick!" she imitated and giggled.

"You're such a little stinker, but I love you, little girl. So much."

She still tried to lunge for the glass, though. The coming years of toddlerdom were going to kill me. I still wanted her to be my cute, snuggly baby, who was sweet as could be, but little miss had a mind of her own.

I wasn't waiting long before Logan and Liam came out. I helped Liam with his skates and shoes while Logan changed from his skates to his street shoes. "Hey, you want to get lunch before these two need a N-A-P?" he asked.

Liam crossed his arms over his chest and pouted. "I don't need nap!"

We cringed in unison. How did he know how to spell?

"Mari's been working on getting him reading," Logan explained. "He's gonna start school next year, so we want to be prepared."

"I don't wanna!" he said and stomped his little feet.

"Liam," Logan said in a warning tone.

I held out my hand to the little boy. "Come on, bud, let's go get lunch together, okay?"

He took my hand and reached out for Logan's other one, and the four of us walked outside together.

"Can we go to Uncle Blaise's?" Liam asked.

I raised an eyebrow.

"He means Eileen's Tavern," Logan explained.

I smiled in understanding. "Okay, yeah, let's go there. Did you know I work for Blaise's daddy?"

"Really?" Liam asked.

"Yup, Uncle Blaise recommended me to help with their math. They hate math, but I'm so good at it," I told him, trying to explain in a way he'd understand.

Logan and I got the kids into their car seats, with both of them babbling away, and we drove over to Eileen's Tavern. I should be working today. I had a ton of things piling up, but with Logan being gone next week, I wanted to spend the day with him. I loved that he made today a playdate with the kids. The way he cared about his nephew pulled at my heartstrings.

It was a fight to get the kids out of the car. Once we got food in them, I hoped they calmed down. I already had the dry cereal ready to go to give to Rosie while we waited for our lunch to be made.

Hal smiled at me when he saw us coming inside. "I thought you weren't working today?"

"Nope. I'll work later, but we're coming in for lunch."

Hal nodded at Logan. "Oh, hey, Logan. Let me grab your seats."

"Thanks."

Hal seated us and grabbed a highchair for Rosie while Liam sat next to his uncle. I gave Rosie her Bulldog plushie and cereal to distract her, and Liam colored from the kids' activity paper. Eileen's Tavern didn't cater to kids, but they weren't unwelcome, especially since a sports bar got loud enough that kids being noisy didn't bother people.

Hal took our order, and our food came out record fast. Liam was happy with his chicken tenders while I fed Rosie mac and cheese, my salad having gone untouched.

"Lil, let her feed herself. You need to eat," Logan said.

That meant she was going to eat with her hands and make a mess, and I didn't want that.

"She's got it," Logan said. "Right, little miss?"

Rosie made a noise of agreement, so I took a bite of my salad.

Hal swung back around to fill our waters. "Hey, some guy was looking for you earlier," he said to me.

"What guy?" I asked.

He shrugged. "He wouldn't give me his name or tell me what it was about. Just thought you should know."

He dropped off the check and left while I mulled over his words. That sounded very sketchy, but there was little to go on. If it was a client, they would have called or emailed.

"What was that about?" Logan asked.

"Not sure," I admitted.

The center of his brow creased, but I waved him off. It was probably nothing.

We had to leave the bar soon after because we had two kid meltdowns. Definitely time for a nap. We boxed up our lunches and brought them back to Logan's place.

Should I have taken Rosie home to my mom's instead of spending more time with Logan? Probably. But I wanted to milk every hour out of spending time with him before he went on the road.

Liam was exhausted after the skating today, so when I put Rosie down for a nap, he went too after Logan read him two stories. After that, I curled up on the couch with my computer to work, while Logan watched game highlights on his tablet and took notes.

"Is this bothering you?" he asked.

I shook my head. "Nope. Are you taking notes about what you're watching?"

He rubbed the back of his neck. "Yeah. Trying to figure out their strategy so we can beat them this week. Riley's all about looking at our stats and video. He's a great defenseman. I wish I was as good as him."

"You are as good. You're in the league too."

"Yeah, but I'm on a two-way contract, and it's up after this year, so I'm worried they'll not re-sign me next year."

"Look, I don't know hockey, but if your team and coaches are happy with you, that should be good enough."

"I gotta be better. I need stability for Liam. I want a long-term no-move contract, but I have to work hard to get that."

I nodded. "Okay, I understand, but he has stability. Even though you're not around a lot, he knows you love him, and he adores Mari. She'll do everything to take care of him."

He reached out and squeezed my hand. "Thanks for talking me off the ledge."

"Sure," I told him with a smile.

"Thanks for coming today. It was fun," he said after a few minutes of silence had passed between us.

I grinned. "It was. It's nice to bring the kids out with us."

He laid his hand on my thigh. "Can I convince you to stay over again?"

"If you stop touching me like that and let me work."

He gave me a sheepish look and pulled away. "Sorry. I like spending time with you."

It looked like he was going to say something else, but he went back to his tablet. I was aware we were spending a lot of time together, time we said we didn't have, but sitting beside him as we both worked while the kids napped felt so natural. Like I could see myself doing this every day.

I worked for a little while longer, but my phone buzzed next to me. I saw a text from Veronica that got my hackles up.

V: Hey, some guy came looking for you at the shop.

ME: Who?

V: No clue. Just FYI.

The hair on the back of my neck raised. Something was seriously wrong. I didn't know what it was, but something was off. Who was this guy? And what did he want with me?

I pushed away the fear for the time being. Tonight was all about spending time with Logan before he left again. I'd get work done now, and then I'd give myself over to him later once the kids were in bed.

"You're still here?" my sister asked the next morning as I walked into the kitchen dressed and ready to head back to Mom's house.

Logan was rushing around getting dressed in his suit, with the kids clinging onto his legs. He was enjoying it and pretending to be a monster to make them laugh.

"Yeah, they might be a handful today," I said. "They were already so cranky when we reminded them Logan was leaving."

Mari sighed. "Liam acts out when he's gone. He misses his uncle so much. It's cute, but I wish I could tell him how to handle those big emotions."

I shrugged.

She crossed her arms over her chest and raised an eyebrow at me. "But you stayed all day and night again, huh?"

I nodded. "Mmmhmm."

After the kids woke up from their nap yesterday, we spent the rest of the day with them, and then Logan and I got dinner ready and started with their nighttime routine. When we read them a story together, with Rosie in Logan's lap and Liam in mine, it all felt so natural. Then we had adult time in his bedroom.

It all felt so right, and I had to remind myself it felt that way because we were in our single-parent routine. But when he looked into my eyes while he made slow love to me, our souls joined. My heart was getting big ideas, and my brain was screaming at me not to make the same mistakes.

"Lil, admit he's your boyfriend already. You're in a relationship," my sister urged.

I shook my head. We weren't. We don't have time for that. "We're just friends."

She rolled her eyes. "Hey, so off-topic, but Mom said someone was looking for you last night."

I stared at her, frozen in fear. That was the third time I'd heard about this. The only logical explanation I thought of someone not telling people who they were was because it was my father. "It wasn't the sperm donor?"

Mari shook her head. "Mom would have called him 'your asshole father.' She said he seemed cagey."

Was this Seth? Was he spying on me? Having someone come after me? I wasn't sure what to make of it. I got a queasy feeling in my stomach at not knowing.

Logan came into the kitchen with both the kids in his arms. They clung to him like little monkeys. He wore that charcoal grey suit that looked amazing on him, and I laughed when I noticed he had a Mario tie on.

"I have two stage-five clingers," he told me with a smile.

I took Rosie from his arms and put her in her high chair. Mari guided Liam to the table and supplied him with crayons and paper. I went over to Logan and smoothed down his tie. "Who picked this one?"

He laughed. "They both did. Boys are gonna give me hell about it."

I smiled.

"I gotta go. I'll see you when I get back?"

I nodded.

He leaned down and captured my lips in a kiss that ended far too soon for my liking, and then he was out the door.

My sister gave me an annoyed look when I sighed a little as he left. "Lil."

"Don't start," I muttered. I walked over to Rosie and gave her a kiss on the forehead. "Okay, baby, mommy's gotta go do work today. Be good for Aunt Mari, okay?"

She made a little noise of discontent. I crouched down to Liam's height. "Be good while Logan's gone, okay?"

"Okay!"

He seemed so unbothered, and that was likely because he was busy coloring.

I had done some work yesterday, but I wanted to go into

the tattoo shop today. Working remotely was fine, but I liked going into the shop. Part of that was because it was easier than working from my bed. I'd work from home more if I had a dedicated space or even an office to do so. One day, just not today.

I drove home, and while I was getting out of my car, I noticed a man standing across the street. I'd never seen this man before, and I immediately had alarm bells going off as he walked over to me.

"Are you Lily Mathews?" he asked, giving me a friendly smile.

"Yes. Can I help you?"

That was when I realized he had an envelope in his hand, and he stretched it out toward me. I took it, and then he was off, walking back to his car. I stared down at the envelope in my hand, my brow furrowing as I noticed it was from the court system. Did I get a jury summons and never show?

I walked into my mom's house, but before she could say anything to me, I was opening up the envelope.

"You have got to be fucking kidding me!" I exclaimed out loud when I realized what it was.

Tears pricked my eyes. Why was he doing this? First, he flaked out on Rosie every chance he got, and now he was filing for sole custody? None of this made any sense.

I wanted to call Seth and ream him out, but that was not the rational thing to do. He'd use that as an excuse for why he should have Rosie.

"Honey, what's wrong?" Mom asked.

I thrust the papers at her, and immediately, her face fell. "Oh, we're fighting this. Let's call your lawyer."

And all the happiness from spending the day with Logan went out the window because I had to focus on this.

On doing what was right for my daughter. I never, ever kept her from Seth, and the only reason I thought he was doing this was to have power over me. Or because I told his girlfriend he was cheating on her. I wasn't going down without a fight. There was no way he was taking my daughter from me.

CHAPTER THIRTY-ONE

LOGAN

I rolled my eyes as TJ stood on top of the bar. He put his hands up and looked out at all of us. "Alright, boys, let's get fucking LIIIIIT!"

I shook my head at him, but we were all used to his antics by now. I was curious if that was going to change when his twins were born. Blaise said it probably wouldn't because TJ was our loudmouth goof.

We were finally at the end of our Western Canada road trip, and now that we had hit three wins in a row, Coach told us to blow off steam tonight before we headed home tomorrow. It had been a good trip, but I missed Lily and the kids. She hadn't been that responsive to my texts lately. I tried not to think about it too much. She said she had a lot of work piling up before I left. I was being clingy.

Blaise nudged me. "What's up with you?"

I stared down at my phone where she left me on read and frowned. "Nothing," I muttered and took a sip of my beer.

"Something's been up your ass since we left Philly."

"I miss Lily."

He raised an eyebrow. "Yeah? I miss V, too."

I shoved my phone into my pocket. "And she's been leaving me on read. I think I'm being clingy."

Blaise frowned. "Is that usual for her?"

I shook my head.

No, it wasn't. Since the Halloween party at Mac's, we'd been texting non-stop. Even before that, we texted regularly. Her not responding to me while I was on this road trip was weird. Mari got dodgy when I asked last night when I video-chatted with Liam. She'd only say Lily was really busy. Which I totally understood, but I couldn't help but feel like she wasn't telling me something.

"Why's it bother you so much? She's not your girlfriend anyway," Blaise reminded me and gave me a pointed look.

Mac snorted beside me. "Bull fucking shit! She's ya girl. We all saw you at the Halloween party."

I rubbed the back of my neck. "It's not like I don't want her to be."

"Then what's the problem?" Blaise asked.

"Yeah, you two looked cute in the photo you posted the other day," TJ said and nudged me.

A mom at the rink had offered to take a picture of the four of us, and I posted it on my social media before we got on the jet. We looked so happy, like we were actually a couple.

"Why aren't you two official already?" Mac asked.

I sighed. "We're both single parents. With my hockey schedule and taking care of Liam, it's a lot to ask of someone, knowing that I won't be around all that often. She was the one who offered the casual situation."

"She thinks she doesn't have time either," Blaise said. "But you both have been making the time, right?"

I nodded.

"You had a playdate with your kids, so you could spend more time with her," he continued, giving me a pointed look.

Mac pointed at me, and TJ nodded.

Blaise ran a hand through his flow. "She's overworking herself. Seth doesn't even pay her child support. V said she couldn't remember the last time he's seen their daughter."

My jaw ticked at that. V let that slip to me, but Lily hadn't said a word about it. If I ever met her ex, I'd give him a piece of my mind.

"Bro, why are you fighting it?" Mac asked.

"Yeah, man," TJ chimed in. "When I met Max, I was all in for her, and you have the same expression on your face as I do when I talk about her. So what's the problem?"

That she doesn't want me that way. That I was only good enough for my body, but she didn't want to try a real relationship. That would have stung the most.

"Dude," Blaise sighed. "You fucking love her. Just tell her. Jesus Christ, I'm tired of you both fighting it."

TJ nudged me. "Go call your girl and have video chat sex, so you're not wound too tight."

I made a face. That wasn't something I wanted to do. Besides, unlike these guys who were on bigger contracts, I had a roommate. I was glad Cally didn't bring chicks to the room like the guy I roomed with last season. He was young, but with Noah as his mentor, he took his hockey seriously over partying like other rookies did.

I pushed TJ away and downed the rest of my beer. "Alright, alright, get off my dick, you assholes!"

"Go, man," Blaise urged.

I shook my head, put a tip down at the bar, and called a car to take me back to our hotel for the night.

I was exhausted. This road trip had been intense, and I'd played my heart out. I tried not to think about Lily icing me out because it could have been that she was too busy. When I studied video, and she did work at my condo, she mentioned being behind. I felt a little guilty because I pushed her to spend the whole day with me. But I didn't regret spending it with her and the kids.

When I got to the hotel, I went up to the room and took a shower, trying to wash the alcohol off me. I lay on my bed and looked at my text chain with Lily. She hadn't responded since I told her I got to Calgary okay. She had read all of my texts, but she wasn't answering.

I shot her a text.

ME: Hey. Want to get dinner when I get back tomorrow? Been missing you and the kids.

I realized with the time difference, it was late for her, so I wasn't likely to get a response. I flipped through my photos, and a warm sensation filled my chest when I looked at our photos at the Halloween party and then from the other day when we took the kids ice skating. Rosie was still too small, but the idea of me one-day putting skates on her feet kept coming back to me. The boys were right. I wanted Lily to be my girl. I wanted everything with her. Because I fell in love with her.

It happened slowly and then all at once. Like the idea of being away from her tore my heart apart. Maybe it was when she held Liam like he was her own. Or because she was my nerdy dream girl, and not having her in my bed made me cranky. If she wouldn't answer me tonight, I had to tell her how I felt. Maybe then she'd stop icing me out.

"You good, man?" Blaise asked me as we got into his car after getting off the jet. We were home, but I was a man on a mission.

I nodded.

Blaise and I had talked about what I was going to do when we got home. The first stop was the flower shop, then her mom's house. Blaise asked Veronica where Lily was working today, but she mentioned she hadn't been in the shop all week and had been working from home. That had the hair on the back of my neck standing still because Lily preferred to go into the office.

Blaise dropped me off at home, where I took a shower, talked with Liam for a little, and then pinned Mari with an annoyed look. "Where's your sister?"

She frowned. "Mom's. I think. Seth took Rosie."

"Oh. Do you mind staying on for a bit? I need to talk to her."

She nodded. "Absolutely."

"I'll pay you extra."

She laughed. "You don't have to. I think you should talk to her. Life kinda kicked her in the pants."

I rubbed a hand through my beard. "Marigold, I love her."

She beamed. "Yeah, I know! I think she loves you too. She's just scared."

I left soon after, high-tailing it to the flower shop for a bouquet of roses and lilies, perfect for both my girls. I didn't know what was going on with Lily, and it irked me Mari wouldn't tell me either, but this was the moment I laid myself bare for her. If she didn't feel the same way...well, I'd deal with that when it came up.

When I walked up the porch to her mom's row house in the Northeast, I felt anxiety rush through me, but I pushed through and rang the doorbell.

After a few seconds went by, the door opened and Lily stood there with her mouth hanging open at the flowers in my hand. "Hey, princess."

She grimaced. "Hi."

"These are for you. I'm not sure what I did to make you mad, but..."

She took the flowers, and her face lit up. Damn did I love her smile. "Logan, I'm so sorry. It's nothing you did. I've just been so busy."

"Too busy to text me back?"

She frowned. "I'm sorry. I have a lot of crap going on that I didn't want to bother you about."

I ran my hand through my beard, and when I looked at her, really looked at her, I saw the fatigue in her eyes. It bothered me she hadn't confided in me, and I wanted to take the weight off her shoulders. I wanted to be her shoulder to lean on.

I grabbed her hands. "Lily, whatever's going on, you can tell me."

She shook her head and pulled away. "Logan, I...I offered you something casual. That doesn't mean you have to listen to me constantly complain about my shitty ex-husband."

"Princess, I don't want casual. Can't you see that?"

She put a hand to her mouth and stared back at me. "What? But I thought you said...we both don't have time for a relationship."

I grabbed her hand again and kissed the back of her palm. "Since the moment I met you at Blaise and Veronica's housewarming party, there was something about you that felt so familiar. We eased into conversation like we had known each other for years because we have."

"Logan," she interrupted.

"Let me finish."

She clamped her mouth shut and nodded.

"We're fooling ourselves. We're both so busy, but yet we've been making the time. I know my schedule isn't ideal, but I'm willing to make the time for you. For Rosie. Even if it's just stealing a kiss when I wake up during my pregame nap when you pick Rosie up in between jobs. Or a video call while I'm on the road. Because I don't care, Lil."

She put a hand against her heart. "What're you saying?"

"I want to try. I don't want you to brush away the thought of us having something real. Because I love the way you smile at me like I'm the only man in the entire galaxy. And how you treat Liam like he's your own. I love your drive to work yourself harder each day for your daughter. She's not mine, and I'll never replace her father, but little miss has me wrapped around her little finger. I want..." I trailed off, realizing I was word-vomiting all my feelings.

I had to get the words out. That she was my world. She was everything I ever wanted and the only person who understood how hard my life was.

"I want you. And only you. For what we have to be real. Not this weird thing where we tell everyone we're not dating, yet we spend every chance we get together. Because, princess? You're my dream girl, and I never want to let you go. Because I love you."

I let out a breath and silently pleaded with her to say

something. She was still processing it all, but instead of saying anything, she burst into tears.

"Oh, Lily. I'm sorry."

She shook her head and waved me off. "I—you love me?"

I nodded and placed her hand over my heart. "With all my heart and soul."

"More than hockey?" she asked, her lips curving up into a sly smile.

"So much more than hockey."

"And video games?"

"Princess, more than anything. It's okay if you don't feel the same. I'm dumping a lot on you."

"I do! Oh God, I've been waiting so long for someone to tell me those words, to lay themselves bare for me. To believe in our love. I kept pressing down my feelings for you because I knew a relationship was out of the question. I've been mad at myself for how much I miss you when I can't have you completely."

"You have all of me, every last inch."

"Logan, I fell in love with you the very first time you took my daughter in your arms and soothed her."

I cupped her face. "I'm with you, okay? It's not gonna be easy, but I want you, and that means everything. The kids, the toddler tantrums at dinner, the bedtime routines, the waking up with tiny feet against our heads. I want the good, the bad, and everything in between."

She leaned up and met her lips with mine. As we kissed on the front porch of her mom's house, I put every feeling I could into it. Showing her with my body all the words I had already said.

When she pulled away, tears still pricked her eyes, and I

wiped them away with the back of my thumbs. "Now, let's talk about these tears and why you've been icing me out."

She grimaced. "Seth filed for sole custody, and he took Rosie yesterday."

Hot rage bubbled up inside me. "He fucking did what?"

CHAPTER THIRTY-TWO

LILY

Logan's strong jaw ticked. I felt like a dick for avoiding him, but I had been so busy working with my lawyer to figure out our case against Seth.

Logan ran a hand through his beard. "Okay, we're fighting this, right?"

"We?" I asked and cocked my head at him.

"Princess, you need a witness. I'm there. There's no way that asshole's taking your daughter."

I couldn't help the smile that spread across my face. "Oh, Logan. I can't ask you to do that."

"I love Rosie, and I love you, and your shitty ex-husband hasn't seen her in weeks."

I frowned. "I think he's doing it to have control over me. My lawyer thinks we have a good case against him. Especially since he refuses to pay child support."

He cupped my face. "You should have told me."

"I'm sorry. I knew these games were important. I didn't want to distract you. Especially if you're not my boyfriend."

"Um...you know I am, right? That's why I came here as soon as I got back."

I beamed. "So I get to be your gamer girlfriend now?"

He grinned. "So much so."

My heart felt so full as I took the flowers he brought me inside and found a vase for them in the kitchen. He followed behind me, and I smiled as his hands slid around my waist, and he kissed my neck. I moaned at his touch, having missed it while he was gone.

"Mmm. I missed you, warrior. So much," I moaned.

He drug his lips across my skin, his hand sliding up my shirt. "Me too, little wood elf princess."

I turned in his arms. "I'm sorry."

"S'okay, princess. I'm here, and I'm not going anywhere."

I frowned. "I've been trying to keep you at bay because my feelings are so strong. I didn't want to be clingy."

He laughed. "I thought I was getting clingy."

I held up my forefinger and thumb together. "Little bit, but I liked it. Everything's happening so fast, but at the same time not. Do you know what I mean?"

He nodded. "Yes. When we met, it was an instant connection, and that first time we kissed, I was a goner. I didn't know you were my best friend already."

"Really?" I asked, my voice hitching up. I always felt that way too, but it was weird to admit that the only constant in my life was a stranger I'd only known on the other side of a headset.

He nodded. "Might not have known your real name or what you looked liked, but everything clicked once I figured out you were Flower."

As soon as I knew he was Ginger, all the pieces fell together. It wasn't just because we lamented the trials and tribulations of being busy single parents. It had been something so much more.

I cupped his bearded face and looked into his eyes. His blue eyes stared back at me, pouring out all the love he had for me. "Things won't be easy with the kids, but I want to be your girlfriend. I want to be cheering you on behind the glass with the kids in my lap. I want to read them bedtime stories and help you manage a meltdown at dinner time. To be the person on the other side when two little babies get needy and have to be in our bed."

He grinned. "They're quite needy."

I laughed. "We probably need to cut out the co-sleeping."

"Probably."

"I want a partner. Someone who can be with me through the good and bad. I made so many mistakes when I got with Seth."

"I'm here, okay? I might not physically be here because of my job, but I'm always going to be by your side. I'm willing to make the time. For you."

I smiled at him. "I'll make the time too."

He tipped my head up and kissed me again, sliding his tongue against the seam of my lips, and I opened to him, letting him take my mouth. His hands slid down my sides as we deepened the kiss, and then he hiked me up into his arms. We kissed deeper as I wrapped my arms and legs around him, clinging to his strong body.

He dragged his lips down my jaw. "I missed you so much."

"Mmm. Come on, my warrior, show me upstairs exactly how."

"Is that a demand?" he whispered.

"I want you to take me like the animal you are."

His lips curled up into a wolfish grin. "Oh, I will, princess."

And then he carried me up to my bedroom and made good on his promise.

I lay against Logan's chest, tracing my hand against the black and grey rose tattoo on his arm. "She would have been so happy that Liam's in your care."

He kissed my temple. "I hope so."

I looked up at him. "She would. You take such good care of him. It's one of the things I love about you. Liam and Rosie aren't yours, but you don't treat them like they aren't. You've been a better dad to my daughter than her real one."

He frowned. "That's why it bothers me he filed for sole custody. I'm with you in that fight, okay?"

I nodded into his chest. "You said that already. I know."

He tilted my head up toward him and kissed me. I melted into him, letting myself give in to the feelings I had shoved down the past couple of weeks. This man had bared his soul to me, and when he got angry about what Seth was doing, it made me love him even more.

He pressed his forehead against mine when he broke off the kiss. "I love you."

"Love you more."

"More than Dragonspire?" he teased.

"More than all the video games in all the realms."

He grinned, and I loved how his eyes sparkled when he smiled at me. "We'll figure out all this stuff together, okay?"

I nodded. "I'm glad you're in my corner. I didn't want to bother you about what was going on."

He kissed my forehead. "Please bother me about it. I'm

so pissed about that dickweed. I really want to give him a piece of my mind."

"Down boy," I teased. But I loved it. Loved how he was protective of me and wanted to be my rock. "I don't want to keep him from Rosie. She's his daughter."

"I know, princess, but he doesn't deserve sole custody if he's been in and out of her life. We'll figure out what works for her. But he's not getting sole custody. Not on my watch."

If I wasn't already lying down, I would have melted into a puddle. Logan Cullen was so sweet, and he was mine. My perfect gamer boyfriend.

I lay back down on his chest, basking in him being in my bed. We never got quiet moments like this, and I wanted to savor them.

My phone vibrated against my bedside table, and I reached out to grab it. I tilted my head when I saw an unknown number pop up with a text message.

> UNKNOWN: I heard Seth filed for custody. I want to help you. We both know he's a liar.

I frowned at the message. Who was this? I saw the dot bubbles pop up, and then another text appeared on my screen.

> UNKNOWN: Sorry, it's Katie! Let me know if you need a witness. Fuck that guy!

My mouth hung open. I had one conversation with Seth's girlfriend, Katie. I gave her my card, but I never expected her to reach out to me. I didn't even realize they had broken up.

"What's wrong?" Logan asked.

"Seth's ex texted me."

He raised an eyebrow. "Are you friends?"

I shook my head. "We caught him in a lie, and he was cheating on her by telling her he had to take care of Rosie while he was telling me he couldn't take her because he had a 'work trip.' I gave her my card if she ever wanted to talk."

He slipped his hand down and grabbed mine in his own. He rubbed his fingers across mine. "That's why you're so sweet, princess. You always think of others."

"I felt bad for her. But this is the first time she's ever contacted me."

"That's good, right?"

I nodded. "Yeah, just...odd. She wants to be a witness if I need it. I'm hoping it doesn't come to that."

"How so?"

"We had a plan in place; it wasn't working, but that was because of Seth. Maybe we don't have to go to court if we can work it out before then," I explained.

My lawyer had been over this with me again and again as we tried to nail down a date for mediation. If we could resolve the issues, then we didn't have to wait for a hearing date. The courts got tied up easily, and this could be a long process. But Seth was being an asshole, so I had a feeling I'd be seeing him in court.

Logan sat up. "Okay, explain everything to me."

"Huh?"

He put my hand on his heart. "Tell me what we need to do to make sure he doesn't take Rosie away from us."

I don't think I could love this man more.

I sighed. "Okay, it's a lot."

"Don't care. Tell me everything."

So I did, and it surprised me he didn't run for the hills and instead helped calm my nerves like the kind-hearted soul I fell in love with.

CHAPTER THIRTY-THREE

LOGAN

Lily's ex was a fucking douche. I was a hockey player, so that was saying something. He fought us at every turn, refusing to agree to the shared agreement or come to a solution during mediation. We had been stuck waiting months until we got a court date to go in front of the judge.

The past couple of months had been a train wreck, but I refused to let the added stress get to me. I respected Lily for wanting her daughter to have a relationship with her father, but I wished he'd take a long walk off a short pier. Or that I could shove him into the boards. He pissed me off that much, and I never resorted to violence.

"You can't sleep either," Lily whispered in the dark of my bedroom.

"Sorry, princess, nervous about tomorrow," I admitted.

I hadn't been sure if I could attend the custody hearing with her. It may have taken us months to get a date in court, but it was still smack in the middle of my hockey season.

The hockey gods must have been on my side as the date landed on an off day for me. I wanted to be there for her every step of the way.

She put a hand on my chest. "I'm nervous too."

"Don't get mad at me."

She turned toward me, her smile tight with stress.

"I hate your ex."

A light giggle bubbled out of her mouth. "Oh, Logan. I know that. He knows it too."

I raked a hand across my jaw. "He sucks."

"You don't have to tell *me* that."

"I hate how he just wants custody to lord it over you. He could give two shits if he spends time with Rosie."

That stuck in my craw. This douche-nugget was only fighting us to get back at Lily. He didn't care if she had sole custody. Not to mention, he switched weeks a couple of times without warning. I made sure Lily screenshotted all the text messages, like her lawyer told her to. Even though she wasn't pushing for sole custody, having the backup that Seth wasn't agreeing to their previous parenting plan was good to have.

Before she could respond, a noise emitted from the baby monitor. Lily checked it with a sigh.

"I'll get her," I offered.

I was out of bed and padding across the room before she could argue. I walked into Liam's bedroom and found little miss standing up in her crib, grabbing onto the bars. While Lily still lived at her mom's, she slept here a lot when I was home. I had no qualms about it since I loved waking up beside my love.

"What you doing up, huh?" I asked Rosie.

"Da-da!" she squealed at me.

I tried not to grin. There may have been a reason Seth

didn't like me. Rosie kept calling me 'Da-da' no matter how much we corrected her. Little miss was stubborn.

"Logan," I told her. "You'll see your daddy in a couple of days."

She shook her head. "No! Da-da!"

"Logan."

"Up? Da-da up?"

She shook her crib, and I gave in by picking her up, not bothering to correct her again. I hefted her onto my hip; she was getting so big now. I felt a tug on my pajama pants, and I nearly jumped when I saw Liam attached to me. I hadn't even noticed him creep out of bed.

"Okay, you two. You want to sleep in my bed, huh?"

"Yes!" Liam cheered.

I took Liam by the hand, and I brought them into my bedroom. The corner of Lily's lips upturned into a smile at Liam jumping up onto the bed. He snuggled down beside her. To say my nephew was smitten with Lily was an understatement. I plopped Rosie down on the bed and got in on my side.

"You two should be asleep in your own beds," Lily said in her stern mom-voice.

"We wanna be with you," Liam argued.

"Alright, bud," I conceded. "Only if you two go back to sleep." I gave Lily a helpless smile from between the kids, and she shrugged in response. We were total pushovers when it came to these two.

We settled them down, and soon, they were fast asleep, but Lily and I lay awake for longer.

"He hates that she keeps calling you 'Da-da,' but I don't care. I want my baby to be loved, and if she has two dads who want the best for her, that's all I could ever hope for," she admitted. There was a shakiness to her voice like she didn't quite believe it.

I held my tongue. In the back of my mind, I wondered when Seth would disappear. I knew his kind, and finding out he cheated on another girl sold the deal for me on him. He was a Grade A douche-bag.

I reached out for Lily's hand and kissed the back of it. "All I want is for my girls to know how much I love them. I'm with you on this. Whatever the outcome of tomorrow, all that matters is Rosie knows how much we love her."

"God, you're the perfect man."

I laughed. "Not always."

"For me, you are."

"Let's get to sleep, princess. Tomorrow's gonna be a long day."

"You ready?" I asked Lily as we sat outside of the courtroom, waiting for our trial to begin.

She had a pained look on her face.

"You have the better case," her lawyer told her. "The courts want to do what's best for the child, and the fact you want to work with Seth means they'll listen more. But..."

"But what?" Lily asked, panic in her voice.

"Given the evidence that he has not followed through with your informal plan, they could decide to give you sole custody."

I gave her a knowing look. I thought that as well. I squeezed her hand. "Whatever happens, we'll make it work."

"You got a good man here," her lawyer said. "Let's get in there."

We entered the courtroom, and I sat behind in the stands but close enough that Lily knew I was right there if she needed me. I watched as the trial proceeded and clenched my fists as the judge asked Seth questions about why he wanted custody.

Seth was a skinny white guy with tattoos all up and down his arms and a squirrelly look in his eyes. Blaise said he was a weasel, and he hated him for how he treated both our girls. Fuck this guy. He might be Rosie's father, but it didn't mean I had to like him.

"Why do you want sole custody and not a shared plan?" the judge asked.

"Because she's my daughter," Seth answered.

"That's not a good enough answer. Your ex-wife has agreed to a shared custody plan, and that was your informal plan, but her notes have documentation of how you weren't even meeting those and how she's had physical custody most of the time. So I'm going to ask you again, why do you want custody?"

"Because I make more money."

The judge rolled his eyes. "Sit down, Mr. O'Connell. Ms. Mathews, can you please take the stand?"

Lily gave me a look, and I mouthed, 'You got this' as she walked over to the stand.

"Ms. Mathews, I have some questions for you as well," the judge began. "You didn't counter your answer with sole custody. Why's that?"

"I want to do what's right for Rosie. Despite that I'm not with her father anymore, that doesn't mean I want to keep him from her. My dad was a deadbeat. I don't want that same life for my daughter."

"Even though your evidence suggests he has been, as you say, a 'deadbeat.'"

She nodded. "Yes."

"And he has not given you a dime of child support, correct?"

"No, sir."

"You work a freelance job. Do you work outside of the home?"

"Sometimes. I work for different clients, so sometimes I work at their locations, or I work remotely. During the day, my sister watches her with the other child she nannies for. But my work is flexible so that I can do the work after Rosie's asleep."

"So you have childcare in place and consistent employment. You can take your seat."

Lily came back to the desk, where she sat with her lawyer while we all waited for the judge to announce his decision.

"I don't make this decision lightly, but I'm recommending a joint custody order. Now, since Mr. O'Connell has kindly let us know about income, he's to pay child support to Ms. Mathews. Mr. O'Connell, I don't want to be back here fighting you when you don't see your daughter again."

In a second, it was all over, and I watched Lily hug her lawyer. I still thought she should get sole custody, but it wasn't my case to make. I watched her walk over to Seth and say something to him while he sneered at her. I clenched my hands into fists and tried to calm myself down.

She walked away without a second thought and jumped into my arms. "It's over!"

"Let's hope he doesn't flake out on you again," I muttered.

She shrugged. "Now he has a court order to follow. He can't just flit in and out of her life without good reason."

I set her down, and I held my hand out to her. She took it, and we walked out of the courtroom together. If she was happy with the result, I was too. Even if I didn't like that we had to deal with him for the foreseeable future. But I'd stand by whatever my girl wanted to do.

"Let's celebrate," I said.

She grinned. "Okay, but then I have to go to the tattoo shop. I have a ton of work to do."

"Okay, I need to go train with Blaise anyway, but this was more important." I turned to her in the middle of the hallway of the courthouse and cupped her face. "You and Rosie are the most important things in my life."

Her eyes were shiny. "Oh, Logan."

"I love you."

She leaned up on her tiptoes, and I bent down to reach her, kissing her with all the passion I could muster. These past couple of months fighting with her ex had been hell, but I'd do it all over again.

I frowned when I saw the tears on her face after breaking the kiss. I wiped them with the back of my thumbs. "No tears."

She shook her head. "Happy ones. I love you so much. I wish we met — in real life — way sooner."

"Me too, princess."

"So, how do you want to celebrate?"

I grinned. "Player Won?"

Her face lit up. "Hell yes! I'm going to kick your butt in Street Fighter again."

I couldn't help the grin from spreading across my face. I loved my gamer girl so much. She was my ultimate dream girl, and she was all mine.

EPILOGUE

LOGAN

ONE YEAR LATER

"Why did you want me to come look at this house with you again?" Lily asked from the passenger seat of my car.

"I value your opinion," I lied.

I gritted my teeth so I didn't let it be known how nervous I was about what I had planned.

I signed a new multi-year contract with the Bulldogs this season, and I finally felt in good financial standing to find my own place. Renting from Mac had been a blessing, but I wanted a bigger place. A better school district for the kids. Both of them.

Lily had been going with me to look at houses, but she

didn't know I'd already bought the one she loved. It was around the corner from Mac and Tali's and a short drive to the practice facility.

She didn't know any of this because I wanted it to be a surprise. Especially when she saw what I had been working on in the finished basement.

When we pulled up into the driveway, she gave me a confused look, noticing Mari's car was already there. There was a big SOLD sign slapped across the For Sale sign in the yard.

She turned to me with that cute little furrow in her brow. "Logan, what's going on?"

"I have to show you something," I said.

I unbuckled my seatbelt and turned the car off. I got out of it, and Lily reluctantly followed me. She had an unsure look on her face. I walked over to her and grabbed her hand in mine.

She pinned me with her 'mom look.' "Logan."

"Hmm?"

"Tell me the truth."

I played dumb. "About what?"

She gestured to the house in front of us, pointing at the SOLD sign on the lawn. "Did you buy this?"

I grinned. "Maybe."

"Maybe? What's going on?"

I rubbed the pad of my thumb over her hand. "Patience, princess. I'm getting to that."

She gave me a suspicious look but didn't press me. I walked us up to the front door and opened it. Mari and the kids were already here waiting for us.

The house was newly built with a modern, open concept. It was a four-bedroom, which was perfect for each kid to have their own room and a guest room. There was also an office on the ground floor that would be perfect for Lily to work from home. She mentioned she only liked going into the tattoo shop because her work-from-home setup at her mom's wasn't ideal. There wasn't room at my condo either, so working from her laptop on the couch wasn't that comfortable. The office was the perfect setup for her to have the working life she wanted.

"Wow, it looks great already," she said as we walked into the living room.

Mari helped with the furniture delivery last week, but I didn't have everything in yet. The most important stuff was in the finished basement. Not a man cave, but something so much better.

"Come on, I want to show you something." I guided her through the house and toward the door to the basement. I opened it, and we walked down the carpeted stairs.

"Why didn't you tell me you bought it?" she asked. "I love this house. The commute will be killer to bring Rosie here, but..."

Her sentence died on her lips as we got downstairs, and she saw the kids and Mari standing there with big smiles on their faces and a sign the kids made that read 'WELCOME HOME!'

I grinned when I heard her gasp as she looked around the room.

Mari gave me a thumbs up.

The basement had been finished when we toured it, and Lily made a joke about it being a perfect man cave, but that's not what I turned it into. I dedicated one-half of the room as an arcade. Along the wall, I had lines of old-school game cabinets and pinball machines. I even had a bubble hockey setup.

There was a wet bar decorated with Dragonspire

iconography. On the wall behind it was a painting I had commissioned Veronica to create of me and Lily in the cosplay of our characters. Last year we went to Comic Con and upped our cosplay game. Nobody knew I was a hockey player there, just another fan of the video game we loved, and it had been awesome. The other half of the room was our gaming setup. In front of the enormous couch was an entertainment center that housed TVs side-by-side, with both of our consoles hooked up and ready to play. One day I'd build us kick-ass gaming PCs, but for now, we loved our consoles.

"Logan," she whispered.

"What?" I asked with a grin and picked up Rosie as she waddled over to me.

"I told you she'd flip!" Mari said.

Liam ran over to us and tugged on Lily's hand. "Lily! Come play with me!"

"What do you say?" I asked her.

Her eyes were saucers. "What's the question? This is awesome. It's like my dream."

"Come live with me. You and Rosie. Move in, and we can be a family."

Not a shock that after we won shared custody of Rosie, Seth was up to his old tricks. He flaked out on Rosie, missing his weeks and dropping the ball. We'd taken him to court again, but they couldn't do much if he refused to be her father. He was paying child support, even though he grumbled he didn't have to because of my new contract. I had asked Lily if she ever wanted to get married again, and she said it didn't matter. She didn't need a piece of paper to know how much I loved her and the kids. That had been good enough for me, but I wanted the four of us together under one roof.

"Really?" she asked, her voice cracking as she stared up at me.

"Really, princess."

She scanned the room, taking it all in, and turned back to me with a bright smile. "This is awesome."

"You like it?"

"Of course she likes it. She's a nerd!" Mari teased from the other side of the room.

I cupped Lily's face. "I love you. This is what I want for the four of us. What do you say?"

Her entire face lit up. "That I'm going to kick your butt!"

I grinned and watched her walk over to one of the arcade cabinets with Liam. They played together while she taught him all her best moves. Rosie cuddled against my neck, and I gave her a kiss on the forehead.

"Love you, sweet girl. You and your mama."

"Daddy!" Rosie cried, and for once, I didn't correct her.

Seth might be her biological father, but I was the one here every day, drying her tears and holding her until she fell asleep. I'd be the father Rosie needed. Rosie and Liam might not biologically be my kids, but that didn't matter one bit. They were mine, and so was Lily, and I couldn't wait to live together as a happy little family.

"Get over here and play me in this!" Lily called.

I grinned and handed Rosie off to Mari. I watched in awe as my dream gamer girl kicked my ass in Street Fighter. Again. And I couldn't have been happier.

ACKNOWLEDGMENTS

That's another Bulldogs book done. It was a joy merging my love of video games with my love of hockey and romance into this book. Writing Lily and Logan's story was so fun to write. I hope you all love this book. When I wrote Lily in The Fake Out I felt bad for putting her with such a terrible person, that I had to give her a better ending. She gets that with Logan.

Once again I have to thank Becky, Chris, and Jessica for beta reading this book and helping me fine tune it. And of course my critique group of J Lynn, Sophie, and Kat for always letting me vent and run ideas off of. This book wouldn't be in readers hands without you.

And as always to my editor Charlie Knight for helping me finesse this story. I'm so glad you loved this one!

ALSO BY DANICA FLYNN

PHILADELPHIA BULLDOGS

Take The Shot

Score Her Heart

Against The Boards

The Chase

The Fake Out

Risky Play

MACGREGOR BROTHERS BREWING COMPANY

Accidentally In Love

Trapped In Love

Temporarily In Love

THE MURPHY BROTHERS

Protecting Her

Capturing Her

ABOUT THE AUTHOR

Danica Flynn is a marketer by day, and a writer by nights and weekends. AKA she doesn't sleep! She is a rabid hockey fan of the Philadelphia Flyers. When not writing, she can be found hanging with her partner, playing video games, and reading a ton of books.

www.ingramcontent.com/pod-product-compliance
Lightning Source LLC
LaVergne TN
LVHW091111080826
845145LV00008B/1870

* 9 7 8 1 9 5 7 4 9 4 2 6 5 *